TURN LEFT AT DOHENY

A petty criminal cannot escape his sordid past in this tough-edged crime novel.

Down-on-his-luck drifter Wycliffe has come to Los Angeles to scam his dying brother out of his estate. Then he meets a glamorous woman who offers him his first taste of the high life, and finds himself involved with a team of hustlers much more sophisticated and brutal than he is. Wycliffe suspects he's being set up. But for what?

TURN LEFT AT DOHENY

J.F. Freedman

Severn House Large Print
London & New York

This first large print edition published 2014
in Great Britain and the USA by
SEVERN HOUSE PUBLISHERS LTD of
19 Cedar Road, Sutton, Surrey, England, SM2 5DA.
First world regular print edition published 2014 by
Severn House Publishers Ltd., London and New York.

British Library Cataloguing in Publication Data

Freedman, J. F. author.
  Turn left at Doheny.
  1. Brothers--California--Los Angeles--Fiction.
  2. Inheritance and succession--Fiction. 3. Swindlers and
  swindling--Fiction. 4. Suspense fiction. 5. Large type
  books.
  I. Title
  813.6-dc23

  ISBN-13: 9780727897497

Severn House Publishers support the Forest Stewardship Council™
[FSC™], the leading international forest certification organisation. All
our titles that are printed on FSC certified paper carry the FSC logo.

MIX
Paper from
responsible sources
FSC® C013056

Printed and bound in Great Britain by
T J International, Padstow, Cornwall.

To Chris Bell

ONE

Wycliff was going to take the Greyhound. He had enough money, that wasn't the problem. But as he stood in line to buy the ticket from Tucson to Los Angeles, an announcement came over the public address system that the scheduled bus had mechanical problems, and there would be a delay until a replacement could be driven down from Phoenix. That could take all day, so he stole a car instead, a late-model Lexus, from the Ventana Canyon Resort parking lot. Metallic champagne paint job, tan leather seats, Blu-Ray, six-disc CD changer in the dashboard, GPS in the dash. The owner was an attractive middle-aged woman who was getting the full salon treatment: hair (cut and colored), manicure, pedicure, and facial, so she wouldn't be going anywhere for a while. By the time she realized her wallet and keys had been lifted from her purse, he would be long gone.

The wallet contained eight hundred and fifty dollars in crisp bills fresh from the bank, and a bunch of credit cards. He kept the cash and tossed the plastic. Then he unscrewed a set of license plates from another car on the lot and switched them, a trick he'd perfected in his teens. All set now, he drove onto the I-10, set the cruise

7

control to five miles over the speed limit, and nestled in the anonymity of the center lane. One stop to refuel and use the bathroom, and eight hours later he arrived in LA, exiting at the La Cienega turnoff and heading north into West Hollywood.

The stunned look on his brother's face when he walked into the hospital room was one of disbelieving shock, but it instantly morphed into blinding anger. 'What the fuck are you doing here?' he raged at Wycliff.

'I came to see you. What other reason would I have to be in this godforsaken shithole?' Wycliff replied with easy insouciance. He was a bird on a wire; he could come and go as he pleased. Billy couldn't. All the difference in the world.

'None,' Billy answered with unconcealed disdain. 'Including to visit me, I would have thought.'

'I wanted to see you before you die.'

'What you want is my money, you prick.' Billy's mocking laugh sounded like his throat was lined in sandpaper.

'Of course I do. We *are* blood, baby brother. If the shoe was on the other foot...'

'I'd scrape it off, because it would be dog-shit.'

Wycliff smiled. He'd been insulted by pros. This was nothing. He pulled up a chair and sat down. His younger brother was nothing more than a sack of bones. You could practically see the skull through the stretched skin of Billy's ravaged face. He knew Billy would be fucked

8

up, the scourge did that to its victims, but this was way beyond what he had imagined. Holocaust survivors from old *Life* magazine pictures had more flesh on their skeletons. Billy had been a beautiful boy, which was his downfall. Every fag from fourteen to eighty had wanted to fuck him, and he'd let too many do it. At least one too many.

'It's not going to happen,' Billy told Wycliff. 'I've made sure of that.'

'You left it to one of your friends, or some bleeding-heart charity?' Wycliff shook his head in annoyance. 'Get smart for once, Billy. What's yours is mine, and vice versa. That's the law.'

'So get a lawyer and sue my estate. If you can find one that'll take you on.'

'We'll see,' Wycliff answered. He checked out the dull, institutional surroundings. Hospital rooms gave him the creeps. 'They gonna leave you in here to rot?' he asked. 'You don't want to die in your own bed, surrounded by loved ones? Or in a hospice, with people who actually care?'

Billy swallowed and looked away, towards the window. 'They need to stabilize me some more. Than I'll go back home.'

'That's good,' Wycliff told him. 'You don't want to die in a hospital. Bad mojo for your journey to the next life, wherever that may be.' He stood, and stretched. 'Where are the keys to your place? Somebody's got to water the plants.'

His brother's face hardened. 'It's being taken care of. I don't want you setting foot near there.'

Wycliff took on a quizzical look. 'Where am I supposed to crash, then?'

Billy would have laughed again, but he wasn't capable of the effort. 'Like I'm supposed to give a shit? I don't want you here, there, or anywhere. I don't want to see you again, Wycliff. Like, never.'

Wycliff took on a hurt look. They both knew that was a joke. It took more than a dying brother to penetrate Wycliff's feelings.

'I'm all the family you have, bro',' he reminded Billy. 'It might be screwed up both ways, but that's how it is.'

Billy closed his eyes. 'Go away. And don't come back. I can have you removed. By force, if necessary.'

Wycliff got up. 'I'm leaving, so don't worry your pretty little head.' He patted the body under the sheet. It was like touching a skeleton. 'Get some sleep. I'll come back later.'

'Don't.'

Wycliff stared down at him. 'We're blood. Blood transcends everything.'

Billy opened his eyes and looked at Wycliff. His eyes were set so deep into his face it was like they were two dim lamps in a coal shaft. 'Except when it comes to you,' he said, his voice a weak whisper now. He was exhausted; it didn't take much. 'You transcend nothing.'

The man who was taking care of Billy's house stared at Wycliff through the screen door. 'Who are you?' he asked. His tone of voice was suspicious. This guy facing him looked like a biker, or a recently released con. Bad news, either way.

'Billy's brother,' Wycliff answered casually,

with no undertone of threat or violence. He took out his driver's license and pressed it against the screen. 'See for yourself.'

The man, who was older than Wycliff, flabby and balding, fumbled a pair of glasses out of his shirt pocket. The lenses were smudged. He peered at the license, taking a good, long look. 'I didn't know Billy had a brother,' he said suspiciously.

'We've been out of touch. But now he's dying, so here I am.' Solidifying his *bona fides*, Wycliff added, 'He knows I'm here. I just came from the hospital. Cedars.'

The man didn't look happy at this unexpected revelation. 'You can come in, I guess,' he said grudgingly.

The house was a Craftsman off Sunset, where Silverlake bordered Echo Park. It was set back from the street, so there was little traffic noise. The trim was past due for sanding and painting and the pocket front yard needed mowing and watering, but the borders around the lawn had been nicely planted with a variety of dwarf rose bushes, about half of which were in full bloom, so the overall feeling was cheerful. As Wycliff stood on the shaded porch, waiting for the nervous-Nelly house-sitter to unlatch the screen door, he made a quick mental inventory of how much work would be needed to whip it into shape so it could be put on the market. Not much, at least on the outside. This was a hot area for real estate; he'd checked it out on the Internet. Choice territory for young up-and-comers who couldn't afford the Hollywood Hills or

11

parts west. All in all, a pretty, inviting little place. He wondered how big a mortgage Billy was carrying. One of the details he needed to check into.

As soon as the caretaker lifted the inside door-latch, Wycliff grabbed the handle on his side and yanked the door wide open. The pasty-faced man almost fell over from the sudden jolt. 'You don't need to be so rough,' he blubber-lipped.

The man's skittish whimper went in one of Wycliff's ears and out the other. He was in his brother's house, that was all that mattered. This pitiful specimen could stay or go, he couldn't care less. As long as he stayed out of Wycliff's hair and didn't try to pull some kind of squatter's-rights rank. Wycliff couldn't imagine this loser standing in front of him as a sexual partner for his brother. Not that sex had any part in Billy's life anymore. Still, you should care about appearances. Billy had been prime. Plenty of straight women had tried their wiles on him. He had slept with some of them, usually for money, but occasionally just to make them happy, because he liked them, as people. But he never got any true satisfaction from the act. He had been born gay, lived his life gay, and would die a man who loved men.

Except for Wycliff. Billy didn't love his brother. He hated him venomously, all the way back to their childhood. Wycliff knew that, always had. Not that he cared, not a bit. Being hated, or more usually, feared, was the emotion he most commonly engendered in people. When he'd been younger it had bothered him that almost

12

everyone was either scared of him or despised him. But he'd outgrown that negativity, had learned to live with it, and use it. The leopard can't change his spots. We are what God made us, like it or not. He was a heterosexual thug, and his younger brother was a gay angel. Neither was ever going to change, even past the grave.

He dropped his duffel onto the floor. It raised dust-motes in the still air. 'Which bedroom are you using?' he asked Billy's friend, who was backing away from him. 'Billy's?'

'No. I'm in the guest room. Billy's coming home soon,' the man ventured bravely. 'So there's really no room at the inn.'

'He ain't home yet,' Wycliff reminded the man without subtlety.

He took in the surroundings. The house was dirty, you could feel the grunge. Billy hadn't had a cleaning service in for a while; that was obvious. When Billy came home, assuming he did, it should be to a clean house. The least a brother could do.

'I'm gonna change the linen and unpack my stuff,' he informed the man. 'Then I'll get to work. A house ain't a home if it ain't clean, don't you know that?'

Billy's sullen friend didn't answer. He was clearly intimidated by this bully who had burst in on him unexpectedly. He could see the resemblance between the two brothers, but still, that Billy could have a blood connection who had this kind of brutish personality didn't seem possible.

Wycliff was oblivious to the caretaker's feelings. He hoisted his duffel, went into his brother's bedroom, and shut the door.

There was no mop, and he had to be pushy to get the caretaker, whose name was reluctantly given out as Stanley, to go to a nearby CVS Drugstore to buy one, along with furniture polish, Simple Green, bath and toilet cleanser, and other janitorial necessities. He peeled off three of his freshly stolen twenties and thrust the bills into Stanley's sweating hand.

'And pick up a six-pack. Bohemia or Corona. And whatever you drink, for yourself. As long as it isn't Chivas, or something too pricy. Some chips and salsa, too.' He gave Stanley a crude wink. 'You look like a man of refined taste. Any friend of my brother's has taste. Billy don't truck with tasteless individuals.'

Which was true, back when Billy had a regular life as a decorating consultant specializing in Feng Shui. Billy counted movie and recording stars not only as clients but as real friends. You'd see his picture in *People* or *Vanity Fair*, in the background, at some hot party or another. Where were those famous friends now? Wycliff wondered. Nowhere near here or the hospital, he'd bet good money on that.

As he contemplated that discouraging thought, Wycliff felt more kindly towards this shlub. It wasn't easy, taking care of someone who was dying. Someone who had sores all over his body, a victim of the modern plague. He modulated his smile, so that it wasn't as wolfish as normal. 'Go ahead,' he cajoled the caretaker. 'Everything will

14

be here when you come back.' He tossed Stanley the keys to the Lexus. 'You can hold these, so you'll know I won't be going anywhere.' With a sly grin: 'Don't be driving it, though. My insurance only covers me.'

After Stanley came back with the supplies, Wycliff knocked down a beer and a handful of chips, then spent three hours cleaning the inside. There was more left to do, but this was a lot better, and he wanted to get a start on the outside while there was still daylight left. Maybe he'd hire a professional cleaning crew to give the interior a thorough once-over. He didn't like being in a dirty house. He didn't like dirty clothes on his person, either. He had more socks and underwear than he needed, for that very reason. Putting on a dirty pair of socks or underpants made his skin crawl. In fact, tomorrow, once things got more settled, he'd root out a Ross For Less and buy some underwear because he was running low, having packed on the fly. He had friends who sneered at Ross, but not him. Their stuff was first-rate: Ralph Lauren, Tommy Hilfiger, Jockey. No one knows where you bought it once you throw the shopping bag away.

The lawnmower was an old-fashioned manual reel-style, but the blades were sharp and it was a small lawn, so cutting the grass was no problem. It was hot out. Wycliff took off his shirt and worked up a good sweat, feeling the sun lubricate the muscles of his back and shoulders. He pulled weeds from around the rose bushes, let the hose run for ten minutes to water them, and found a usable rotating sprinkler in the garage.

While he took his shower and shaved, the lawn got a good soaking. When he went back outside, now freshly bathed and dressed in jeans, a designer T-shirt, Lucchese cowboy boots in real alligator, and a Fred Segal linen sports jacket he plucked from his brother's closest (they were the same size, or had been), the grass looked much better, like he'd given it a new lease on life. Too bad I can't do that for you, little brother, he thought, as he coiled up the hose. Nurse you back to health with a dousing of tap water.

He went back inside. It was almost eight, getting dark. Stanley was in the living room, sitting in front of the television set, eating take-out from the Burrito King on Alvarado Blvd.

'Don't wait up for me, ace,' Wycliff told him jocularly, like they were old buddies. 'I'm a night owl.' He dangled a key-chain in his fingers. 'I found an extra set of keys, so you can lock the door if that makes you feel more secure. Just don't pull a gun on me when I come in,' he added with as friendly a smile as he could muster.

Stanley stared straight ahead, his mouth stuffed with chorizo, tortilla, and beans. 'Tomorrow we'll go see Billy,' Wycliff went on. 'Cheer him up. Friends and family, the best medicine.'

Stanley's doleful look was a clear sign he wasn't buying Wycliff's bullshit, but he just kept chewing and watching *Wheel of Fortune*. Wycliff gave a cursory glance at Vanna White's tightly wrapped behind as she turned three squares over to the letter E, and went out the door.

TWO

Wycliff didn't know how long he'd have to nurse his cash until he managed to convince his brother that the estate should go to him and he could legitimately dip into it, but a drink at a nice bar wouldn't break the bank, so he treated himself to a Johnnie Walker Red, water back, at the bar in the famous Chateau Marmont hotel where the hip movie stars hung out, according to the gossip rags he leafed through in the checkout stands at the fast-food restaurants he normally patronized back in Arizona. He didn't see any stars, but it was still early. No self-respecting actor or actress would show their face until at least eleven, that much about show business he knew. He could nurse his drink, maybe have one more (although at twelve bucks a pop drinks were damn pricey; Johnnie Black, which he preferred, was twice as much, so he passed on that), and stargaze like a pro. Covertly, with feigned nonchalance.

He heard the woman before he saw her. She was behind him, at the other end. 'Tanqueray on the rocks.' Her voice was low and silky, with a touch of tobacco in the throat, like an old-fashioned movie star's. 'With a squeeze of lime, please,' she instructed the bartender. The way she said *please* it was like a queen talking to a servant.

Wycliff rotated slowly on his stool so he could see what she looked like without seeming to be too obvious, although with hardly anyone else in here, any move was obvious. So what, he thought. It's a bar. That's what people do in a bar, besides drink. Check each other out.

The woman was alone. She was sitting at the end of the bar, where it was darkest. Glancing at her sideways, he could see that she was older than him, by more than a few years. Five or ten, maybe even fifteen. In this light, it was hard to tell. Good bars keep the lights low.

It took Wycliff a moment to realize she was looking at him. Not just looking, but openly staring. For a man who was normally the epitome of cool around women, it was strangely disconcerting. He wasn't sure, but he might have flinched, just for a second.

'I wouldn't mind some company,' the woman said, her voice carrying just far enough to reach his ears, but no deeper into the room. If the bartender had heard her, he didn't acknowledge it. He placed her drink in front of her, took some damp bills off the bar, and moved off.

Well, she wasn't hustling him, at least not for this round, Wycliff thought, still looking her over. Although she was an older woman, she was very good looking. More sexy than pretty, which was even better. Wycliff picked up his drink, left a dollar for a tip, walked down to the end of the bar, and sat on the stool next to hers.

Up close, he recognized her, or thought he did.

She definitely looked familiar. Movie-star familiar, although he didn't know which one. Damn, he thought, his first night in LaLa land and here he was, about to have a drink with a genuine Hollywood actress. Maybe she was a real star, or at least a well-known celebrity. Wycliff's viewing habits were more television than movies, so although he could have easily recognized Jennifer Aniston (too young) or Marg Helgenberger (closer, but still too young) on sight, even a well-known film actress probably wouldn't register on him, unless it was Julia Roberts or what's-her-name, the perky little chick from *Legally Blonde*. Too bad, he thought; if he could have said 'Hello, *fill in the blank*,' it would have meant points. On the other hand, he didn't think Jennifer or Marg or any actress of their stature would invite him to have a drink with her. Still, he was a good-looking guy, and everyone knew these actress chicks were weird.

'Don't say it,' she warned him, before he could open his mouth. She stirred her fresh drink with the tip of her pinkie and licked it.

'Say what?' he asked. God damn it, who was she?

'That I look familiar. It's the oldest line in the book. A man of your caliber can do better than that.'

Saved by the bell. 'I wasn't going to,' Wycliff responded. He flashed a smile. 'Give me some credit.' He hesitated a moment; now what should he say that wouldn't peg him as a rube from the sticks? Thank God he'd copped his brother's cool linen jacket. Otherwise, he'd look like he'd

19

just dropped in from a truck stop in Clovis, New Mexico. He should have left the cowboy boots back in Arizona.

'Good.' She smiled. One of her front teeth was chipped a little. On her, it looked sexy.

Lauren Hutton. That was it. Except it wasn't. The tooth had thrown him off.

'So what were you going to say?'

Well, now he had to answer. Whatever came out of his mouth wouldn't be right, he knew that for sure. He took a mental breath. What the hell – sometimes you've got to dive in without knowing how deep the water is under the surface.

'Not that you look familiar, but that you look like...' Wycliff hesitated again. Somehow he knew that the next two words out of his mouth were going to make or break this evening, and maybe, by extension, his entire West Coast sojourn. He took a wild guess. 'The woman from *The Forty-Year-Old Virgin*.' A funny damn movie. A forty-year-old male virgin in the United States who wasn't a priest or gay. How weird could that be?

'Catherine Keener,' the woman tossed off with a shake of her head. Her hair was medium length, just touching her shoulders. It was the color of mink, streaked with thin silver lines, like subtle pinstripes on a three-thousand-dollar suit. 'I get her once in a while,' the woman continued. 'But no. Not her. Not Annette Bening, either. I don't know why they get grouped together, except they're about the same age.' She leaned in towards him, an unmistakably intimate

20

gesture. 'Charlotte Rampling.'

Wycliff stared at her. His expression tele-graphed *who*?

'Before your time,' she said, 'unless you're a movie buff. She's sixty-plus now, but she's still stunning. Like Catherine Deneuve. Timeless.' She took a sip of her drink. 'I'm not quite that old yet, but I hope I look that good when I am. Half that good.'

An opening. 'You look damn good now, how-ever old you are,' Wycliff told her, hoping it came off as a compliment. He'd been sitting here for less than a minute, and this woman had him off-balance already. He was going to have to bone up on actresses fast.

The woman touched two fingertips to Wycliff's wrist. Her fingertips fluttered against his skin, like a butterfly on the wing. Her touch was velvet. He started tingling, all over. 'That's nice of you to say, since you are younger than me.' She took a tiny sip from her drink, put the glass down, and made a quick tongue-flick across her lips. Her lipstick was dark crimson. 'You look familiar to me as well,' she told him.

Since he didn't know anyone in LA except his brother and the sad sack house-sitter, that was pretty much impossible. Was she flirting with him? He couldn't see any harm in playing along, if it floated her boat.

She ran her fingers along his coat-sleeve. 'Maybe it's this jacket. Linen, isn't it?'

He had no idea. 'I guess,' he answered. 'Check the label if it matters to you.'

'Darn, I hate it when this happens,' she said.

'It's right on the tip of my tongue...' She stopped talking and stared at him, her eyes widening. 'No, it couldn't be. It must be the jacket.' She took another sip of her drink. 'This is probably a ridiculous shot in the dark.' And then she said his brother's name.

Wycliff's jaw hit the bar.

The woman thought she had confused him. 'I'm sorry,' she apologized. 'We're talking actor look-alikes, not real people. I should have said Christian Bale.'

Batman. He knew that one. He didn't think he looked much like Batman.

'He's my brother.'

Now it was her turn to be confused. 'Christian Bale is your brother?'

He shook his head *no*.

Her eyes widened in the darkness like a cat's. 'Billy is your brother? I was right.' She leaned in and scrutinized him more closely. 'You *do* look like him!' she said with a delighted squeal. 'I'm not hallucinating, after all.'

Wycliff's hand shook as he lifted his drink to his mouth. He and Billy did look alike, true enough; although where Billy was almost delicate, like Bambi, he was more on the rough-edged side, the raging-bull type. Their looks matched their personalities, always had, right from the cradle. But yes: put them side by side, you'd know instantly they were brothers.

Which was a testament to the power of their father's genes, because he and Billy weren't full brothers, only half. Same asshole of a father, but different mothers. Their father was one of those

22

charming, handsome bastards who made a good first impression, good enough to get plenty of attractive women into his bed. That was his only claim to fame, his prowess as a swordsman. He had passed that feature down to his sons; the only positive legacy he gave them.

Wycliff didn't remember his own mother at all. She flew the coop while he was still in the cradle, practically, having had it up to here with the constant abuse, both physical and mental. (Wycliff didn't remember that, either, of course, but the stories were family legend, recounted not only by aunts and uncles and cousins, but by the old man himself, as if being a bully was something to brag about.)

Shortly after his own mother's departure, the woman who would bear Billy came into the picture. She, too, was a shadowy figure, and like her predecessor, she didn't stick around long. Wycliff had been old enough by then to have vague memories of her. She was pretty and smelled good, he remembered that. Smoked cigarettes, could match the old man whiskey shot for shot. Had men over when the old man wasn't around. She was tough, tougher than him. She stood her ground when he tried to beat her down, even bested him at times. One memory Wycliff had of those days was waking up in the morning and finding his father snoring like a drunken bear on the living room couch, having been banished from the connubial bed.

And then one day she was gone, too, never to return. She was no dummy: she cleared the bank account out first, leaving father and sons high

23

and dry. And years later, to add insult to injury, the brothers discovered that neither of their mothers had been married to their father, which made them not only brothers, but bastards.

So they'd had shitty childhoods, but not overwhelmingly terrible. They lived with relatives most of the time, who were decent enough people. The boys were kept together, and never had to go to foster homes. Not so bad a childhood. Wycliff knew kids who had it worse. They had survived. Except one of them, fortunately not him, wasn't going to much longer.

Wycliff didn't dwell on the past. It had no allure for him. The present, particularly right now, was much more promising.

So this woman knew Billy, and he'd happened to stumble in here, and she saw him and made the connection. There was a logic to this mystery after all. Wycliff's breathing slowed down and became less shallow. For about five seconds. Then he thought, hold your horses! You didn't fall out of the tree last night, you dumb shit. Of all the gin mills in the world, this woman happens to be in this one, where he, a stranger from out of town, drops in for a drink, in a strange city full of bars? What if he'd gone to the Argyle, or the Roosevelt, the Dresden Room, or any of the hundreds of places he'd seen on E Television? This chance meeting seemed awfully convenient. Way too convenient.

'Are you following me?' he asked her. 'You're following me, aren't you?'

She laughed. 'I was here first. You just didn't notice me.' She touched his arm again. 'How is

your brother? I haven't seen him for some time.'
She paused. 'I heard he wasn't well.'

'He's dying.'

She gasped. 'Is it...?'

'AIDS,' he confirmed. 'Full-blown.'

She looked stricken. 'That's what I heard. I'm so sorry.'

'Me, too.'

The woman knocked her drink back in one long swallow. 'Let's go where we can have some privacy. If you feel up to it.'

Private time with this woman, that wouldn't be a hardship, as long as she didn't slip some drugs in his drink, or whatever they did out here. Was this some kind of setup, despite her disclaimer? If it was, the joke was going to be on her, because most of the money he'd nicked from the woman in Tucson was hidden in his rolled-up underwear back at the house. If this mystery woman was looking for an easy score, she had picked the wrong pigeon.

What the hell, Wycliff thought. Going for it was his style. Always had been, always would be. He drained his Scotch (it hadn't been that generous a pour, anyway). 'Lead the way,' he told her.

She rested her hand on his arm for support as she got off her stool. Wycliff felt the heat from her hand to his arm. She wasn't scalding, but she was definitely a warm-blooded creature.

'I'm Wycliff,' he said, introducing himself.

'Call me Charlotte.'

'Nice car,' she remarked, when the valet brought

25

the Lexus around and opened the passenger door for her. She was wearing a slit skirt, so a nice bit of leg showed when she slid onto the creamy leather seat. Her legs were excellent, Wycliff noticed. He wondered if the rest of her body would measure up. The question was, would he find out? And if he did, then what?

He got into the car, palmed a tip to the valet, and pulled out into traffic, heading west on Sunset. 'Where to?' he asked her.

'Straight ahead,' she answered, adjusting her seatbelt. 'You'll turn left at Doheny. It isn't far.' She turned on the radio and found a soft jazz station. Not Wycliff's kind of music, but this was her party, until he figured out what she really wanted. As he drove down the congested Strip he looked around at the occupants of the other cars and the people who were walking, talking, and hanging out on the sidewalks. They all looked like they belonged. In this car, with this woman beside him, he looked like he belonged, too.

Her condo was a compact two-bedroom in a six-story building a block south of the Strip. She gave Wycliff the numbers for the security code and directed him to a spot in guest parking, and they rode the elevator up to her floor, one below the top. She led him down the corridor to her door. He followed her inside.

Right off, Wycliff could see that the place had been decorated by a woman who had taste and money. Modern, but not sterile. It fit the woman the way her dress did – it showed her off to her advantage while still holding something back.

26

'Nice place,' he complimented her.

'Your brother was my decorator.'

So she was a client of Billy's. It made sense she would recognize him. Her connecting the two of them was legit. 'Billy has good taste,' he said, looking at the room more carefully. Everything fitted perfectly.

'The best.'

For a moment, Wycliff was startled. Had this woman and his brother been lovers? Another piece to be fitted into the puzzle? Whatever the deal was with her, he needed to play it cool and slow.

There was a narrow balcony off the living room that was framed with floor-to-ceiling smoked-glass doors. The woman walked across the room, slid open a door, and stepped outside. The sounds of the city hummed up.

'On a clear day you can see to the ocean.' She was in silhouette from the moonlight, her back to him. 'That's why you live in a place like this,' she said, still looking out. She turned to him. 'Do you want a smoke? A drink?'

Wycliff wasn't going to make any decisions like that. Her place, her game. 'Either,' he answered. 'Or both. Whatever you're having.' He threw her one of his good boyish grins. 'I'm easy.'

She smiled back. 'I doubt that. But I'll take what you tell me at face value, until you show me otherwise.'

The Scotch she poured him was single malt. It tasted peaty, like he was drinking liquid bog. Wycliff liked that kind of Scotch, but it was expensive, so he didn't drink it very often. There was one ice-cube in it, like he'd requested. She was drinking gin and tonic, mostly tonic. She was pacing herself. He needed to be careful not to drink too much, too fast.

They sat outside on deck chairs. The night was warm and there was almost no breeze. She had American Spirits, so that's what they were smoking. Not a brand he favored, there wasn't enough flavor, but he wasn't complaining. This was going better than he could have expected or anticipated in his wildest imagination. And this was his first night in town.

The silence lay on them comfortably for a few minutes. She had kicked her heels off and was resting her stockinged feet on the railing. She rattled the ice cubes in her glass. 'I'd offer you some grass, but I don't know you well enough yet,' she said. 'I have to be careful.' She laughed, deep in her throat. 'I pick up a strange man in a bar, bring him home, and sit alone with him drinking. Not too careful, I'd say.'

'I'm not going to hurt you, if that's what you're worried about,' he told her. He was sincere; he wanted her to believe him. 'That's the last thing on my mind.'

She smiled at him. 'I know. You're Billy's brother.'

She was a force of nature in bed. Her firm, lush body had been sculpted by a great plastic surgeon, but so what? It's the results that count, and these results were stellar.

They sat up in her bed, smoking and drinking,

28

white wine now. Another thing to like about her: she smoked in bed. He couldn't remember the last woman he'd done that with.

'Where are you staying?' she asked him.

'At my brother's.'

She nodded, as if that's what she'd expected. 'Is anyone else there?'

'A caretaker.' Wycliff made a snap decision. 'But he's moving out, now that I'm here.' His fingers brushed her thigh. It felt like silk-covered ivory. 'Tomorrow.'

'Good,' she said.

Meaning? he thought. But she didn't elaborate, or question him further on the subject. Instead, she produced a tightly rolled joint and they smoked half of it, washing it down with the wine. Wycliff was in a groove like none he'd ever been in before. And why not? He was in bed with a beautiful, sexy, and yes, mysterious woman, smoking killer weed, drinking excellent wine, driving a fine set of foreign wheels (which he figured he could hang on to for a few more days before he had to dump it), had cash in his pocket, and to top it off, all this was happening in Los Angeles, home to the stars. The only comparison he could think of was Vegas, but Vegas was deliberately artificial, where you went to hide your naughty stuff – *what happens here, stays here*. This was the real deal, he was sure of it. The warm, musky, sensual body lying next to him was proof of that.

'So what's your agenda for tomorrow?' the woman asked him. 'Do you have one?'

They were dressed now, sitting in her living room. It was late, after midnight. They'd had sex again and drank another half bottle of wine, but slowly, over a couple of hours, so Wycliff was clear-headed. Not completely, but good enough. He'd be extra-careful driving back to Billy's place. His ride was hot and his license was bogus. A stupid DUI bust would blow his whole deal, which was way better now than it had been a few hours earlier.

'Go to the hospital in the morning,' he informed her. 'That's it, for now.'

'Good for you,' she said, as if giving him her seal of approval. 'Brothers need to stick together, especially in a crisis.' She took another cigarette out of her pack and lit it, blowing a smoke ring up at the ceiling. 'That leaves the afternoon free for us to go shopping. You need some decent clothes of your own, you can't wear your brother's stuff, it isn't your style. And don't worry about what it'll cost. It's on me. A loan, until you get on your feet, since you're new here.'

She was going to fuck him cross-eyed and outfit him too? What had he done to deserve this?

The puzzle. He had to remember that. She wanted something from him. What was it? Something illegal? If that's what it was, how dangerous would it be? He had to find out before he got in too deeply. Illegal he could handle; he had made a living scamming the system. But real danger, the kind that could get you killed or sent away for a long time, was something to be avoided at all costs. It was okay to be out on the edge, but not so far out that one stumble and over you went.

Be careful, he cautioned himself. Don't be another chump that got taken by a woman, no matter how alluring. Like what Glenn Close did to Michael Douglas in *Fatal Attraction*. He shivered, thinking about how it ended. He looked over at Charlotte, who was reclining on her sofa, smoking her cigarette. She was wearing a fluffy white Terry robe that sported a Four Seasons hotel logo on the breast pocket. Don't be one of those crazy ladies, he prayed as he stared at her.

She stood up. 'You have to go now. Pick me up tomorrow at one. I'll be waiting for you outside.'

Their good-night kiss at her front door was the perfect way to end the night. 'I hope I won't regret this,' she said.

'Regret it how?' Again, his antenna went up.

'All of it. And what's to come.' She licked his ear. It felt like he'd been zapped by a lightning bolt. 'I'm not as much a *femme fatale* as you're thinking I am. I'm too old to be now, if I ever was. I'm flattered you wanted to sleep with me, to tell you the truth. Not every young man would, especially one as attractive as you.'

And if a pig had wings... 'You're wrong about that,' he said. 'You're a beautiful woman. Your age doesn't matter.'

She smiled. 'I hope you keep thinking that.' Gently, she pushed him out the door. 'I need to get my beauty sleep. I don't think you'd feel the same about me if you saw me in the morning.'

31

'I bet I would.'

'That's sweet.' She gave him a quick peck on the cheek. As he turned to go, she stopped him. 'I don't think you should tell your brother you met me. Not yet.'

Maybe they really had been lovers, Wycliff thought, before Billy got sick. His brother could swing both ways. Especially with a woman this attractive. Even though she was old enough, he thought with a kinky flutter, to be his mother.

'Fine with me,' he agreed. 'You'll be my secret.'

She smiled. 'And you mine.'

THREE

Wycliff didn't have to give Stanley the boot. The forlorn caretaker had flown the coop on his own. He left a self-pitying note in what looked like a girl's handwriting: *I hope you're happy now, you narrow-minded shithead. Don't forget to water the plants.*

'Narrow minded?' Wycliff said out loud. 'That's the best you can do?' This dipshit had seriously underestimated his bigotries. 'Hell, son,' he declared pridefully to the room, as if he were working an audience at Caesar's, 'I'm an equal-opportunity, jack-of-all-trades prick! My brother didn't hip you about me?'

32

Whatever, good riddance to that sorry loser. I am in business! Wycliff thought gleefully. He had his own pad (at least until Billy came home, if he ever did), a primo set of wheels (short-term, but for now his ass was going to be riding on baby-soft leather), plus he'd connected with a rich, erotic, mystery woman who was going to lead him to who knows where? Something crazy, he knew that, for sure. But exciting.

This had been one hell of a day, he thought, as he stripped down to his Jockeys and crawled into his brother's bed, now laid with freshly washed sheets. He had come out here to try and wheedle, guilt-trip, threaten, whatever it took to get his dying sibling into cutting him into some of his estate. If Billy had offered him five grand to go away and never come back, he would have taken it in a heartbeat. Now, in less than twenty-four hours, he was way ahead of the curve.

Times have been lean, he thought to himself. Now they're going to be fat.

'You didn't waste any time,' Billy said sourly. He was propped up in bed on two fluffy pillows. He had been shaved and bathed and was wearing fresh pajamas, but he still looked awful. 'Stanley called and told me this morning. The poor man was in tears. He really extended himself for me, and you pissed all over him.'

Cried like a girl, Wycliff thought derisively. 'His choice, not mine,' he replied, faking like he really was sorry. It was a lame attempt that wouldn't have fooled a deaf man, not that he gave a damn. 'I would've been happy to share.

33

There was plenty of room for both of us.'

'Not enough for him, with you,' Billy corrected him. 'For anyone with you.'

Wycliff shrugged off the insult. 'We all have our demons.'

'Except yours are way more visible than other people's. Yours scream out.'

Wycliff thought of last night, with Charlotte. 'Some people like me the way I am,' he said, almost boastfully. 'Some people like it a lot.'

'Sick people.'

'You're about as sick as they come.' It was almost too easy, toying with Billy like this. He needed to rein that in. Eye on the prize. But he couldn't help digging. 'Are you saying you like me like I am? I thought it was the opposite.'

Billy's head lolled to the side, as if there was virtually no musculature in his neck to support it. 'Fuck off.'

It was ten in the morning. Wycliff had slept like a brick. After he woke up he took a long, scalding shower, cooked himself a bacon-and-eggs-and-coffee breakfast, dressed in his best remaining outfit, and read the *LA Times*, which he found on the front porch. Breakfast and the paper at home like a civilian, he thought, as he scanned the comics. There are benefits to living the square life. It was too bad he wasn't cut out for it. It must be nice, not to be living on the edge all the time.

Starting today, his life was going to be different. Change was in the air.

'Any word on when they're going to let you come home?' he asked.

Billy glanced at him, then away. 'No.'

'Haven't seen the doctor yet today?'

'He was by. We didn't talk about that.'

Wycliff looked at his brother more closely. They're never going to let this poor bastard out of here, he realized. He's going to die in this miserable place. That sucked. Billy was going to die anyway, and not in months, but weeks. Why not let him have the dignity of doing it in his own bed, in his own home, with his friends attending? Wycliff knew why: money. They could come on all pious about taking care of the patient better here, and they probably were sincere, he had to give these people some credit, they lived with these sick and dying victims day in and day out, but still, they got paid for it. The institution got paid by the patient, by how many beds they filled. Altruism only goes so far. It doesn't pay the bills.

'Whose decision is it?' he asked his brother.

'What decision?'

'When you can go home.'

Billy looked at Wycliff in surprise. 'It's up to the doctors,' he said. 'When they think I'm strong enough.'

Wycliff's brow furrowed. 'Strong enough for what? To bale hay? You're never going to get any stronger. And I know you good enough to know you don't bullshit yourself about stuff like that, it's too important.'

In truth, he didn't know that about Billy. He barely knew anything at all about his brother. But he knew it anyway, it was part of their shared DNA.

Billy's exhale was like stale air leaking out of a punctured tire. 'Strong enough to take care of myself.'

How stupid was that, Wycliff thought? 'You're never going to be. Wasn't that the point of Stanley? I'm sure there are dozens of your friends who would be happy to help you out.'

'Not dozens, but some,' Billy answered. He sounded embarrassed that more of his old friends wouldn't come to his aid. 'But at the stage I'm in, only family is legally permitted to be in charge of your care at home.'

They stared at each other. 'And I'm the only family you've got,' Wycliff said.

Billy held his look for a moment; then he turned away again. 'Right.'

Wycliff could hear the air-conditioner humming. It helped, but not enough. 'I could do it,' he said. 'They'd have to let me sign you out, wouldn't they?'

His brother started laughing. It came from his chest, like nails on a blackboard. The tortured laugh turned to a hacking cough.

Wycliff looked down with alarm. 'Jesus, man, don't check out on me now.' He leaned over and pulled Billy away from the bed, holding him against his chest, pushing rhythmically on his back. 'In and out. Come on.'

Billy got control of his breathing. He swallowed in deep gulps of air. 'Where did you learn to do that?' he asked in surprise.

'I worked in a hospital once.'

Billy stared at Wycliff with suspicion. 'I didn't know that.'

'What you don't know about me would fill the *Yellow Pages*. You hardly know anything about me,' Wycliff said. 'And vice versa.'

Billy nodded. 'To answer your question: yes, you could sign me out. You're the only one who can.' He licked his lips. 'So now we both know when I'm going to get out of here.'

Wycliff walked over to the window. The room was on the ground floor. The view, what little there was of it, was of the parking lot. 'Maybe I will,' he said, staring out.

Billy started laughing again, but caught himself before it became a hack. 'You're going to take care of me? That'll be the day. You have no idea of what that would entail.'

'As a matter of fact, I do.'

'Dealing with dying men who can't even wipe their own behinds?' Billy snorted. 'I can just picture you emptying bedpans and dressing open sores.'

'I've wiped plenty of butts in my day, believe me. And worse.'

That was true, every word. What Wycliff left unspoken was that the hospital had been in the Dade County, Florida jail, a notoriously tough place to do time. Volunteering for hospital duty had cut Wycliff's sentence of a year for kiting bad checks to four months. To shave two thirds off his time, he could endure cleaning shit and piss and vomit off sick men. Besides, the hospital was the only safe haven in the jail. In the general population you joined a gang for protection – in his case it would have been a skinhead gang, you stick with your own race, especially in a jail where most of the prisoners were Latino or black – or you became some heavyweight's jailhouse girlfriend. Wycliff was a pretty big guy, and under normal circumstances he could take care of himself, but inside that joint he was woefully inadequate. He had lied to the jail authorities about having worked in a hospital in the army. He knew they wouldn't check up, they needed all the willing help they could get.

He did his time and managed to survive a jailhouse virgin, but the experience seared him. He never wanted to face the prospect of being in that position again, because he knew that if there was a next time, he might not be so lucky. That was why he was careful, vigilant. Why he was going to be cautious regarding Charlotte.

'I've got a few deals going,' he told Billy. 'I don't know how long I'm going to be around. Of course, if things were different between us...'

Billy stared at him. 'You think I don't know your game, you moron? I could read you in Braille. The moment I signed any money over to you, you'd fly the coop like a hawk.'

'Then don't.'

'Don't what?' Billy asked with suspicion.

'Don't sign anything over. I'll get you out of here, take you home, take care of you. If and when you want to do anything for me, that will be up to you.'

Billy's face hardened with suspicion. 'What if I never do?'

'Then I helped my baby brother live his final days out with some dignity.' He smiled. 'Maybe God will reward me.'

'God doesn't know you exist.'

'Well,' Wycliff said, 'then that's a good reason to do it.'

FOUR

Charlotte, wearing a wide-brimmed hat that shaded her face against the sun, was waiting outside her building when Wycliff pulled up on the stroke of one. Even though her daytime outfit was more subdued than the one she had worn last night she still looked great, even better than he remembered. A beautiful, wealthy, mature lady who could shame most women half her age.

As he looked at her, his inner voice, the hard-earned voice of self-preservation, warned him: *do not forget how you met her, the out-of-nowhere improbability of it.* She was playing a game and he didn't know the rules. Hell, he didn't even know what the game was. He had to play it super cool. Don't let your emotions control your brain. Easier said than done.

'You look very nice,' he complimented her. 'Better than nice.'

'Same to you, cowboy,' she told him cheerily. She gave him a kiss on the cheek. Her perfume made him light headed.

'Where to?' he asked. Wherever she wanted to go, he was ready to follow.

'Culver City. There's a wholesale men's outlet

there that has the same selection as Barney's, at half the price. I only pay retail when I have no other choice.' She smiled. 'Somewhere in the past I must have Middle Eastern blood in my veins. The souk has always fascinated me.' She pointed out the window. 'Take this street to Venice Boulevard, then go west.'

Wycliff didn't know what a souk was, but he wasn't going to show his ignorance by asking. She already had him pegged, rightly, for a rube.

Charlotte fastened her seat belt and ran the manicured fingers of one hand along the smooth leather. 'How long have you had this car?'

'Not long.'

'I didn't think so.'

Meaning she was on to his heisting it? Or that it was so new he couldn't have had it long? He glanced over at her, but her face didn't reveal which choice was the right one. Lexuses were for women, anyway. He was more the BMW or Audi type. The M3 Beemer would be a great ride, but a car that hot could be a red flag. No need to advertise his presence. A nice 5-series sedan would do just fine. With the big engine. Never mind, he already had a gorgeous older woman for a lover, a hot set of wheels, and a new wardrobe on its way. What was next, winning the lottery?

'Penny for your thoughts,' Charlotte said, breaking his reverie. The tone of her voice indicated she already knew them.

'You,' he told her. That was easy to say, because it was true, so he didn't have to come up with a lie, his more normal MO. 'My brother

40

coming home. A beautiful day. Life could be worse.'

'Or better,' she answered. 'Or both,' she added, somewhat cryptically. 'Turn right at the next light.'

The jewelry store was on a quiet side street on the eastern edge of Beverly Hills. Wycliff parked around the corner, per Charlotte's instructions. As they got out, she reached into the back seat for one of the new sports coats she had bought him, a navy-blue Brioni. 'Put this on,' she said, slipping it out of its plastic bag. 'And your hat, too.'

She had known precisely the look she wanted for him. One dark suit for special occasions, a couple of sports coat and slacks combos, shoes, shirts, neckties, and accessories: Armani shades, Rolex Oyster Perpetual watch (a good knock-off), and a Dodgers hat (*'you are in LA now, darling'*).

He did as instructed. Charlotte nodded her approval. 'Are you packing?' she asked casually.

He jumped. *'A gun?'*

'No, a hatpin. What else would I be asking about?'

He shook his head, flustered. 'No.'

She snapped open her large Gucci purse and pulled out a short-barrel S&W revolver, the classic FBI model. Wycliff had fired one at a shooting range in the Arizona desert when he was testing various under-the-table pieces (as an ex-felon, he couldn't buy a gun legally). He had wound up purchasing a Glock 17, a sweet agent

41

of destruction, but he'd had to pawn it to cover the rent, and he had not yet raised the scratch to redeem it. This little S&W was considered old fashioned, but it had plenty of kick. You hit your target with it, they're going down.

'Take this,' she told him. 'Just in case.'

He recoiled. This relationship had suddenly vaulted to a higher plateau. 'In case of what?' he stuttered.

'In case the Martians invade us.' She thrust the gun into his hand. It felt heavy, solid. 'Put it away.'

He slipped the gun into his waistband at the small of his back and looked over his shoulder to see if there was a tell-tale bulge under his sports coat. There wasn't.

They walked around the corner to the store's entrance. The reinforced steel door was locked. Charlotte pushed a buzzer. A moment later, the door lock clicked open. Charlotte turned the knob and entered, Wycliff on her heels. 'Keep your hat on and your hands to yourself,' she told him as the door silently closed behind them with an authoritative *thunk*.

The store was plush. Low lighting, thick wall-to-wall carpeting, a pair of matching oxblood-colored leather club chairs. A select display of women's jewelry – bracelets, earrings, rings – nestled behind the locked display cases. Reflexively, Wycliff looked up to the ceiling. A surveillance camera was tucked in one of the corners behind the counter, aimed downwards. SOP for a place like this. An old con he had befriended in the joint, who specialized in high-

42

end burglaries, had hipped him to the fact that most of the cameras were dummies, their mere presence usually enough of a sufficient deterrent to discourage theft.

There were no other customers in the store. A muscled-up security guard (ex-cop or military, Wycliff figured, from the fit look on him, not one of those cheesy mall cop wannabes) was planted against the far wall, his holstered gun prominently displayed on his hip. It was identical to the Glock Wycliff had once owned, and now didn't. He glanced at the automatic with envy. This dude's piece was definitely bigger than his.

A swarthy middle-aged man in a Versace suit, his skin-tone identifying him as Middle Eastern, entered from behind a closed door at the rear of the store. 'Mrs Cooper!' he greeted Charlotte warmly. He cast an inquisitive look at Wycliff.

'My associate,' she introduced Wycliff, without offering up a name. Meaning, they both understood, my bodyguard. 'In case I buy that diamond-and-emerald ring today and take it with me. I do covet that ring,' she trilled. Her voice had taken on a subtle southern accent.

'An exquisite piece,' the owner agreed. 'It's in my safe. I'll bring it out for you.'

He went into the back room to get it. 'I love this store,' Charlotte declared. 'So tastefully decadent. Lordy, what the rich spend their money on.'

'Like you?'

'That's rude.'

'You're here to buy a diamond ring, aren't

43

you? Expensive enough you want me armed for protection.'

She looked at the security guard, who was out of earshot at the opposite side of the room. 'Keep your voice down. In fact, stay quiet altogether.'

That stung. 'You brought it up.'

'Oh, I'm sorry. Did I hurt baby's delicate feelings?' She leaned towards him. Her voice, soft and husky, was barely more than a whisper, but the force was intense. 'Cool it for now.'

Wycliff was in over his head, and her sudden toughness towards him confirmed it. He took a step back, glancing as he did at the rent-a-cop, who stared back at him with opaque eyes.

The proprietor returned from the back. He set a piece of dark velvet cloth on the counter and unfolded it.

The ring, set in platinum, featured a large oval-shaped diamond in the center surrounded by several emeralds. Charlotte looked at it with a discerning eye. 'Beautiful,' she murmured. 'Absolutely stunning.'

'One of the finest I've come across in a long time,' the owner agreed.

Charlotte delicately picked the ring up. 'May I?'

'Of course.'

She slid the ring onto the second finger of her left hand, which was otherwise unadorned. 'This is beyond perfection.' She extended her hand and looked at it adoringly. 'How much is this piece of heaven on earth?'

The owner smiled. 'Six hundred thousand

dollars. The same figure I quoted the last time you visited us.'

Wycliff felt the blood rushing to his head. That rock was worth over half a million dollars? How much was the rest of the inventory in this story worth? Tens of millions, had to be.

Charlotte held her hand out to him. The ring was dazzling against her pale skin and blood-red nails. 'Buy it for me, would you, darling?' she said. 'I would be *ever* so grateful.'

Wycliff's knees buckled. Charlotte laughed. 'Don't stop breathing. I'm just funning on you.' She turned back to the store owner. 'The others you showed me. May I look at them as well?'

'Certainly.' He retreated to his office again.

'What do you think?' Charlotte asked Wycliff. She held her hand up and looked at the ring on her finger. 'Should I buy it?'

The question staggered him. 'Jesus, don't ask me. Six hundred thousand dollars for a ring? For Kobe Bryant, maybe, but not regular mortals.'

She gave him a penetrating look. 'You have to set your sights high, darling. That's what dreams are for. I've been a dreamer all my life. A dreamer and a schemer. You can't have one without the other.'

Wycliff knew about dreams. And he certainly was hip to the scheming side; most of his life had been devoted to one scheme or another. Not at this level, but he understood where Charlotte was coming from. *Maybe that's been my problem. Maybe I haven't schemed at a high-enough level. If you are going to fail – which I always have – you might as well fail high.*

45

Maybe she could teach him how.

The owner emerged from the back room with a long, narrow jewelry box. He opened it to reveal half a dozen rings, all featuring large diamonds as their centerpieces. Carefully, he took the rings out of the box and placed them on a soft cloth on the counter.

'Can I examine them more closely?' Charlotte asked.

'Of course.' He took a loupe from his pocket and handed it to her.

She took the ring off her finger and put it on the cloth next to the others. Then she placed the jeweler's glass against her eye and brought one of the new rings up to it, slowly turning the ring from side to side.

This is not this lady's first rodeo, Wycliff thought, as he watched her examine the ring. She knows what she's doing and she checks everything out. Which brought him up short. If Charlotte was this vigilant in examining a piece of jewelry, she would be as meticulous in finding out everything she needed to know about a human being. His instincts told him that she had an agenda, and that he was part of it. Be careful, he warned himself. You don't know these waters. There could be sharks lurking under the surface.

Charlotte put the second ring down and shook her head ruefully. 'This is what happens when you climb Mount Everest. Every other mountain is a molehill in comparison.' She picked the first ring up again, looked at it fondly, put it down. 'Don't get me wrong, they're all beautiful. But they aren't...' She didn't need to finish her thought.

'Yes,' the owner agreed. He was on her wavelength.

As she handed him his loupe it slipped from her fingers, sliding across the counter and onto the floor. 'I'm sorry,' she apologized, bending over the counter to see where it had landed. 'I hope I didn't scratch it. There it is,' she pointed.

'Not to worry,' the owner assured her as he retrieved the eyepiece from the floor.

Charlotte pursed her lips in concentration. 'I have to have that ring,' she declared. 'I have a meeting with my accountant on Monday. I will beat him over the head with an ax handle until he agrees to let me have it. It is my money, after all.' She was building up a good head of steam against the absent financial advisor. 'What are stock certificates? Pieces of paper. You can't admire them, you can't wear them, you can't turn your friends green with envy over them. That ring will surely appreciate, don't you think?'

'Absolutely,' the owner assured her. 'It will double in value in five years or less. I give you my blood oath.'

She laughed. 'That won't be necessary. Just don't sell it out from under me.'

'I promise I won't.'

Charlotte turned to Wycliff. 'Isn't this fun?' Her eyes were sparkling.

Fun? Wycliff thought. His heart was pounding, and it wasn't even him who was laying a small fortune on the line. 'Yes,' he told her. That was what she wanted to hear. 'It's fun.'

Juan, the *hermano* in Pacoima who owned the chop shop, was a walking slab of concrete, sporting jailhouse tattoos all over his arms and neck. 'So you know my man Aaron Montoya, over there in Arizona?'

'Yeah, we've done stuff together in the past,' Wycliff affirmed. *Stuff* meaning the occasional B&E. Aaron had given him this dude's name, in case Wycliff ever needed to do business on the west coast. 'He's good people,' he said.

'The best,' Juan agreed.

The Blue Book on the Lexus was $39,500. Juan offered seven large. 'Which is generous, bro', this car's already on the national hot list.' Wycliff didn't hesitate – he snatched the bills out of the man's hand like it was the last pork chop on a boarding-house platter.

'In the market for fresh wheels now?' the big man asked.

'Yes,' Wycliff answered, 'but cleaner than this one. I've got to play it extra safe.'

'Copy that,' Juan agreed. 'Anything particular you got a hankering for?'

'BMW,' Wycliff answered. 'An Audi S4 would be fine, too.'

The chop-shop owner whipped out his cell phone and speed-dialed. 'Richard, it's Juan. Dude of my acquaintance just blew into town, needs a car with paper that'll pass for legit. Something of the Germanic persuasion would be his first choice. He's cool, I'll vouch for him.' A moment of listening, then: 'On his way.' He snapped the phone shut. '2010 3-series Beemer, cherry ride. The paperwork will get you into Fort Knox. My man will work a sweet deal for you.' He brought up a ball of phlegm and hocked it onto the concrete floor. 'Hey, Chuy,' he called across the room to another behemoth, who was taping a Porsche for priming. 'Take a break and give this dude a lift over to Richard Ortega's.'

Wycliff and the owner shook hands. 'Nice to do business with you, partner,' the man said. 'You come across another car to unload, you know where to find me. I particularly can use Escalades and E-class Mercedes.'

Wycliff smiled. 'I'll keep that in mind.'

Twilight was fading into evening when Wycliff pulled into the driveway of his brother's house in his new ride, a metallic-platinum BMW 335i. He carried a sack of groceries and his fresh-from-the-store wardrobe inside and turned on some lights. The house was warm and inviting. If you had to die, this would be as good a place as any to do it. Billy would be at peace here, in his own, familiar surroundings. With a loving family member at his side.

After he and Charlotte left the jewelry store, they had a late-afternoon drink at a wine bar in West Hollywood, then he brought her home. She had an engagement in the evening. They would get together again tomorrow. She didn't tell him what the engagement was and he didn't ask, although he was mildly curious. Maybe she was seeing another man. For all he knew she could be married and had some kind of arrangement with her husband. He didn't think that was the case, but with this woman anything seemed possible.

She was trouble – that he did know – in spades. What kind of trouble was the question. As long as she didn't put him in a hot box, he would swing with it. She was glamorous, great in bed, and had money: everything he had always wanted in a woman. Even her age was a positive. There was no chance of a long-term relationship. Theirs was not going to be an open-ended affair. She would use him for what she needed him for, he would get whatever he could out of it, and they would move on. Hopefully, trouble free. Wycliff had never been in a relationship that hadn't ended badly. Maybe this would be the one that would break his losing streak.

He fired up the Weber's on the back patio and grilled a couple of center-cut pork chops, which he ate with potato salad and an ear of corn, the food washed down with two cold Bohemias. A Camel filter and a slug of Gentleman Jack for dessert. He would not smoke inside, he would maintain the interior as a sterile chamber for his dying brother.

The Dodgers were beating the Diamondbacks on Billy's hi-def big-screen Sony. Wycliff sprawled out on the couch until the game was over, then remained there, out of *ennui* more than anything else, as the local news segued into commercials for Cialus, women's roll-on deodorant, Wal-Mart.

He was bushed. He reached for the remote to turn the set off.

'*In Beverly Hills, a brazen robbery in a*

50

jewelry store.'

His hand froze on the controls.

The newscaster continued: *'An unidentified woman, who the police speculate is a professional at this type of theft, stole an expensive ring from an exclusive jewelry store this afternoon. The woman had been in the store before, trying on the ring, and when she returned, accompanied this time by an unknown man who authorities assume was part of the sting, she was able to divert the store owner's attention long enough to take the ring and leave before the theft was noticed. Cosmo Kalajian, the owner of the store, estimates the value of the stolen ring at over half a million dollars. According to a statement issued by the Beverly Hills Police Department, unless the ring turns up in a pawnshop or another jewelry store it will probably not be recovered.'*

Dumb-ass doofus! Wycliff silently cursed himself. The gun Charlotte had foisted on him should have been an alarm bell in his head, warning him this woman was not some housewife treating herself to a trinket. If there was ever a time for a stiff shot of Gentleman Jack, this was it. He turned off the set, pried himself off the couch, and walked into the kitchen. The telephone rang. He jumped in startled panic, his heart pounding in his chest. The phone rang again, loud, shrill. It's not for you, he told himself. No one knows you're here.

Which was not true. His brother knew. Stanley, the former occupant, knew. And of course, Charlotte knew. Who else? He had not told anyone else; had he? His mind was racing. He couldn't remember. Hell, he could barely breathe.

A third ring. The ring tone was loud, like a hammer hitting an anvil. Maybe Billy's hearing had deteriorated because of his illness and the phone was turned up extra high.

Wycliff couldn't stop himself. He tore the receiver off the hook.

'Are you watching the evening news, by any chance?'

'Yes,' he choked out. He felt his blood heating up in his chest. What would happen if it actually boiled inside him? Would he blow a gasket? More likely, a heart attack, which right this moment did not seem that far-fetched.

'You have nothing to worry about,' Charlotte told him, her voice maddeningly calm and assured. 'You're fresh off the shelf here. No one knows you exist, except me.'

He wanted to reach through the line and strangle her. 'This caper of yours could put me in prison.' His throat was constricting, he could barely force the words out. 'There was a video camera! We're on tape! Why in God's name did you involve me?'

'Don't be a baby,' she scolded him. 'If there actually was a tape, they would have shown it. And you were wearing a hat, so your face was covered. I'll explain everything when I see you.'

'Is that why you called?' he bleated. He sounded like the lamest little bitch in the world.

Charlotte's voice, in contrast, was molten honey: her self-control was infuriating. 'I called to make sure you don't act rashly, like making a beeline out of town.'

That very thought had been coursing through his mind.

She punctuated the silence. 'Are you still there, Wycliff?'

He groaned. 'Yeah, I'm here.'

'Take two aspirin and go to bed. You'll feel better in the morning.'

The phone went dead in his hand. He stared at it like it was a dead rat. Numbly, he dropped the receiver back onto the cradle.

He couldn't call her back, he didn't know her phone number. He didn't even know her real name. Anything about her, truth be told. *She's setting you up, dummy. For a big, goddamned fall.*

There was nothing he could do about it. His instinct, which flashed in big neon letters, was to cut and run. And that was the one thing he could not do. Not because of her. He didn't owe her squat. She had spent a few hundred dollars outfitting him. From what he had seen of her lifestyle, she could easily afford it.

The reason he couldn't leave was his brother. He had given Billy his word that he would get him out of that miserable deathtrap of a hospital and bring him to his own home, so he could die with some dignity. They were polar opposites, him and Billy. Cain and Abel. But this time around, the evil brother would not slay the good one.

Wycliff didn't think he could fall asleep, but he conked out as soon as his head hit the pillow. His dreams were turbulent. He was being chased by pursuers unknown, he was looking for something or someone he could not find, the world was closing in on him. All in vivid color and violence, like an X-rated comic book.

The knocking on the door sounded like a rifle shot. He sat bolt upright. He slept commando, so his first move, once his brain unscrambled enough to realize this was not a nightmare, was to grab his pants and struggle into them.

Three more raps. Not hard knocks, like cop bang-bangs. Three steady tattoos.

The revolver that Charlotte had thrust upon him was on the side table next to his wallet and keys. He snatched it up, cracking the barrel to make sure it was loaded; a fundamental detail he had neglected to do earlier. Another rookie mistake.

It was loaded, fully. Five copper-jacketed .38 bullets, all snuggled in their chambers. He wasn't looking for trouble, but if it came, he was prepared.

All the lights were off. Thank God for that, the darkness gave him cover. He slipped out of bed and crept from the bedroom to the living room.

The front door opened directly in from the street. Holding his breath, he tiptoed around the perimeter of the room, hugging the walls, until he was next to the window that overlooked the street. He pressed his face against the glass and peered out.

He jerked the door open. Charlotte, clad in a raincoat over bare legs, stood on the threshold. Her hands were in her pockets to keep them warm from the chilly late-night fog. She was wearing just enough makeup to smooth out the rough spots.

'This is how people get shot,' Wycliff rasped at her.

Her look to him was one of infuriating calmness. 'Can I come in?' she asked. Without waiting for an answer, she stepped past him. He slammed the door shut behind her as she walked into the center of the room. 'Nice,' she commented, looking it over. 'What do you have to drink?'

There was a bottle of white wine tucked in the back of the refrigerator. He popped the cork and poured two glasses. Charlotte gracefully lowered herself into a Herman Miller Eames lounge chair, crossing one regal leg over the other. Wycliff perched on the couch across from her. She took a sip of wine and placed the glass on the side table.

'Here's the lowdown on that television story,' she said. 'It's a load of crap from start to finish.' She held up her left hand. The ring glistened on her finger. 'Beautiful, isn't it?'

Speechless, Wycliff gaped at the rock.

'It's also worthless,' Charlotte told him. 'Any reputable jeweler would take one look at it and kick you out the door.'

Wycliff's head was spinning. 'Then what was the point?

Charlotte laughed. 'Money, my darling. Money is always the point.'

She explained: 'That owner has been trying to run with Harry Winston and Tiffany for years.

Before the economy tanked in 2008 he managed to keep his head above water, but once the bottom dropped out...' She pointed her thumb to the floor. 'Even though the economy has recovered, he didn't. The customers don't come to him anymore.'

Wycliff was lost. This was moving too fast for him.

'What do you do when your business goes kaput?' Charlotte asked rhetorically. 'You sell off your inventory for whatever you can get for it, dimes on the dollar if you're lucky. But you're still under water, so you burn the building down and collect the insurance. Except this poor shlub doesn't own the building, so he's shit out of luck there.'

She smiled. 'And that's where I come in. The shady lady walks out with the ring and the distraught owner calls the police. They investigate his claim, and validate it. His insurance company will bitch and moan, but ultimately they will pay up. They'll negotiate a price well under the stated amount, but it will still be hefty.'

She took another little sip of wine – she was careful not to drink too much. He had noticed that about her the first time they met. 'What the smarty-pants insurance doofuses don't know,' she continued deliciously, 'is that the ring they appraised two years ago and my ring aren't the same. The real ring was sold on the black market. To a Chinese buyer, I presume, they buy everything. This one' – she held up her hand again to show him – 'is one hundred percent bogus. Glass and silicone. What you win when you knock over the bowling balls at the county fair.'

She put her glass down. 'Everyone goes home happy. The insurance company low-balled the owner on the premium, he puts his illegal gains in his bank account, and my fee covers my expenses for a year. It's a win-win, all around.'

Wycliff's mind reeled. Charlotte was all woman, but she sure did have brass *cojones*. They were birds of a feather. The difference was that she flew high, and he didn't. Not yet. If he hung with her, though, maybe he could learn how to soar.

There was something off with this, though, and he had to find out what it was. 'Why did you need me if it was all a set-up?' he asked her. 'You didn't need my help to pull off this caper. You could have done it just as easily on your own.'

She nodded in agreement. 'No,' she admitted, 'I didn't need your help. But I did need something from you. Something more important than you standing behind me with a gun in your pocket.'

'What was that?' he asked. He wasn't sure he wanted to hear the reason.

'I needed to find out if you had the balls to be a player. That you wouldn't cut and run.' She smiled. 'You stood firm. You passed the test.' She paused. 'This time.'

She sat up straight. 'One thing I have to know,' she said sharply. 'You didn't touch anything in the store, did you? I specifically told you not to.'

He had kept his hands to himself, per her

instructions. He hadn't even opened or closed the store's door, even though, as the man, he should have. Charlotte had done that. She had done everything.

'No,' he answered. 'I didn't touch anything. No fingerprints, if that's what you're worried about.'

'Good boy.' Her tone was like an owner's complimenting a dog that had been trained to roll over and play dead.

She had nothing on under the raincoat and he was butt-naked under his jeans, so stripping down for action was quick and easy. As before, their love making was an explosion.

Her cab was idling at the curb. He walked her outside. 'Pick me up later today,' she told him. 'Not too early, I need my beauty sleep. We'll continue with your makeover.' She kissed him on the tip of his nose. 'I love playing Henry Higgins. For most of my life I've been Eliza.'

Not for the first time was Wycliff clueless regarding what she was talking about. He waited until the taxi drove down the street and out of sight. Then he went back inside, made sure all the doors were locked, and poured himself a stiff bourbon nightcap.

FIVE

The salon on Rodeo Drive was way classier than the one in Tucson where he had pinched the Lexus. That was Arizona; this was Beverly Hills, California, where the world learns what class is all about. Charlotte had said nothing about his new wheels when he picked her up outside her condo, except to remark that this car was more his style. Where or how he got it was seemingly of no concern to her.

The receptionist at the front desk confirmed his name in the appointment book. 'Last-minute cancellation, lucky for us,' Charlotte informed him. 'Usually it takes weeks to get a booking.' She instructed his stylist on precisely how she wanted Wycliff's hair to look, then left him to have her nails done.

Two hours later, after a shampoo, rinse, cut, blow-dry, and color highlights, Wycliff arose from the chair a changed man, at least on the outside. When the finished product was revealed in the front and back mirrors he gaped at himself in slack-jawed disbelief. This dude in the reflection was as sleek as a seal. His hair color, for his entire life a muddy brown, was now the shade of dark mink, with subtle blond highlights. As a bonus, his scraggly beard had been shaved as smooth as a baby's ass. He had not seen his unadorned face in over fifteen years. Not a bad-looking guy, if he did say so himself.

Charlotte beamed her approval. 'Lovely, Fernando,' she complimented the stylist, as she handed him a sheaf of bills. 'You are a true miracle worker.'

She hadn't used a credit card. He remembered that yesterday, she had paid cash for his new wardrobe. This woman leaves no trail.

Dazed and dazzled, he let her lead him outside. He couldn't remember the last time he had felt the sun on the back of his neck. 'A huge improvement,' Charlotte complimented him. 'Now you don't look like a Barstow truck driver.' She took his jaw in her small hand and twisted his face one way, then the other. 'No one will recognize you from your old look.'

Meaning he couldn't be matched up to a surveillance tape if there turned out to be one. That was a heavy load off his shoulders. She wasn't one step ahead of him, she was in front by leaps and bounds.

'Lordy Miz Claudy!' Billy exclaimed breathlessly. He could barely get the words out, he had so little lung power. 'This can't be you.'

Wycliff, standing at his brother's hospital bedside, was sharply dressed in a slick guyabara shirt and black linen slacks that Charlotte had picked out for him. 'It's me, pal,' he confirmed. 'The me that was always there, just waiting for the right time to get out from under.'

'From under the right rock.'

Christ, Billy, let it go already. He didn't say so out loud. He knew all too well that after a lifetime of hostility, that was hard to do. Yet somehow he was learning to do exactly that. It was amazing how much better it felt. Hopefully, his brother would learn that, too. It would help him find peace in his final days.

Billy squinted at him through weak eyes. 'Man, what a change.' His diseased-gum grimace was wolverine. 'You have a rough-trade kind of appeal, Wycliff, now that you've lost the cave-man look. If you wanted to go on the gay hustle, you could make serious money.'

'Not my thing, but thanks for the compliment.' The thought of having sex with a man repulsed him. Scared the shit out of him, too. A fate that could await him if he ever wound up back in prison.

Billy's release papers were in order. The hospital attendants bathed, shaved, and dressed him for the last time, then wheeled him down the corridor to the elevator. Wycliff trailed behind. The entire on-duty staff, including the doctors, formed a congratulatory farewell line. Some of the women dabbed at their eyes.

Outside, waiting for the valet to bring the car around, Wycliff handed Billy a pair of sunglasses. 'Your eyes are weak,' he said, repeating one of the instructions Billy's doctor had given him. 'They can't handle harsh light.'

Billy fumbled the glasses onto his face. He was so gaunt they made him look like Mr Magoo. 'Thanks,' he muttered. He was breathing in short, panting bursts. Wycliff unscrewed a

61

bottle of Evian and handed it to his brother, who drank in thirsty gulps.

The BMW, all bright and shiny, arrived at the curb. 'Is that yours?' Billy asked suspiciously.

'Lock, stock, and pink slip,' Wycliff answered breezily. Not exactly true, but so what? His brother wasn't about to run a DMV check.

'I thought you were down and out. You must be doing better than I guessed.'

If you only knew... 'Way better.'

He lifted Billy up out of the hospital wheelchair and deposited him in the front passenger's seat, securing the seat belt as if for a child. He tipped the valet, made a minor adjustment in the rear-view mirror, and pulled away into the traffic flow. Billy stared out the window as the car purred down Beverly Blvd. 'I never thought I'd see this again.'

Wycliff glanced over. 'See what?'

'The rest of the world, outside that hospital room.'

'Makes you appreciate the little things.'

Billy looked at Wycliff. His brother he had never really known and now hardly recognized. 'Yes,' he agreed. His voice was thin and strained. 'It really does.'

Wycliff parked in the driveway and got out. 'Wait here,' he said. As if this poor bag of bones could go anywhere without being assisted. He went into the house and came out a moment later pushing a wheelchair. He opened Billy's car door, lifted him out, and set him in the chair, making sure he was secure, so he wouldn't fall over.

'Brand spanking new,' he told Billy. 'You can rent one, but I didn't want you sitting on someone else's dried-up sweat. You need as much of a germ-free environment as possible.'

'How do you know all this?' his brother asked. He couldn't keep the suspiciousness from his voice. A new hairstyle and wardrobe didn't make up for a lifetime of lies and deceit.

Wycliff wasn't going to let Billy's hostility get under his skin. If the shoe had been on the other foot, he would have reacted the same way. 'I've been reading up on it. The hospital workers gave me advice. The hospice people, too.'

That was true, but there was a large omission in his accounting. His practical knowledge about cleanliness had come from his on-the-job training in the Florida jail hospital. Men died there needlessly and stupidly from routine infections that could have been avoided if the staff paid attention to simple stuff like washing their hands and autoclaving their instruments.

He wheeled his brother up the walkway to the front door. 'Ready?'

'I've been ready since the day they carted me out of here. Waiting for this has felt like forever.'

'Then welcome back to your home.' Wycliff opened the door and wheeled his brother inside.

The hospice contingent, two women and a man, had arrived early in the morning. They had converted the living room into an at-home hospital room: hospital bed, oxygen canisters, all the necessary implements required for a patient who was already in bad shape and would only get worse. A new window air-conditioner had been installed to keep the temperature a steady 72 degrees. Even though the house had been cherried out and updated, the wiring was iffy for handling the extra power an air-conditioner would pull, so Wycliff had done a heavy-up on the electrical system to make sure it wouldn't overload. Back when he had tried to get his life in some kind of order, he had been a journeyman electrical assistant. He could wire a building pretty good. He prided himself on that skill, one of the few accomplishments he had done in his life he could boast on.

Billy appraised the set-up from his wheelchair. 'Oh, man,' he said softly.

'The president of the United States wouldn't get it any better,' Wycliff told him.

The flowers were the sweet touch. After the hospice people had finished and left, Wycliff had gone to Trader Joe's and bought half a dozen cheap bouquets, which were displayed in vases set about the room. They filled the air with a fragrant redolence.

He helped Billy out of his clothes and into a new pair of pajamas. His brother was so weak he couldn't undress or dress himself. Wycliff handled him like he was a newborn as he lifted him onto the bed, which had an egg-crate mattress pad on top of the regular mattress, to prevent bed sores. He could feel the bones under the skin, which was as fine as parchment. The bones felt like dry twigs. One slip and his brother could break a leg, a hip. Had to be careful not to let that happen.

They sat together for the afternoon, watching daytime TV. The television had been set up so Billy could watch it comfortably from his bed. He dozed on and off. When he woke up, Wycliff heated some soup he had stocked up on from Whole Foods. Everything his brother ate or drank was going to be organic. His death was inevitable, but if they could hold it off an extra week, a month, that would be a victory.

The first relief attendant, a wiry Filipino, showed up at four. He would work an eight-hour shift, so Wycliff was free until midnight. Hiring help was expensive, but Billy's estate could afford it. He had discussed the costs and arrangements with Billy, and once Billy had been assured this wasn't one of his brother's shady scams, he had called his lawyer and made the financial arrangements. All the money would flow through the lawyer: Wycliff wouldn't touch a cent. That was fine with him. If there was a payoff for doing good it would come after Billy died, and it would be big. Jeopardizing that possibility was stupid. You don't jump over dollars to pick up dimes.

'Any special instructions?' the attendant asked in a slight sing-song accent, scrutinizing the layout.

'Just keep him comfortable and happy,' Wycliff said. 'The medical chart is in the kitchen. My cell phone, his doctor's.' He bent over his brother, now awake and watching Oprah. 'I've got to go out for a little bit. I won't be gone long,' he promised. 'Anything you want me to pick up?'

'No.' Billy scrunched his dry bloodshot eyes, one of the multitudes of painful afflictions he was suffering from, with more on the way as he regressed further. Life's a bitch and then you die, Wycliff thought. He gently tilted his brother's head back and gave him a squirt of Liquid Tears in each eye. Billy blinked from the soothing drops. 'Thanks.' His voice was a wheezy gasp.

'Don't exert yourself,' Wycliff cautioned him. 'You need anything, that's what Diego's here for.'

'His name is Diego?' Billy asked, painfully craning his neck to look at the caregiver, who was in the kitchen boiling water for tea.

'Hell, I don't know what his name is.' Latinos were Jose, blacks Rufus, Filipinos Diego, Chinese Chan, whatever. He didn't think of his attitude as racist; it was simply an easy way to deal with a bunch of foreigners who wouldn't mean anything to him, once this was over.

Billy sagged back on the fluffy pillow. Just that much exertion had exhausted him. Wycliff patted his brother's hand. He could see the veins throbbing through the skin. 'You're home, man. Where you're supposed to be.'

Real tears formed in his brother's eyes. 'Thank you,' he whispered.

SIX

Charlotte took him to dinner at a sushi restaurant in Little Tokyo. 'You've never experienced a meal like the one you're about to have,' she promised him. Wycliff didn't know if that was a good thing or not.

The restaurant was a narrow hole in the wall, a front-to-back Formica counter with a dozen plain wooden stools. You practically had to squeeze in sideways between the stools and the opposing wall to get by. The calendars and posters on the walls were in Japanese, featuring pictures of tourist-looking sites. A small overhead television was playing a Japanese soap opera without English subtitles. No one seemed to be watching.

The lone sushi chef behind the counter, a stern-looking older man, was dressed in a traditional white sushi coat. His jet-black hair was bound up in a blue-checked bandana. A dazzling array of raw fish was geometrically arrayed in front of him. The waitress, a young woman with tiny porcelain features, wore tight black slacks and a white blouse of some synthetic material that clung like Saran wrap on her skinny frame. She had a row of earrings in her left ear, including a long dangler with a pearl in the center. She

67

tottered up and down the aisle in gravity-defying high-heeled shoes, dispensing hot moist towelettes and drinks.

All the stools were occupied except for two in the center, which had *reserved* placards on the place mats. When Wycliff and Charlotte sat down, the waitress whisked the signs away.

'*Konnichiha,*' Charlotte greeted the chef. He grunted back at her. She picked up the sake list, looked it over, and pointed out her choice to the waitress. 'You drink sake, don't you?' she asked Wycliff as she washed her hands briskly. She folded her towel and placed it to the side. 'Its wine, made from rice.'

He followed her lead on the hand washing. 'Yes,' he answered. He'd had it a few times. He preferred whiskey or beer, but the Japanese stuff wasn't too bad.

'And you eat sushi, I assume. You'd better, for what a meal here costs.'

He watched as the chef placed two pieces of raw fish on rice patties and put them on a wooden board in front of the man sitting next to Wycliff. The fish was dark red. It looked like it had been alive five minutes ago. The patron looked familiar, from a television series, Wycliff was pretty sure. What was the name of that show? He couldn't place it, but he recognized the face.

The unknown celebrity picked up the first piece with his thumb and forefinger and looked at it like he was going to cry with joy. He ate the morsel in one bite, paused a moment, then did the same with the second. 'If this isn't heaven, it's damn close,' he said to his companion perched on the stool next to his, a beautiful woman who definitely looked well known. Another television star? From one of the reality shows, like *American Idol*? Wycliff wasn't about to make an ass of himself by asking them who they were, but he would have liked to know. Eating elbow to elbow with a television star and his hot lady friend who is also probably famous, you don't get opportunities like that back in Tucson or any of the other places he had lived in.

What the couple was eating was another matter. Wycliff could feel his stomach talking to him. He did not like raw fish. The one time he had tried it, he had thrown up later. If he had known this was where Charlotte was taking him he would have told her to save her money.

'I've had it,' he said, answering her question. 'But I don't care much for it.' He tried to make a joke. 'Where I come from, civilized people cook their food.' They had to have some cooked food here, even if it was plain rice.

'Where you come from they eat road kill, so I wouldn't be judgmental if I were you.'

She was laying it on extra thick, but he knew what she meant – another dig at his past life. 'I try not to judge,' he said. 'My pot's blacker than just about anyone else's kettle.'

'That's a good quality to have. You do have some redeeming features.'

The waitress brought their sake and poured two tiny cups. Charlotte raised hers in toast. 'To acceptance,' she offered.

'I'll drink to that.' He clinked his cup to hers

69

and downed the liquid in one gulp. The taste surprised him, it was good.

'You order for me, I wouldn't know one dish from the other,' he told her. 'But cooked, okay?' He didn't want to barf in front of whoever this unknown celebrity was.

Charlotte shook her head. 'You don't pick and choose here. Chef gives you what he wants you to eat. You might not think it from the looks of this place, but people make pilgrimages from all over to eat here. It's a harder reservation than Mozza.'

Another fancy restaurant, Wycliff assumed, from the way she said the name. He looked at the surroundings. Pretty drab. A Denny's had more personality.

This was not the first time she had pointed out to him that she had the necessary clout to get into the hotshot places. He wondered if she knew Jack Nicholson. He had always wanted to meet Jack, just to shake hands, maybe converse for a minute about the Lakers. The Joker seemed like a real person, not some plastic Hollywood creation.

'So it's going to be all that raw stuff?' He could feel bile rising in his mouth.

Charlotte put her sake cup down. She didn't slam it, she would not make a scene here, but the gesture was emphatic. 'Yes, the fish will be raw. That's what sushi is.'

'I don't know...' He felt like such a wimp.

She turned to the waitress. 'Excuse us to chef for a moment.' She snatched her purse from the counter and marched out. Wycliff followed, bestowing an excuse-her smile on the famous celebrity, who wasn't paying them any attention.

Outside on the sidewalk Charlotte had taken on the grim face of a third-grade nun about to lay down the law with a ruler. 'Are you trying to make me look like a fool?'

He was startled. 'No.'

'Then what is with your antisocial attitude?' She was fuming, but still under control.

He threw up his hands defensively. 'Back off. Take a chill pill.'

She glared up at him. 'A chill pill. How original. After all I've done for you, a little appreciation should not be too much to ask. Not embarrassing me in public should not be too much to ask.'

Wycliff had had as much as he was going to take for tonight. 'Stop right there,' he said, putting up his hand like a traffic cop. 'I appreciate what you've done for me, Charlotte, the clothes and fancy haircut and all that. You're great in the hay, too, I certainly appreciate that. But what I do not appreciate is being mocked. I've had enough of that to last me a lifetime. And I do not appreciate being used as a dupe in whatever scams you're running, or planning to run.'

His assertiveness threw her off-stride. 'Keep your voice down,' she hissed, looking around to make sure they weren't being overheard.

'Fine,' he said. 'I'll talk low. But you need to listen up carefully. I am not going to let you set me up for a fall. Not you, not anyone.'

'I'm not setting you up.'

'Then what gives? Something stinks, and it

ain't that fish back in there.'

She took his hand in hers. 'I don't want to upset you.' Her voice was soft now, soothing. 'I want it to be good between us. Like it has been.'

Her hands felt like velvet, like all of her felt. God, how he wanted that velvet. 'So now what?' he asked her. Don't make me go back in there, he pleaded silently.

She turned on a dime, now all sweetness and light. 'We blow this joint,' she said. 'I want you to be happy, darling. Because if you're happy, so am I.'

The New York strip ran bloody on the plate, exactly the way he liked it. The crispy-skinned baked potato was smothered in butter and sour cream. The shrimp cocktail appetizer, the crusty sourdough bread, the full-bodied Napa cabernet: this was his kind of eating, the meal he would order if it was his last dinner on death row.

The Pacific Dining Car, Charlotte informed him as the maitre d' led them to a booth, was the oldest and best steak joint in town. What passes for royalty in Los Angeles – the mayor, the governor, rich developers, sports and music stars – came here to eat and greet. It was everything Wycliff liked in a restaurant: thick leather booths, old-hand waiters gliding around the room, the smell of luxury.

She wasn't having a steak, too much cholesterol. For her, grilled sand dabs with sautéed spinach on the side. She stared at him over the rim of her wine glass. 'How's your steak?' she asked solicitously.

'Perfect.'

'Even better than sushi?'

He could smile about that fiasco now. 'Even better.'

He had cheesecake for dessert. He was full after the heavy meal, but she pressed it on him after he told her cheesecake was his favorite dessert. 'You don't have to finish it. Eat a few bites, for the pleasure. It's a house specialty.'

Another lesson to learn from her: you don't have to eat everything on your plate. Leave a bite, so you don't look desperate.

The coffee was good and strong. They took their time over it. He passed on a brandy. Learn restraint, like Charlotte. No time like the present to start. Tonight was turning out to be full of lessons.

She put her coffee cup down and dabbed at her lips with the napkin. Her lipstick left a pale blood-red impression on the bleached cloth.

'Do you know why we're here?' she asked.

Because I don't like raw fish and you were savvy enough not to cram it down my throat. But that wasn't what she meant. She didn't mean here, here. She was coming from some deeper place.

He didn't know the answer, so he threw the question back at her. 'Why *are* we?'

'Don't laugh at me when I tell you,' she said. 'Promise.'

That sounded heavy. Vulnerability was not an aspect of this woman's personality that she had revealed, at least up to now.

He held up two fingers in the Boy Scout salute. 'Promise.'

'That first night we met, back at the Marmont bar. Do you remember?'

That night was chiseled on his brain for eternity. 'Of course I remember.'

'I was feeling sorry for myself that night. I'd had a string of bad luck, personally and professionally. I'm not going to bore you with ancient history, let's just say I was down in the dumps. And then, there you were.'

Now she was going confessional on him? From the very beginning she had been the alpha dog, he the underdog. Keeping him off-balance was one of the ways she controlled him. Letting her hair down didn't feel right. Out of character.

He should have ordered that brandy.

'I looked at you and thought, that's an attractive man, although rough around the edges, which I'm usually not attracted to. I prefer sophistication to brute energy, Cary Grant rather than Bruce Willis, but the aura you were sending out wasn't threatening. Masculine, but not frightening. I instinctively knew you weren't someone who would hurt me. Female intuition, whatever. Even so, approaching a strange man in a bar is not something I would normally do.'

She was flattering him. It felt good. He still wished he'd ordered that brandy.

'But then I made the connection about you and your brother and it all clicked. Billy is sweet and good and masculine, but he's gay. He's not available for a woman.' She coughed nervously, deep in her throat. 'I don't know how many women fell for that man, knowing it was a hopeless cause, but I'm sure the number is legion. Even women old enough to be his mother, like me.'

Wycliff believed her. His brother had been beautiful. Why shouldn't women get turned on by him, even if he would not, could not, reciprocate?

'I never made a play for him. Not only because we worked together as designer and client, but because it would have been disrespectful. The age difference was an obstacle, too. But I loved him. I know other people who knew him, worked with him, and they all loved him. He was transcendent, a modern-day Billy Budd, if you know who I'm talking about.'

He didn't, but he kept his mouth shut. She was rolling. He didn't want to stop the train.

'Anyway, that night at the Marmont bar. I see this man who turns me on, which is unusual for me, I'm the opposite of impulsive, as you know by now, and then it hit me who you were related to. I wasn't positive, but I had this strong feeling about you, and like I said I was feeling punky, and I thought Billy is a good man, so you must be, too.'

She reached across the table and touched his hand. 'Is it all right for me to tell you these things? If it isn't, say so. I don't want to make you uncomfortable.'

'No,' he told her. 'It's okay.'

That was a lie. It *was* uncomfortable, her opening up like this. Scary, too, like she was inside his head. But it was also an ego boost, being the object of a woman's desire. Especially this woman. True, she was older, but bottom line, she was ageless. Some women, he was beginning to realize, will be sexy forever. Charlotte was one of them.

She fiddled with her napkin some more. 'I could use a nightcap. You'll join me, of course.' She signaled the waiter. 'Two Remy's, please.'

After the waiter left, she continued. 'I was nervous. Would this attractive man want to get together with a woman my age? It was dark in there.' She laughed. 'But not that dark.'

She had been nervous? He thought he had the corner on that market.

Their cognacs arrived in heavy snifters. The waiter refreshed their coffee cups and glided away. Charlotte raised her goblet in toast. 'To right now.' She clinked her glass to his and took a sip. He drank, also. The cognac went down smooth.

'But you did,' she said. 'You were willing to get to know me.'

'Yes, I was.'

Her smile seemed to be genuine. 'So that's your answer.'

He had lost the original train of thought. 'Answer to what?'

'Why we're here. Because we're attracted to each other.'

He thought about what that meant. If it meant they liked to sleep with each other, then yes, they were attracted to each other. He understood how an older woman, no matter how sexy she was, dug getting it on with a younger man. Not only for the performance, but for the ego-boost as well.

But there was more to them than a good roll in the hay. Charlotte had a plan for him. He didn't know what it was, but for sure it was more than she was copping to. The jewelry heist was a prime example. He had given her a pass on that, but not again. If he so much as caught the faintest whiff of another set-up it was *adios*, the party's over. This was a dangerous woman. That was part of the attraction, the combination of sex, age, uncertainty. He was alive around her, more than he had ever been with a woman. But he couldn't let his cock overrule his brain. That could be fatal.

He knew he could be manipulated, but he was not a complete fool. He had survived life up until now – not always well, but he was still standing on his own two feet – and he was planning to keep on surviving. He could be slow in figuring shit out, but he was no dummy. He was not going to play the fool for her.

They went back to her apartment and made love. They couldn't linger, because he had to be back at the house by midnight to relieve the caretaker, which was good, because he needed to put some distance between them to give him time to sort out what he was thinking and feeling.

Billy was asleep. The caretaker was watching television, with the sound muted. 'Everything is in order,' he whispered as he gathered his stuff. 'I changed his diaper, so you won't need to until morning.'

Wycliff had not performed that function yet. He knew how – when he'd told Billy he had done it before, he hadn't been lying – but changing your own brother's diaper was different from changing an anonymous hospital patient's. He had never seen his brother naked, as an adult. He would not only have to change the messy diaper, he would have to wash and wipe Billy, powder him, smooth on lotion so he wouldn't chafe. The thought creeped him out, but there was no alternative. He had signed on to be his brother's keeper. For everything, not just the parts you want to cherry-pick.

He sat on the back porch, lights out, smoking and drinking beer. A cool breeze came from the direction of the reservoir. Sounds of crickets and bullfrogs came out of the darkness, and up in Griffith Park, a pack of coyotes howled call and response. It must be nice to have a place of your own to come home to, he thought. An anchor, some certainty. He'd never had that. He had lived a transient life since he had bailed from the family homestead as a teenager. That had been okay when he was young, but he wasn't that young anymore, he was slowing down, he could feel it in his blood, his bones.

He had nothing. You have to face the facts, no matter how harsh a light they shine on you. No home, no savings in the bank, no future, no vision of one. A few grand that would burn a hole in his pocket fast enough, a semi-legitimate car, a sexual partner with an agenda that was as much a mystery to him as the day he had met her.

And a dying brother who despised him. What a parlay.

That tearjerker story Charlotte laid on him tonight in the steak joint sounded good when she was weaving it but it didn't hold up, now that he could think about it objectively. It was a fantasy, smoke and mirrors. The question was, why him? Because she needed a dupe and knew he was a patsy from the minute she had laid eyes on him? He could be his own worst critic, but in this instance, coming down on himself didn't feel right. There had to be a better reason for her to have made a move on him. Something about who he was, specifically.

What was that? The answer was crucial. It tied into Billy somehow, he felt that in his gut. The other imperative was finding out who *she* was, for real. Not some movie star look-alike or however else she was camouflaging herself.

He needed information. To stop his brain from itching, and to survive.

SEVEN

The bathwater was warm, but not too hot. You had to be as careful controlling the temperature as if you were bathing an infant. Ever so carefully, Wycliff lowered Billy into the tub, cradling the back of his brother's head in his hand. Billy moaned. Any movement was painful, because his muscles were atrophying. They were like rubber bands that had lost their elasticity and would snap if stretched too much.

Billy's body sank into the water like a bag of pebbles. Wycliff made sure his head was above water. He propped a washcloth behind his neck to cushion his fragile skull from the porcelain rim.

Earlier, he had fed Billy his breakfast – oatmeal and tea – and undressed him. It was the first time he had seen his brother naked since they were little boys. He had to swallow hard to keep from gagging. Bones protruding everywhere. Skin the color of burnt candle, dry and clammy to the touch. Black and blue marks turning yellow from where he had bumped into anything.

The queasiest moment had been undoing the diaper. He placed a towel underneath first, in case there was leakage. His brother stared at him, unblinking, as he peeled back the adhesive straps and slid the cloth away from Billy's abdomen and ass. The shit-stain was minimal, more liquid than solid, like baby poop. He dropped the messy diaper in the covered trashcan which would be emptied several times a day. Then he washed his brother's cock, ass, scrotum, and the parts in between with a warm washcloth. Billy's shriveled pecker looked like a blind, newborn bird's head.

Billy managed to smile (more a grimace) while Wycliff cleaned his nether regions. 'So you're a closet queer after all. You've been repressing the urge for years, haven't you? How does it feel?

Does it turn you on?'

'Extremely,' Wycliff replied, dead-pan. Billy's penis felt like a dead worm. 'I never realized what I was missing.'

Billy couldn't counter-banter; he was too exhausted from even this miniscule effort. He closed his eyes and drifted into semi-consciousness.

'You look as spiffy as the King of Spain,' Wycliff said, as he finished dressing his brother in his daytime outfit of T-shirt, boxers, and cotton booties. 'Or in your case, the Queen.' He propped Billy up on the bed. Later, when the relief man came, they would change the sheets.

'Har de har har.' Billy ran his hand along his jaw, which Wycliff had carefully shaved. 'Do you cut hair, too?' he jested. 'I'm looking ragged. Can't have my fans seeing me at anything but my best.'

'You wouldn't like the results. Give me your barber's name, I'll bring him over.'

Billy's face twisted. 'She won't come. She doesn't want to see me looking like I do now, instead of how I used to. I get a lot of that.'

That stung Wycliff. It must sting Billy more, he thought. 'Fuck 'em if they can't take a joke. I'll get somebody good to buff you up, don't worry.'

Billy looked up at him with grateful spaniel eyes. 'Thanks.'

Wycliff, embarrassed, turned away.

81

EIGHT

Charlotte was out of commission for the evening. She didn't say why, and Wycliff didn't ask. He fleetingly thought about driving over to her apartment, wait for her to come out, and tail her to where she was going, but decided not to. He didn't know what kind of car she drove or if she took cabs or limos, one of the many holes in his lack of knowledge about her. Maybe she was entertaining another man. Seeing female friends. Options that didn't involve him. He could sleuth her another time. Tonight he wanted to be around people his age who were healthy and vibrant.

He had been in LA for almost two weeks and had barely seen anything. Venice was supposed to be a cool place. It would be nice to actually see and smell the ocean. He Googled clubs and other local attractions on Billy's Powerbook and printed out the list, along with a map of how to get there. After making sure Billy was settled in with the caretaker, he hopped in his car and headed towards the beach.

The heavy commuter traffic crawled like a slug. Wycliff didn't mind, he was happy just to be out and about, away from sickness, impending death, and Charlotte's mysterious shenanigans. He smoked a couple of cigarettes with the windows rolled down for ventilation and listened to country music booming out of his car's excellent sound system.

He lucked into a parking spot on Washington Blvd, less than a block away from the pier. He got out of the car, locked it with the remote, and fed the meter with quarters. The setting sun was low over the ocean. His cheat sheet was folded up in the back pocket of his jeans. He consulted it, looked around a minute to get his bearings, and strolled along the sidewalk.

The ice-cold margarita in the surfer-themed bar went down fast and smooth. He dropped a twenty on the bar and let the change ride. Playing it casual, he swiveled on his bar stool and checked out the room. More guys than chicks, which did not bode well, and none of the women looked like they were anxious to be picked up. It was early – the whiff of going-home-alone desperation was not yet hanging in the air.

Not to worry. If he scored, good deal. If he struck out, there were other ways to enjoy an evening at the beach. Get something to eat, have a few drinks (in moderation, he had to be careful to avoid getting a DUI), rub elbows with people his age. He was out in the world. It felt good.

He switched to beer, Sierra Nevada on draft, and nursed the tall schooner until it was obvious there were no pickings to be had here. He left a couple singles for a tip and walked out into the night. It was cooler by ten or fifteen degrees than it was inland, and the breeze blowing off the ocean raised goose bumps on his bare arms, a far cry from hot, bone-dry Arizona, where the only bodies of water were rich people's swimming pools. He had done a stint cleaning pools, one of the dozens of grunt jobs he had drifted in and out of over the years. Plastic-surgery-enhanced housewives, slathered in oil, tanning with their bikini tops unfastened, would lie on towels at poolside, cock-teasing the hired help. He had scored a few of them, but they had been hollow victories. The women weren't screwing him as a specific person, they were getting off on ten minutes of exciting danger. More excitement than they got from their husbands in a month, as one of the more candid ones had confided to him.

His own house with a swimming pool was one of his ultimate dreams. Adorned with hot babes around the clock, like Hugh Hefner. He wondered if they still had the wild parties at the mansion he had read about in Playboy. If you were rich enough to have your own house with a pool, the women would flock to you.

Lots of fantasies. That's all they had ever been. But now, for the first time in his life, he indulged in thinking that some of them might come true.

The sun was almost down now, a sliver of orange lollypop on the horizon, sending rainbow waves across the cumulus sky. He walked onto the pier, which was thinning out as night-time approached. A smattering of pedestrians; some locals still fishing, groups of teenagers loitering, waiting for something exciting to happen. Latinos and blacks as well, which he hadn't expected; he'd always thought the ocean was white man's territory. Most blacks can't swim,

84

that's a scientific fact. He knew LA was gang capital of the world, but he thought the action was inland. Maybe they were spreading out to here, the world one big gangland. He didn't want any part of that. He wasn't scared, he could take care of his business, but he needed to keep his nose clean. No hassles, nothing to call attention to himself.

Wycliff reached the end of the pier and looked out over the water. The sea was black-green, churning, the foamy waves pounding the pilings. He inhaled salt spray into his nostrils. He would buy a bathing suit and the next time he came here he would plunge in, swim out past the breakers, and body surf until he was wasted. California dreaming was becoming his reality.

He fired up a smoke. The nicotine rush felt good. He looked out over the horizon as the sun hesitated in one last gasp of suspension, then slid below the horizon.

'Got a light?'

He turned. The speaker had come up unawares behind him. One of the Latino teenagers he had passed by earlier. The boy was medium-sized, with some pudge on him. Low-riding khakis, JC Penny wife-beater. Arms adorned with blue-ink homemade tattoos, probably acquired during a stay in juvenile hall or the county jail, although he didn't look old enough for adult prison. His look to Wycliff had no threat in it.

Wycliff tossed the kid his pack of matches. 'Keep them.'

'Thanks, man.' The kid pulled a skinny blunt from behind his ear and lit it. He sucked in deeply, held the smoke, exhaled with a whoosh. He held the joint out to Wycliff. 'Want a taste?'

Smoke marijuana in a public place with a Latino gangbanger? That would be the smartest move of the day. For all he knew, the kid was a plant.

'No, thanks,' he declined casually.

'No *problema*, big man,' the kid replied. He had a cocky smile on his mouth. He glanced behind him. His friends were looking at them by studiously not looking at them.

They must think I'm a mark, Wycliff realized. Was he throwing off that vibe? Some out of place tourist, ripe for plucking? The last image he would have thought he projected. He was taller than any of them by a good three inches, probably outweighed the heaviest one by at least twenty pounds, and was still in reasonably good shape. It had only been a couple of weeks since his last job working construction in Tucson. But there were four of them against his solo act. It wouldn't be much of a contest.

Stay cool. Don't acknowledge threat. Above all, do not show fear, these jokers can smell fear better than an airport security dog can smell Afghani heroin stashed up a courier's ass.

He flicked his cigarette butt into the ocean and pushed off from the railing. 'Take it easy,' he said, his voice low and calm. He started walking away from the kid towards the street. The pier was dimly lit, and less populated than it had been only a few minutes ago.

'You, too,' came the voice from behind his back. 'You take it easy.'

Just keep walking. And listen and watch. The kid's compadres were off to the side ahead of him. A few stared at him with blank expressions.

He reached them. Walk easily, no hurry. Don't look around. Listen for footsteps coming up behind. Keep walking at the same pace.

He did not hear footsteps. What he heard was laughter. Snickering.

They had been fucking with him, and he'd let them. His armpits tingled with humiliation flop-sweat. Good thing he wasn't carrying Charlotte's revolver, he might have done something he would regret.

Reaching the street at the foot of the pier, Wycliff couldn't resist the urge to look back. The boys had not moved from where they had been. They were not paying him any attention. They had gotten their rocks off by messing with his head, so he no longer mattered to them. Or maybe they were just a bunch of kids hanging out who could give a shit less about some lame older guy. Maybe the offer of weed had been a friendly gesture, nothing more.

It's okay to be paranoid, but you have to have a reason. There had been no threat. He felt like an asshole.

The night air, in combination with the two earlier drinks and his panic attack, had roused his appetite. He spied an Ernie's Taco House halfway down the street, a duplicate of one he had eaten at in North Hollywood. He hadn't gotten ptomaine poisoning, a good-enough recommendation.

The place was your typical Mexican restaurant: red fake-leather booths, bad paintings (some of them actual black velvet, including the worst Elvis he had ever seen), a long bar that took up the entire far wall. The back bar was stocked with dozens of various tequilas for every taste and pocketbook, along with every other kind of booze known to man. The Mexican waiters wore red jackets, white shirts with black ties, black slacks. They crafted their pompadours with pomade.

He made a quick visual survey of the possibilities. None of the available women were worth hitting on. On the drive here he'd had this film loop running in his head like how it played out in a beer commercial: lots of hot chicks, all gorgeous and available for a stud like himself. Well, he might be in LA, home to the stars, but this was real life, not make-believe.

He had picked up a woman in a bar on his first night in town – an encounter that had given him a false sense of entitlement. Except he had not picked her up, she had been the aggressor. And their encounter had not been your standard wham bam thank you ma'am roll in the hay go your separate ways. Charlotte had not chosen him for his looks or charisma or prowess in bed. She needed him to help her pull off some agenda as yet unknown to him, something that would be far dicier than the jewelry-store theft, to which he had been a bystander, a distraction.

So he wouldn't get lucky tonight. That was all right with him. The pressure to score was off.

The enchilada/relleno combo with beans and rice hit the spot. The margarita he washed it down with added to the satisfaction. Sated, he ordered a coffee, passing on dessert, although the flan was tempting. He wasn't doing physical labor now and wasn't going to for the foreseeable future, which hopefully would be never, so he had to come up with another way to stay fit. He could join a gym, there was a 24-hour fitness center a few blocks from Billy's house. That would be a good place to meet women. Hard bodies running on the treadmill, climbing the Stairmaster, crunching their abs on the Nautilus machines. Tomorrow, when he had a break from his caretaking duties, he'd check it out.

It was still early. He had a few hours left until he had to drive back to Billy's house. It would be dumb not to use what free time he had left. Charlotte might want him at her beck and call every night, starting tomorrow. He was powerless to say no to her, no matter what.

He checked his Google map. Santa Monica, another area he wanted to check out, was the next city over. He got into his car and headed up Pacific Ave. As he drove, he vented at himself. Damn those kids. Double damn him for letting them get his goat. This is how your brain gets messed up when you're living on the edge. A snake under every rock, an assailant hidden behind every shadow.

Life on the edge was getting old. He needed normalcy, a respite from his nerves being constantly frayed. He had responsibilities now he had never had before. He was a caretaker entrusted with helping his brother reach the end of his life in peace and dignity. That was a solemn duty. He couldn't fail at it. He had made a promise and he had to keep it. Maybe he shouldn't have made that promise, because being responsible for anyone other than himself was foreign to his nature. But he had done it, and for once in his life, he was going to keep his word.

His nerves were still jumping. A nicotine hit would settle him down. He reached into his shirt pocket and pulled out his pack of Camel filters. Empty. He must have smoked his last one on the pier. At the time, he had been too discombobulated to notice.

The AM/PM Minimart a block away was lit up in neon beer signs. He parked in front, made sure the doors were locked, and went inside. The lighting was florescent-zombie harsh. On guard because of Charlotte's jewelry store caper, he looked up at the ceiling. Security cameras at all four corners. Robbing a convenience store was an amateur play. They don't keep much cash in the register, the surplus automatically goes into a safe. Anyone with experience knows that. Only junkies and punks would try to knock off a place like this, which made them dangerous locations to be in, because those assholes don't know how shit works, and can go off half-cocked.

There were a few other customers in the place. None of them looked like trouble. He waited while the woman in front of him paid for a refrigerator keg of Old Milwaukee and a roll of Tums with a debit card, then took her place at the counter and told the Pakistani clerk behind the counter he wanted two packs of Camel

Filters 100s. 'And one of those two-dollar lighters,' he added, pointing at the display window.

'You shouldn't smoke those.'

He turned around.

The woman was about his age. She was dressed in nurses' scrubs and orange crocs over athletic socks, her face washed clean of makeup. Her reddish-brown hair, a tangled bush of wiry curls, was pulled back in a utilitarian ponytail. She looked weary, probably coming off shift.

Instinctively, he checked her out. She was not conventionally pretty, certainly not in any way that appealed to him. Her nose was pointy, her pale complexion was splayed with freckles, her chest was small and her hips were ample. A good body for having kids, maybe, but not one he'd want to parade on his arm.

'Cigarettes kill you,' she said. 'I've seen the results. They aren't pretty.'

'You can get killed lots of ways.'

'But why increase the odds?'

She had spunk. He liked that in a woman. 'What are you, Mother Theresa?'

'Hardly.' She stretched and yawned. 'Just putting in my two cents. Not my business.'

He looked at her more closely. Her lips were full and soft. Even without lipstick, they were kissable. 'What hospital do you work at?'

'St John's.'

'Where's that? I'm new around town.'

'Right here in Santa Monica. Where are you from?' she asked.

'Tucson, Arizona, most recently.'

'I've never been there. What's it like?'

'It's okay if you like blast-furnace heat. Here's better.'

The clerk put his merchandise on the counter. 'Twelve seventy-three,' he said. Wycliff ignored him. 'What do you do there, at St John's?'

'I'm a nurse. I work with cancer patients.'

'Hence the two cents. I guess you see some pretty ugly...' He stifled *shit*. 'Stuff.'

'Twelve seventy-three,' the clerk impatiently repeated.

Wycliff stole a look at her left hand. Ringless, although that could be a false reading. People who work with their hands often don't wear rings, because they can get tangled up in equipment. A co-worker on a house remodel last year had lost a finger when his Marine Corps ring was snagged in a cross-cut saw. The blood spatter had been humongous. They packed the digit in ice and took it with him to the hospital, but it was too late to sew it back on.

'Can I buy you a cup of coffee?' The words came out unexpectedly.

Startled, the nurse looked at him suspiciously. 'Thanks for the offer, but I don't think so.'

He wasn't going to go down without a fight. What did he have to lose? 'You realize you could be responsible for me if I don't buy the cigarettes, don't you?'

'How do you figure that?'

'If I don't buy these cigarettes I might not die, which would mean you saved my life. Where I come from, you save someone's life, you're tied to them. Forever.'

She laughed. It was a good laugh, from her gut. 'I thought you were from Arizona, not Sicily.'

'Same difference. Seriously, if I pass on the smokes, can I buy you a coffee? One coffee, not even a refill.'

She considered the trade-off. And him. 'Okay.'

He followed her car, a ten-year-old red Honda Civic with Obama/Biden stickers plastered on the rear bumper, to a local coffee joint on 4th street, away from the congestion of the 3rd St Mall. A sparse crowd, huddled over their laptops. *Kind Of Blue*, the sound turned low, played on the stereo. The woman ordered a double-shot latte with half and half – 'It actually helps put me to sleep, believe it or not' – and he opted for a traditional cappuccino, waving off her offer to pay for her own. They carried their drinks to a quiet area in the back and sat next to each other on a lumpy sofa.

'What brought you to Los Angeles?' she asked him, opening the conversation.

'My brother lives here.'

'Where?'

'Silver Lake. Over by—'

'I know where Silver Lake is,' she interrupted, but sweetly. 'I trained at Hollywood Presbyterian. That's a nice area.'

'It is,' he agreed. He didn't know how to small talk a woman like this.

'So you're out visiting?'

'Not exactly.' He was uncertain of how deep into his situation he should go. He had just met her.

She sipped her drink and slipped her feet out of her crocs, flexing her toes through her socks.

'He's sick,' he explained. 'I came out to check up on him.'

'That's brotherly of you,' she said. 'How is he?'

'Not well.' A vision of Billy flashed in his mind. Ash complexion, bones showing through skin, eyelids fluttering like hummingbird wings. 'Pretty bad, actually.'

A look of genuine concern crossed her face. 'What does he have?'

'Complications from AIDS. His doctors tried different drug combinations on him, but they didn't work. They're not a silver bullet every time.'

It was as if all the air had been sucked out of the room. The woman opened her mouth as if to say something, but nothing came out.

'He's almost gone,' Wycliff told her. 'It won't be long.'

Her hands shook. She put her coffee cup down. 'I'm so sorry.'

'Thanks.' He didn't know what else to say. He wasn't good at dealing with emotion.

'So you came out to be with him.'

He explained his mission, the sanitized version. They had not seen each other for a long time, different lives, different career paths, as it often is with siblings. He knew Billy was sick and he was just finishing a job, so he had some free time. He drove out, not expecting the horror he found.

'Tubes coming out of everywhere, open sores.

It was a disaster. I almost threw up, the first time I saw him. I had no idea.'

She reached over and placed a hand on his briefly, then withdrew it.

'He was going to die in there,' Wycliff continued. 'The hospital wouldn't let him come home unless he was in the care of a family member. One of their million bullshit rules. They care more about their rules than they do human beings.'

She recoiled at hearing this. 'That's not true. Not always,' she amended truthfully.

'In his case it was.' He smiled at her wanly. 'He didn't have a nurse like you looking after him, that's for sure.'

She blushed. He was feeling more at ease with her now.

'They didn't know about me,' he continued. 'Billy hadn't told them. He didn't want to burden me. We're each other's only kin. There's no one else.'

'That's tough,' she said. 'So you showed up from out of the blue?'

'Way out.'

'Was he surprised to see you? Happy?'

'He was surprised, for sure. But he was damn glad I was there. It was like he was drowning and suddenly got thrown a life-preserver.'

She clucked sympathetically. 'I can imagine.'

'Yeah, it was a tearful reunion,' he told her, laying it on thick. 'Very emotional.'

'He must have been thrilled beyond words.'

Thrilled was not a word Wycliff would have used to describe their first encounter. 'It was pretty heavy, absolutely.'

He embellished his résumé, telling her that he was a general contractor, mostly remodels these days: people can't sell their houses, so they're sprucing them up. He was doing good business, he had to keep on adding extra crew.

'I was working seven days around the clock,' he said. 'I needed a break, so out I came.' His face clouded. 'Lucky I did. I don't know what would have happened to my poor brother if I hadn't shown up.'

'He was very fortunate,' she agreed. 'To have a brother like you who would take responsibility for him. Not everyone would do that. It's hard, taking care of someone who's dying.'

'He's my brother.'

She looked behind him.

'Did I drop something?' he asked her, turning to see what she was looking at.

'Your halo. It must have slipped off.'

It was a good thing he hadn't taken a swallow of coffee, because he would have choked on it. 'Not hardly.' If this woman knew the real him she'd be making tracks so fast her dust would raise dust. 'Maybe devil. Certainly not angel.'

'Don't be modest,' she said. 'I'm a good judge of character. You're a good man. I can tell.'

They drank their coffee in silence. He checked the time on his cell phone. 'Got a late date?' she teased him.

'I have to be back at the house by midnight to relieve the hospice worker.'

'Sorry. I was joking.' She finished her latte and put the cup down. 'I'm enjoying being with you.

I don't want it to end.'

'Does it have to?'

'Not if you'll call me.'

That was unexpected. 'I'd like to,' he told her.

'Then I'll let you go. But only if you promise to call.'

'I promise.'

'I don't know your name,' she said. 'First names are enough for now,' she added quickly.

He understood where she was coming from. Single woman, on her own in the world. If she had misjudged him and he turned out to be a crazy stalker, she didn't want him to be able to find her too easily.

'Wycliff.'

'That's a new one on me.'

'Old English. Very posh.'

'So you're royalty out slumming?'

He almost laughed out loud. 'Not hardly. My mother had dreams.'

'Parents dream for their children.'

'Since I don't have any, I wouldn't know. She bailed when I was an infant. I have no memory of her, not even pictures.'

'That's awful. I'm sorry.'

If you knew my old man you wouldn't think so. 'Win some, lose some.'

'So your brother is older than you?'

Wycliff shook his head. 'Younger, a couple of years. Same father, different mothers. His flew the coop real soon, too. We were raised mother-less, the two of us.'

'Is your father still alive?' She caught herself up. 'I guess not, if you are your brother's sole

97

relative.'

'No, our father isn't alive. The prick died a long time ago.' How or when, he didn't know and didn't give a shit. 'No one cried at his funeral.'

She flinched. 'That's awful.'

'Ancient history.' He smiled to assure her he didn't carry a dark cloud about that around with him. He changed the subject. 'You need to tell me your name, now that you know mine.'

'Amelia,' she said. 'Like the lost pilot. It means industrious. When I was little I thought it was the name of a flower. Something pretty, that smelled good.' She laughed. 'It's more like a piece of machinery.'

Nurses were industrious. She was pretty enough, in her own way, and he was sure she smelled good.

She gave him her phone number, which he laboriously inserted into his ancient cell phone. She did the same on her iPhone. He should get one of those, he thought with envy, as he watched her fingers dance over the keyboard. Moses in the desert had used his model.

They walked outside to their cars. As she reached hers and opened the door she rose up on her toes and they kissed. It was a good kiss.

'I'll be holding my breath, waiting for your call,' she teased him.

He wasn't the type to play it cool. 'You won't be waiting long.'

NINE

Billy was asleep. 'He had a real good appetite,' Ricardo, the hospice worker, told Wycliff. Wycliff called him by his proper name now, since he was part of the team, not just another minority to ignore. 'Chicken and rice, my specialty,' Ricardo boasted. 'He cleaned his plate. You wouldn't know he was sick. There's some in the fridge, in case you're hungry.'

Wycliff was heartened to hear this news, although his mind was elsewhere. 'You're doing a great job, Ricardo. See you tomorrow.'

'A different aide tomorrow,' Ricardo corrected him. 'Luis. Your brother will be in good hands,' he assured Wycliff.

Wycliff was grateful. These people gave their all for coolie wages. 'I know that,' he told the caretaker.

'You had a call.'

'Who?' Wycliff asked, off guard.

'The lady didn't say. Just left a message and a number. She said you would know who.' He handed Wycliff a sheet of paper with a note scribbled on it.

Wycliff glanced at the note and stuck the paper in his pocket. 'Thanks.'

He closed the door behind the man and locked

it. Then he reached into his pocket, took out the crumpled note, and read it again. *Call me when you get this*. A 310 area-code number.

It was late, almost midnight. The call could wait until morning.

He checked Billy to make sure everything was okay. His brother's breathing was deep and regular. He's sleeping like an innocent newborn, he thought with unexpected feeling. It was the drugs, he knew, but Billy's expression in repose was so beautifully calm. If he was dreaming, he wasn't having nightmares.

He poured himself a stiff Maker's Mark over ice and took it outside to the back porch. The crickets serenaded him. A cigarette would be soothing, but he didn't have any, he remembered, as he settled into the porch rocker swing. He had promised Amelia he wouldn't smoke, a vow he would honor at least until tomorrow. Or maybe longer, depending on how things progressed between them. A woman would have to cast a powerful spell to get him to quit smoking. He didn't know if he could, he had been smoking since he was in his early teens. He had tried to quit numerous times, and had never been able to.

Call me when you get this. He knew that Charlotte would not be denied. He could ring her up at one, two, three in the morning, she would answer her phone. And if he didn't call, he would hear about it.

She picked up on the second ring. 'What took you so long?'

And a pleasant good evening to you, too, he

thought resentfully. 'I was out. I just got back.'

'Where were you?'

'Just out.'

'There's no such thing as just out. Where were you?'

What was this crap? He wasn't a teenager on curfew. 'I went to Santa Monica. I wanted to see the ocean.'

'How was it?'

'Wet.'

He could hear her indulgent chuckle on the other end. Was she on her patio, smoking and drinking some exotic liqueur? Or maybe she was in bed, slathered in beauty cream. Either place, she could be smoking, she didn't have petty rules. He wished he had a cigarette.

'Is the hospice worker there?' she asked.

'No, he's gone home.'

'So you can't come over.'

'I'm here by myself.'

'That's a pity. Because I really want you.'

His loins started coming to attention, even though he didn't want them to. He needed to give his penis a lobotomy. 'I want you, too,' he told her. Not a lie, but not the naked truth, either.

She *was* smoking, he could hear her inhale. 'Who were you with?'

'What?' The phone in his hand felt like it was vibrating.

'In Santa Monica,' she answered, as if talking to a school child, 'or wherever you were. Who were you with?'

He fortified himself with a hit of booze. 'No one.'

Another inhale over the wire. He could picture her French-inhaling, sucking the smoke into her lungs and expelling it out her nostrils, like an old movie star on Turner Movie Classics. 'If you say so.' Meaning, I know you're lying.

He didn't rise to the bait.

'Can you arrange for someone to relieve you tomorrow, during the day?'

'I don't know. It's one in the morning, I can't call anyone now.'

'I'm sure you can work something out. These people are professional do-gooders, that's their job.'

He started to explain that he didn't know if there would be someone available on such short notice, but she had already hung up.

TEN

Sadie, the hospice supervisor overseeing Billy's care, arrived early in the morning to check up on her charge. Billy was awake and alert. Sadie took his vital signs and questioned him about how he felt.

'Good,' he told her. 'Way better than before.'

'There's nothing like being in your own surroundings,' she said knowingly. She smiled at Wycliff, who was observing from a respectable distance. 'With family.'

'Amen to that,' Billy agreed.

She finished her exam, made sure the oxygen supply was working properly for when Billy had to use the respirator (as a precaution, he always had a mask on at night while he slept), and that he had all his meds and was taking them properly.

'See you in a couple of days,' she said cheerfully, as she gathered her stuff.

Wycliff walked her out of the room. 'Can I talk to you for a minute?' he asked quietly.

He had to work, he explained, as they spoke quietly in the kitchen. Billy was doing better than expected. He was going to live longer than the doctors had anticipated (which he was thrilled about, of course). Billy's care was being financed from his estate, but Wycliff had to pay his own bills, and his money was dwindling.

'Can he afford more help?' Sadie asked. 'If he can, I can get you as much as you need.'

'He can afford it,' Wycliff assured her.

An hour later another aide, a large, pretty-faced Guatemalan woman, was on the job. Her name was Raquel. 'Like the movie star,' she told him with a broad wink. She settled in with Billy, and Wycliff took off.

Wycliff punched in the security code to Charlotte's parking garage, rode the elevator to her floor, and rang her doorbell. Her revolver was in his front-right pants pocket, hanging low like a second cock. He was glad he'd had it the other night, but now he needed to be shed of it. If he was caught with a firearm, there would be hell to pay.

The door swung open. Charlotte was wearing a frilly dressing gown and high-heeled bedroom slippers with peek-a-boo toes. She had done her makeup, but her hair was still wrapped in a towel. 'Sorry for running late, darling,' she said, kissing him on the neck and adding a love bite. 'There's fresh coffee and croissants on the kitchen counter. I won't be long.' She disappeared into her bedroom.

Wycliff had spent all morning gearing up to confront Charlotte about her high-handed attitude over the phone last night, and in the blink of an eye she had disarmed him. Feeling off balance, he poured a cup of coffee, blew on the rim to cool it, and took a sip. Rich and smooth. Delivered from some fancy deli, he assumed, since there was no coffee maker present. Women like Charlotte did not cook. A microwaved cup of tea would tax her limit.

The pistol in his pants felt like a radioactive rock. 'I brought your gun back,' he called to her.

'Put it in the top drawer of the chiffonier by the front door,' came the muffled reply.

What the hell was a chiffonier? It must be the three-drawer chest against the wall, because there was no other cabinet by the door. The delicate piece looked like it was from China or some foreign country. Probably an expensive antique, Wycliff thought, since his brother would have selected it.

He opened the top drawer. A faint scent of Charlotte's perfume wafted up from a bundle of scarves that was inside. He took the gun out of his pocket and stuck it in under the scarves. He felt relieved not to be carrying it around any-more.

'Darling, would you come zip me up?'

He walked into the bedroom. Charlotte was lying on the bed, naked.

'Let's not quarrel.'

The croissants and coffee were just the opening course. Charlotte had ordered in an extravagant picnic lunch. Roast turkey and honey-baked ham sandwiches, salads, olives, pickles, an assort-ment of organic cheeses, along with thick slices of rich chocolate cake, all wrapped up in fancy packages like gifts bestowed upon royalty. A bottle of Riesling, real china and silverware, and crystal wine glasses complimented the spread. The feast was all carefully arranged in a fancy Williams-Sonoma wicker picnic basket.

They drove to the top of Coldwater Canyon and headed west along Mulholland Drive. After about a mile, Charlotte directed Wycliff to an empty building site that overlooked the entire LA basin. The entrance to the property was protected with a heavy, locked chain. Charlotte got out of the car and opened the lock with a key she fished out of her purse.

'The developer is a friend,' she explained. After Wycliff drove through, she relocked the chain and got back in the car. 'We're all alone,' she said brightly. 'No one can disturb us.'

The day was clear and warm, barely a cloud in the sky. They walked to the edge of the bluff and spread a blanket out on the lush, wild grass. Charlotte handed him the bottle of wine and a corkscrew. 'Be a darling and do the honors, please.'

They ate their lunch sprawled out on the blanket. 'Down there,' Charlotte said, pointing a perfectly-manicured finger, 'is Portuguese Bend. If we had a telescope you could see almost to San Diego. And that way' – she pointed in the opposite direction – 'is Point Conception, all the way up in Santa Barbara County. We'll go to the wine country there some weekend, where they filmed *Sideways*. It's lovely there. Very romantic.' She wiped her fingers on a cloth napkin and took a sip of wine. 'After your brother...' She didn't finish her sentence.

That's my life, Wycliff thought. Billy now, without him after he dies. Everything – Charlotte, the new woman (if anything came of that relationship), the unknown future – was centered around his brother. Until Billy died, everything else was on hold.

Which didn't mean life doesn't go on. It was, in a fury. Bringing Billy home from the hospital and taking responsibility for him, meeting Charlotte and getting immediately involved with her, with the excitement and the danger she brought, now maybe with Amelia, too, along with his remarkable physical remake, not to mention making good money boosting cars. Everything in his life had changed almost beyond recognition since he had arrived here on hardly more than a wing and a prayer. And there were going to be lots of other changes; he felt it, he knew it.

He was ready for change, but he had to be careful. Charlotte had opened new and exciting worlds for him, but she was dangerous and unpredictable. The crazy jewelry store caper was hard proof of that. He had to be vigilant with her, on guard.

As if reading his mind, Charlotte asked, 'What are your plans, Wycliff? Do you have any?'

Her question caught him off-guard. 'Like what?' he parried.

'Like anything,' she returned. 'What was it you did back in Arizona? Some kind of construction work, if I recall correctly?'

'Yeah,' he mumbled.

'For yourself? Others?'

'Both,' he answered, trying to be as vague as possible. He didn't want to go into his shabby past. He was shedding himself of it, like a snake that grows a new skin and leaves the old one behind.

She persisted. 'Are you going to do that here?'

'I don't know. I'll worry about that when the time comes. Right now, I have a full-time job.'

'Yes, you do,' she agreed, 'which you're doing admirably. But at some point, you have to think of your future. Your brother is going to die soon. That's terrible to acknowledge, and I know how awful you feel about it, but you have a long life ahead of you. You can't bury your head in the sand and pretend that somehow everything will take care of itself, because it won't.' She took another sip of wine. 'Take it from someone who's been there,' she said, sounding authoritative. 'You don't want to leave the important things to chance. You need to plan ahead, Wycliff. You'll be sorry if you don't.'

It was nice to be told he was going a good job taking care of Billy, not that she could know anything about that, since she wasn't there. But the rest of what she said, that sunk in. He had been a scrambler and a scuffler all his life. He had survived, but that was all it was: baseline survival. That way of life had been tolerable then, because he hadn't experienced any better. But now he had, and because he had, he couldn't go back to the life he had led. It would be unbearable.

What was he doing to do after Billy died? Something with Charlotte? Was that what she was hinting at, not too subtly? 'I hear you,' he told her. 'I've been thinking about it.' He smiled at her, turning on the charm. 'You got some suggestions you want to lay on me? You've been pretty good so far, telling me what to do with myself.'

'Perhaps,' she answered coyly. 'It will depend.'

Maybe now they were getting down to concrete specifics. 'On what?'

'Many things.' She unwrapped the slices of cake and set them on plates. 'We can talk about that later. For now, let's enjoy these beautiful surroundings.'

They cleared the food and utensils off the blanket and made love with the sun shining down on their naked bodies. The sex was great – it was always great – but his mind was wandering. What actually was her plan for him? Of course she had one, she wasn't wining and dining and fucking him just because it felt good.

She was too calculating to do anything just because it felt good.

He was riding a tiger, and he couldn't get off. Which was all right, for now at least, because he didn't want to. The ride was way too exciting.

'I won't be able to see you tonight,' she said. 'I wish I could, but I have an obligation I can't get out of.'

It was mid-afternoon. They had driven back to her condo. 'Will you be with your brother tonight?' she asked him.

'Yes,' he answered. 'That's where I'll be.'

'I'll see you tomorrow, then.' She reached into her purse and took out her cell phone. An iPhone, of course, like Amelia's. He was the last Neanderthal left on the planet. 'I don't want to call you on your brother's line anymore, now that he's there. You and he need your personal space. Let me have your cell number.'

He recited it to her and she programmed it into her phone. 'See you tomorrow, darling,' she said. 'Don't do anything naughty.'

He walked to the elevator. He could feel her eyes burning a hole in his back until he got in and the doors closed behind him.

ELEVEN

Billy was out of bed when Wycliff got home, sitting in the living room in a special adjustable recliner the hospice people had brought over. Raquel, the new caregiver, had shaved and bathed him and dressed him in a long-sleeved crewneck cotton shirt and dark blue sweat pants with parallel white stripes running down the legs. The house smelled of fresh vacuuming and lemony air-spray.

The most unexpected and pleasant surprise was that Billy was holding a tall cool one, clenched in his fist. He raised the bottle in toast. 'Care to join me, big fellow?'

Wycliff broke into a happy grin. 'Hell, yes.'

He snagged a cold Corona from the fridge, popped the top, and clicked the bottle to Billy's. 'Hair of the dog.'

'Back at you.'

Raquel beamed as she watched the two of them banter back and forth. 'Don't he look handsome?' she cooed.

'Gorgeous,' Wycliff agreed. 'How's about you give me a bath now, so I can look handsome, too,' he flirted.

She giggled. 'You don't need my help to bathe your own self, mister.'

He kept the banter going. 'Not as good as you could.'

She gathered her stuff. 'My old man wouldn't go for that. He's Samoan. They get real jealous.'

The only Samoans Wycliff knew of played football in the NFL. Their necks were as big as his thighs. 'Just kidding,' he said, backing off.

'See you, Billy boy.' Raquel gave Billy a sisterly kiss on the cheek. 'Enjoy the rest of your day.'

'Thanks for everything.'

She waved good-bye and left. 'Looks like you made a conquest,' Wycliff remarked as the door closed on her bodacious ass.

'She's a nice person.' Billy took a sip of beer, swallowing slowly, his Adams apple a bobbing walnut in his withered throat. 'So many people are being nice to me.' He paused. 'Thanks to you.'

Wycliff swigged a mouthful of his own brewski. 'No biggie. You would have done the same.'

Billy shook his head. 'No, I wouldn't have. Not in a million years.' He closed his eyes, either in fatigue or thought, Wycliff couldn't tell. 'I still can't believe this is happening. Me here in my home, you, all of it. I owe you.'

'No, you don't,' Wycliff answered quickly. If his brother knew what was really going on in his life, he wouldn't be so quick to heap on the praise.

'I'm learning a lesson from you, big brother. Something I would never have thought could happen.'

'What is that?' Wycliff asked, genuinely curious. Him teaching anybody anything, that would be a first.

'That the leopard can change his spots.'

If only. 'But he'll still rip your throat open if you turn your back on him,' he reminded his brother.

'Not if he's been defanged,' Billy rejoined, as if to assert that had already happened.

One beer and Billy was ready to get back into bed. Wycliff carried him into the bedroom, undressed him down to T-shirt and shorts, and positioned him comfortably, resting his head on a mound of pillows.

'Any movies you want to watch?' he asked. 'You've got Direct TV, you can order up whatever you want, right into your set.'

'Anything? Bulgarian folk-dance documentaries? Instructional videos on Navajo basket weaving?'

'I don't know about the Bulgarian ones, but the Navajo, definitely. I think that's number ninety-nine thousandth on the request parade. Seriously, what do you want to watch?'

'Check to see if they have *Magnificent Obsession*.'

Wycliff had never heard of that one. 'When did it come out? Is it recent?'

Billy shook his head. 'It was released in 1954, starring Rock Hudson. The art direction was to die for.'

Wycliff knew who Rock Hudson was – the homosexual movie star from back in the days when being a gay actor was the kiss of death.

Wycliff knew he had died of AIDS, one of the first ones to admit it publicly.

'I don't know if the list goes back that far,' he said, trying to stay nonjudgmental. 'We can check if you want.'

Billy's expression was more grimace than smile, the skin across his face stretching like it had been shrunk by a voodoo doctor. 'I'm kidding you. See if you can bring up the earlier episodes of this year's *Mad Men*. Same decadent period from when Rock was in his heyday, but now you can show the nasty stuff on screen. I missed it while I was in the hospital. They don't carry the premium cable channels unless you're in the VIP section.'

Halfway through the first episode, Billy slipped into sleep. Wycliff muted the sound just as the front doorbell rang, announcing Ricardo's arrival to take over for the evening shift.

'I didn't think you were going to call.'

'I said I would.'

'People say all kinds of things they don't follow through on.' Amelia's hand touched Wycliff's across the table, her fingers lingering for a moment before she withdrew them. 'I'm not playing it very cool, am I?'

'Playing it cool's for phonies.'

'That's refreshing to hear. I guess you're not too cool yourself, since you didn't wait the prescribed three days before calling me.'

'I'm about as uncool as they come, Amelia.'

She laughed. 'Saying that makes you extra cool. You know all the lines, don't you, Wycliff?' she teased.

They were in a corner booth in Ye Old King's Head Pub in Santa Monica, a block off Ocean Blvd., drinking their second black and tans. Not a tourist joint (except on St Patrick's Day), the clientele was mostly expatriate Brits and Micks and darts aficionados. A spirited darts game was in progress on the other side of the large room. The sound system was tuned to a classic rock 'n' roll channel (right now playing Del Shannon's 'Runaway'). The song caught Wycliff's ear. *Crime Story*: now that was a great TV series. He'd been a kid glued to the TV set twenty-five years ago, watching the blood and gore and glamour. The life on the tube was so much better than the one he had actually been living in those days.

That wasn't true now, though, especially with this sweet woman sitting next to him, their legs lightly touching, thigh to thigh. She was in jeans and a light sweater, her hair in a ponytail like last night's, but more artfully pulled together, with a ribbon rather than a rubber band. The touch of makeup she wore was barely noticeable. She doesn't need any, he thought, as he sipped a layer of foam off the top of his fresh schooner.

'I wish I actually was cool,' he responded to her joshing. 'Usually when I try to be witty I wind up putting my foot in my mouth.'

Amelia sipped from her own mug and wiped her lips with a lady-like napkin swipe. 'I don't believe that. Not after that brilliant come-on last night.'

'Beginner's luck.' He grinned awkwardly.

What he had with Charlotte was a wild and crazy fantasy. This woman was the real deal.

'Could've fooled me,' she told him.

They exchanged basic information. She lived not far from here, in a small apartment complex. She had her own place, she could finally afford the rent without a roommate, after years of school and getting her career up and running. One pet, a cat from the rescue shelter. Wycliff wasn't allergic to cats, that was one issue they wouldn't have to deal with, fortunately. She had once dated a nice man, she told him, a radiologist (her mother would have been over the moon), who almost went into cardiac arrest when she brought him home and the cat jumped into his lap.

She had offered to meet Wycliff somewhere between here and Silverlake but he didn't mind the drive, he wanted to be close to the ocean, to the pulsing energy he felt radiating from it. And he wanted to stay clear of Hollywood, West Hollywood, and Beverly Hills, because of the one-in-a-million possibility he might run into Charlotte. Charlotte would never set foot in a down-and-dirty Santa Monica bar, so he was safe here.

There was no logical reason he should avoid Charlotte, but there were powerful emotional ones. In her mind, she owned him. He thought back to last night, the phone call demanding to know where he had been, if he had been with anyone, the demands to get more relief help for Billy so he could be at her beck and call. A woman scorned could be lethal. The graveyards

115

were full of men who had not remembered that fundamental rule.

'Where are you?' Amelia asked, breaking into his dark reverie.

He flinched. 'Here.'

'You seemed to be somewhere else.' It wasn't an accusation, more a question.

'Sorry,' he apologized. 'I've got a lot on my mind.'

'Of course you do,' she said, honestly sympathetic. There was no phoniness to her. How strange was that?

'But I'm with you now,' he told her. 'Nowhere else.'

They walked along the dirt path that meanders alongside Ocean Ave. and overlooks the wide beach and the ocean, the water dark now, the waves glowing iridescent in the moonlight. Tentatively, like a junior high-schooler on his first real date, he reached for her hand and she took it in hers and they strolled easily, not feeling a need to talk, enjoying the night, the breezes, the buzzing traffic hum, the other evening walkers. They stopped at the protective railing near Montana Avenue and stared out into the ocean's darkness, and as he turned to kiss her she was turning to him.

Her second-floor one-bedroom on 12th St was small, cheery, and feminine without being frilly. A large bay window offered an expansive view of the street. Her cat, a Burmese mix, stared unblinkingly at him from his perch atop a bookshelf.

'Is he the jealous type?' Wycliff asked, staring back at the cat. 'Or is it a she?'

'He is an excellent guard cat,' Amelia answered. 'So don't try anything cute.'

'Can I pet him?' He reached towards the cat.

'Sure. Who needs five fingers?'

He jerked his hand away. Amelia laughed. 'I'm kidding. He's a real pussycat, in the good sense of the word.'

Wycliff plunked down on her couch while she put a kettle on for tea. The sofa was draped with an Indian-style blanket overlaid with earth-tone colors and zigzag patterns. It was probably second hand, he assumed, as were the other pieces of furniture, no two pieces matching, but bundled all together, they worked. For sure she hadn't had a professional help her decorate.

He felt comfortable here. He could be himself, whoever that was. Or was going to become.

Amelia joined him with two cups of tea-bag tea and a plate of Pepperidge Farms Milanos. 'I'm no Martha Stewart,' she told him without apology, 'my schedule's too hectic. The last anything I baked was probably in Girl Scouts.'

Wycliff couldn't care less about that. That's why grocery stores were invented. 'Did they teach you how to tie knots?'

'Any particular kinky fantasy you have in mind?' she asked as she blew on her tea and took a sip.

He almost dropped his own cup. 'Well, let me think—'

'That was a joke, buster. I'm pretty vanilla. Probably too tame for you.'

Or just right. A comeback such as *you won't know until you try* bubbled up in his mind, but he swallowed it. He didn't want to push her. And of course, there was Charlotte. 'I'm sure you're good at it,' he said, and immediately thought, Christ, how lame was that.

'What a compliment!' she said, laughing. 'You are such a silver-tongued devil.'

He put his cup down and reached for her and they fell into a clumsy embrace, tangled up in each other's arms and legs, sliding off the sofa onto the floor. Rearranging themselves, they went at each other like dogs in heat, wet, sloppy kisses, hands grabbing hunks of hair, bodies pressing hard, his hand under her sweater, caressing her breast through her bra. She rubbed his chest, his thighs, pulling him tighter to her.

Breathless, they came up for air. 'The bed will be more comfortable,' she gasped, taking his hand and leading him into her bedroom, where they fell onto the bed, making out like bandits.

'I'm not sleeping with you tonight.'

They were side by side, on their backs. They had been kissing for fifteen minutes without coming up for air. Their clothes were still on, except for their shoes. His cock in his jeans felt like a stalactite.

'I don't know you well enough yet,' she told him. 'And I'm having my period.'

'That's okay.'

'It's not that I don't want to.'

'It's okay,' he told her again, cutting her off. He turned to kiss her again.

118

His cell phone went off. The ring froze him, his mouth inches from her lips. It rang again.

'Aren't you going to answer it?' Amelia asked. 'It could be about your brother.'

He hadn't thought of that, but it was true. The caretakers had instructions to call him immediately if anything unforeseen happened. He took the phone out of his pocket and looked at the ID: *Private Party*. Not a hospice worker, their names would be displayed. Which left only one other possibility.

'Who is it?' Amelia asked.

'Didn't leave a number. Probably a telemarketer. They've perfected the art of calling at the most aggravating time to a science.'

The ringing stopped as his voice message came on. He thumbed the sound down to vibrate, in case there was a second call. Which there was, immediately on top of the first one. He could feel the phone vibrating against his leg. Chinese water torture couldn't be worse than this.

Amelia cupped the back of his head in her hand. 'Come here, you.'

He hadn't had a nicotine craving this intense in years, going back to when he was in jail, where smoking was prohibited. Talk about cruel and unusual punishment. This was worse, because the torture was self-inflicted.

He sat in the dark in his car, which was parked in Billy's driveway. He had a few minutes before the clock turned midnight and he had to go in to relieve Ricardo. He was going to call Charlotte; *not* calling her wasn't an option. But he was dreading the guilt tripping, accusation by implication. He had planned on doing it from outside Amelia's apartment, but then he had a terrible thought: what if Charlotte could tell where he was, from his cell phone? He was a dummy about electronics, he didn't know if a cell phone could act like a GPS, pinpointing your whereabouts down to a specific address on a specific block. So he hadn't called then. Now he had to.

Charlotte picked up on the second ring. He knew she wouldn't go to sleep until he called her back, no matter how late.

'Thanks for returning my call.' Her voice was neutral; not sweet and loving, but not harsh or accusatory, either. 'I was beginning to worry about you.'

'I'm fine,' he muttered.

'I'm happy to hear that. Where have you been? You weren't at your brother's.'

How in the world did she know that? Was she spying on him? An educated guess? A microchip she had secretly implanted in his brain? 'I was out. I'm here now, though. At his place.'

'Safe and sound. You are, aren't you? Safe, at least.'

'Yes,' he told her through clenched teeth. 'I'm good.'

Off-handed: 'So where were you again?'

Christ, he thought, she's relentless. 'Just out. Dinner, couple of beers. Nothing special.'

'If it was nothing special, then why can't you tell me where you were?' she continued, maddeningly rational. 'Unless you're hiding something from me, which I can't imagine you would do.'

He could feel the sarcasm almost literally oozing through the airways, into his telephone, and onto his skin, like sap dripping off a tree. 'And why didn't you answer when I called?' she went on. 'Were you preoccupied with something else?'

Some *one*, not some *thing*. 'I was in a restaurant. It's rude to talk on the phone in a restaurant.'

'What manners. I didn't realize you were such a quick learner, darling.'

Managing to keep up: 'That's because you're such a good teacher.'

The sarcasm dripped even thicker. 'Why thank you, Mr Charming. So you were where?'

He was not going to let her trip him up. 'Out, like I said.'

'Have it your way. I'll see you tomorrow evening.' An order, not an invitation. 'We're going to have an adventure.'

An adventure. He couldn't imagine what it might be, but he wasn't looking forward to it. He felt exhausted. Sparring with Charlotte was draining, the intensity of their love making turned inside-out.

'See you tomorrow,' he told her, hanging up before she could keep the conversation going any longer.

Billy, wide awake, was in the living room, watching Charlie Rose. 'This one was a pistol tonight,' Ricardo told Wycliff as he beamed at Billy. 'Polished off *two* heaping plates of food.

121

We're going to put meat on those bones, I'm telling you.'

'Yeah yeah yeah,' Billy laughed. He gave Ricardo a frisky waist-pinch.

'Be good,' Ricardo bantered to Billy as he was leaving. 'Don't do anything I wouldn't do.'

'Would that I could, Ricardo Ricky,' Billy answered, as he waved good-bye.

Two days and they're best friends forever, Wycliff thought. Billy had always made friends easily, going back to when he was a toddler with beautiful tow-head curls. Unlike himself, who was world-class at alienating anyone he came in contact with. Although Charlotte had sure as hell cottoned to him, in her own strange way. Amelia, too. Maybe he wasn't scaring people off any-more.

He sat alongside his brother, watching the tube. 'What do you do when you're out at night?' Billy asked. 'You got something going on the side?' he teased.

'Not hardly,' Wycliff answered, fending him off. 'Just cruising around.'

'Cruising is dangerous terminology to use with someone like me,' Billy goosed him verbally. 'Maybe the leopard really has changed his spots.'

Wycliff shook his head. Not long ago a state-ment like that would have raised his hackles. Now it was water off a duck's back. 'Naw, I'm still plain-vanilla straight. Not the adventure-some type.'

That, of course, was bullshit. What he had going with Charlotte was like the colors in the rainbow, including psychedelics and neons, all exploding together.

'Your loss. But you still have time.' *Unlike me* went unspoken. His brother's tank was about to run dry. He didn't know diddley about Billy's life, but he'd bet dollars to doughnuts the ride had been pretty damn wild.

It was nice, bantering with his brother like this. They had never been able to. Accusations and curses had been their common language. Looking death in the eye can bring a lot of fundamental changes, he thought insightfully. Not only bad ones, but good ones, too.

Billy turned to him. 'Do you get high?'

'You mean marijuana?' Wycliff asked, taken aback.

'No, dude, hot fudge sundaes.'

'Of course,' Wycliff said. 'Doesn't everyone?'

'Everyone I know, but I don't know everyone. You want to smoke? It helps me sleep, and toking alone isn't sociable.'

'Sure, I'm good. You holding?'

Billy pointed to a hutch in the corner. 'Baggie, pipe, and lighter in the second drawer.'

Wycliff found the goods and brought them over. 'You do the honors,' Billy said. 'My hands get to shaking. Don't want to spill any of this excellent sensimilla.'

Wycliff packed a loose bowl. He put the pipe to Billy's lips and lit it. Billy sucked in a greedy lungful, held the smoke for a few seconds, then expelled it with a chest-rattling cough. Wycliff held his brother's glass up so he could drink water through a straw. Then he fired up the pipe again and took a deep hit himself, the smoke banging his lungs. Immediately, he could feel a buzz.

'How do you score?' he asked. His brother spoke the truth: this was righteous weed. 'You have a dealer, someone you can trust?' That would be useful to know, if Billy was willing to share the info.

Billy, gasping for breath, was still able to cackle like a rooster. 'This is medical marijuana. Totally legitimate, courtesy of the voters of the sovereign state of California. Is this a great country, or what?'

Wycliff had never been inclined to think that way. Usually, it was the opposite. But a secure roof over his head, cash in his pocket, a lover who might be dangerous but exciting, and maybe a real relationship, too, knock wood? Not to mention free dope, courtesy of his brother? His life was still far from great, but right now, it was pretty up and walking good.

TWELVE

The woman looked to be in her mid-to-late thirties. She'd had her breasts done, plus other work; no mortal woman's cheekbones are that striking. Small waist, slender hips, well-rounded behind. The diamond on her ring finger was almost the size of a golf ball. Her stylishly disheveled blond hair was held together in a loose twist with a pair of chopsticks. She wore designer jeans and a silk blouse, unbuttoned partway down to show off her assets under the lacy bra. Three-inch heels. She had probably spent an hour putting herself together so she could look like she had just rolled out of bed.

Wycliff looked her over. She was sexy enough, in a Las Vegas showgirl kind of way. Attractive, not so much, because she was copping an attitude, acting out in public and not caring if anyone picked up on it. Less than a month ago he would have been dripping saliva down his shirt at the thought of bedding a hottie like this woman, but his horizon now was a lot higher than when he had hit town. He already had one incredible woman in hand, with another one maybe about to happen.

Be thankful for what you have, he reminded himself. Don't get greedy. He had come a long way in a very short time. If a couple of months ago anyone had told him he would be where he was at this moment, he would have called for the guys with the butterfly nets. Yet here he was, styling like a fresh prince. Count your blessings.

It was a couple minutes before eleven. Raquel had come to the house at ten to spell him for a few hours so that he could take care of a much-needed piece of business, which was about to transpire at a Verizon store on Little Santa Monica Boulevard, in Beverly Hills. No more pre-historic equipment for him: he was getting his own brand-spanking-new iPhone. He had called around to half a dozen locations until he found an outlet that had the phones in stock.

The store was busy. He had signed in and taken a seat, waiting for a sales person to become available. He had been here for fifteen minutes and there were still two customers ahead of him on the waiting list.

From where he was sitting he could see outside to the store's parking lot. The woman had pulled up in a midnight-blue Porsche Cayman. She had parked at the far end of the lot away from other cars, so it wouldn't get dinged up. To Wycliff's taste, the Cayman was the cherriest car on the road. He was happy with his Beemer, but if he could have any car, that Porsche would be the one. More than a Ferrari, Bentley, Maserati, cars that cost two, three, ten times as much. He didn't need the most expensive car in the world. That little bomb parked outside would be perfect.

The woman was on her cell as she stormed into the store and she kept her jabber going, even though she was in public. She had taken the chair right next to Wycliff's after she signed in, so he couldn't help but hear her end of the conversation, which was juicy. She was a recent widow who had been married to a man considerably older than her (confirmation of Wycliff's assumption that she was a trophy wife). She had been screwed in his will. Not only had all his money gone to his children, but, more importantly, now that she was no longer married, her credit rating had plummeted. She was in the process of negotiating to buy a new residence for herself (his kids had gotten all his property, too, including the house in Bel Air she had lived in with the deceased), and she was trying to scam her potential lender by withholding the information that she was no longer the spouse of a multi-millionaire. From hearing her side of the agitated conversation, Wycliff surmised that some underling in her accountant's office had accidentally blown her cover, and she was frantically scrambling to put Humpty Dumpty back together.

'Do whatever you have to do to fix it,' the woman told the person on the other end in bitter anger, 'or I will tie you bastards up in court for the next ninety-nine years.' She ended the call and slumped back, eyes shut tight, quivering like a hard-ridden thoroughbred.

Then she started crying, silently, her body shaking violently. Wycliff, startled and alarmed, looked around. Was anyone besides him watching her breakdown? A quick survey of the room told him no. She was alone in her grief. Plastic breasts, bullshit attitude, whatever else was phony about her, her emotions weren't fake. This woman was hurting for real. He felt the need to reach out to touch her, a hand on her shoulder, something minor to ease the pain, if only for a moment. But he hesitated. It wasn't his place to do anything.

His name was called. He glanced at the woman again but she was oblivious to him, absorbed in her sorrow. He got up and walked to the waiting salesperson.

It took half an hour to purchase the new phone, have his data transferred from his old one, choose a personal ring tone (the opening bars of the theme music from *The Good, The Bad, And The Ugly*), and get walked through a basic tutorial by the technician, so he became absorbed in his own business and lost track of the woman who had turned to mush in front of his eyes. As he left the store, though, he saw that her car was where she had parked it, so she was still inside. He hoped she had been able to pull herself together.

'Excuse me!'

He stopped and looked behind him.

The woman had come out of the store and was striding urgently towards him. She was wearing sunglasses, but he could see mascara smudges under her eyes from her tears. He waited for her to catch up. Her shades reflected the sun as she looked up at him. 'Do you drink?' she asked abruptly.

That was a weird question. 'Sure,' he answered.

'I mean now. In the morning.'

At one time or another Wycliff had knocked a drink back at every minute of the day and night, but he normally didn't drink early. That was for lushes, men (and the odd woman) you see go into a bar at six in the morning for their pre-work fix, or stagger out of one before the sun had risen. 'I've done that,' he admitted.

'Would you? Now?'

'Now?' he repeated, thrown off-guard.

'You were eavesdropping on my demented conversation in there, so you know I'm not doing very well. You weren't being rude,' she

128

continued, letting him know she wasn't angry that he had violated her space, 'you couldn't help it, I was out of control.' She ran her hands through her unkempt hair. 'I need to unwind, I'm really...' Her sigh was more like a moan. 'I need a drink, and I don't want to drink alone.'

He followed her in his car down South Beverly Drive. She hung a right on Pico, drove west for several blocks, then pulled over at a meter. Wycliff found an open spot further down the block and parked. The area was populated with small stores, ethnic restaurants, a couple of hole-in-the-wall bars. The woman tottered slightly on her high heels as she trotted up to him.

'You'll need quarters. The parking cops are merciless around here.' She handed him a dollar in coins, which he fed into his meter. 'We can get more change inside if we need it.'

How much drinking was she planning on, he wondered? He was on a schedule, he had to get back to the house. He would lend a sympathetic ear for as long as it took him to drink a bloody Mary, then make his exit.

The bar was long, narrow, and dark. A few hard-core habitués, solitary drinkers, took up space on stools. One bartender, no waitress. The woman led him to the last table in the back. 'What are you drinking?' she asked.

'I'll have a bloody Mary.'

'Two bloody Marys,' she called to the bartender. 'Extra Tabasco.'

As he did whenever possible, Wycliff sat facing the door. The woman slid in across from him and took off her shades. Her makeup was smeared, her eyes bloodshot. 'Do I look as bad as I feel?' she asked, staring him in the face.

'You've looked better, I'm sure.' He didn't know this woman from Adam, and in half an hour or less they would part company and he'd never see her again, so he could give it to her straight.

She tried to force a smile, but couldn't. 'At least you're honest. That's a long-gone commodity nowadays.' She coughed, trying to clear her throat. 'Who am I to talk? I'm more full of shit than anyone, pardon my French.'

Wycliff had nothing to say back to her, so he didn't. Coming here with her had been a waste of time. He should be on his way back to his brother's house, where he was actually needed. This woman wanted someone to vent at, and he was standing there with his thumb up his ass, so she had bagged him, and he'd let her. He didn't desire her except as an idle fantasy, the kind men enjoy dozens of times a day, but he also knew that if she had been a plain Jane he wouldn't have followed her here.

She glanced at his unadorned fingers. 'You're not married.'

'No.'

'Ever been?'

He shook his head. 'No.'

'You're smarter than me. I didn't even get a kid out of it. All I got was' – she waved a bejeweled hand in the air – 'stuff.'

The bartender set their drinks down at the end of the bar. The woman got up and brought them back. She picked up her glass and looked into it as if she was trying to see into a crystal ball.

'What do you do, if I may ask? I'm not trying to get personal or anything.'

The lie came out of his mouth so easily now he was beginning to believe it. 'I'm a contractor. Housing. Remodels.'

'Would I know you? I've remodeled some houses and flipped them. My husband and I.' She quickly amended: 'Late husband.'

Wycliff took a small sip of his drink. Properly done, spicy with a nice bite of horseradish. 'No,' he told her. 'I'm from out of state. I'm not licensed in California.'

She looked deflated, as if hoping their paths might have crossed. 'Oh.' She sampled her own drink, nodded approvingly, took another swallow. 'What are you doing here, then?'

They weren't going to get personal. He'd make sure of that, even if she didn't. 'I'm visiting a relative. My brother.' That admission couldn't get him into trouble.

'Are you going to be around long?'

Now it was getting too personal. 'I don't know. I'm playing it by ear.'

She studied him over the rim of her glass. 'You look like a cop. Were you, ever?'

He laughed. 'Not hardly. Why do you ask?'

'Because if I unburden myself to you – I kind of did, already, back at the phone store – I want to know I'm not going to get busted.'

'I'm not a cop,' he assured her. He wasn't going to get personal from his end, but where she seemed to be going sounded interesting. No

131

harm in listening. 'What are you afraid of?'

'Anything. Everything. The whole enchilada.' She leaned in towards him. 'Can I trust you?'

His impulse was to say *no, you can't*, but he didn't. 'You won't get in trouble with me,' he told her.

She stared at him as if trying to make up her mind. 'I shouldn't have asked you that, because I don't trust anyone these days, certainly not a stranger.' She smiled. 'A tall, handsome stranger, across a crowded room.'

Wycliff couldn't help but smile back at her. 'Thanks for the compliment.' Be nice, he reminded himself. She's hurting. 'You're very good looking yourself.'

Actively flirting now: 'Even with these raccoon eyes?'

'On you, it's sexy.'

She shook her head. 'Oh, God. I'm such a sucker these days. I am the neediest woman on earth. So now that you know that, you can go.'

This was fun. Just keep it light. 'I haven't finished my drink.' He held up his glass for proof.

'A billion people starving in China,' she came back. 'That's passé, isn't it? The reality is here, in places like New Orleans and the Jersey shore.'

Wycliff had missed his share of meals, recently enough to remember. He ate the olive off the toothpick. The woman reached across the table and took one of his hands in both of hers. Her hands were soft, the hands of a woman who had people working for her to do the heavy lifting.

'I want to tell you a few things about me,' she said. 'I'm not going to unburden my life story on you, just some recent history. Can you take it?'

'I can take anything you can throw at me,' he told her. Superficial woman. What he had lived through, what he was living though now, made any bullshit she could lay on him feel like a feather. 'Do I want to? That I don't know.'

The woman reared back in surprise, staring at him with fresh eyes. 'That's calling 'em like you see 'em. I respect that.'

He was trying to drive her away, but his coming on straight was having the opposite effect. He should have anticipated that. Played it cool, said *yes* or *no* to her questions, finished his drink, boogied on down the road. Now they were dancing.

In for a dime, in for a dollar. 'Talk to me.'

'Have you ever killed anyone?'

They were on their second bloody Marys. The bartender poured with a heavy hand. Wycliff wouldn't have a third. Looking at the woman, he could tell that the alcohol was affecting her. She had spilled some of her drink on the table, and giggled as she mopped it up with a cocktail napkin.

What to answer? Play with her, play it straight? Was she joking around, or was there an undercoat of seriousness there? 'Deliberately?' he decided to answer.

Her eyes tried to focus on him; came close. 'Is there any other way?'

'Lots of them. You could kill someone by

133

accident, in a car, for instance. You can kill legally, in the line of fire, if you're a cop or a soldier. Protecting a loved one against a murderer or rapist.' He ate the cocktail olive. 'That wasn't what you meant, was it?'

She took a second to recalibrate. 'I hadn't thought about the variations.'

'Anyway, to answer your question. I've never killed anyone. Deliberately or any other way.'

Her look back at him said *I'm not sure I believe you.*

They weren't going to get personal? This was walking right up to the line. He had to make sure he didn't cross it, if he hadn't already. 'I'm a lover, not a killer.'

'Talk is cheap,' she teased. She dipped her finger in her drink, sucked it slowly, staring at him.

Time to hit the road. Wycliff drained his glass, set it down. 'Thanks for the drinks, and the conversation. Hope your day turns around.' He stared to slide out of the booth.

'I'd pay a hundred thousand dollars.'

That stopped him in his tracks. 'What did you say?'

The woman looked around the bar. She and Wycliff could have been invisible, as far as the other patrons were concerned. 'You could use a hundred thousand dollars, couldn't you?'

'Everybody could use a hundred thousand dollars.'

'Sit down. Please. I'll make it short.'

Get out of Dodge, moron. He lowered himself back into the booth.

'Do you want another drink?'

Wycliff shook his head. 'You don't need one, either.'

'Needing and wanting are two different things, but you're right.' She twirled the sizzle stick between her fingers. Her nails were long, well manicured; she wasn't a nail-biter. Under the table, though, her leg was jitterbugging.

Was she serious? The phone conversation he'd overheard had been nasty. Who did she want to knock off? Did she hatch this crazy idea this morning, or had it been brewing, spreading its poison inside her? And if it had, had she hit on anyone else before him? That is, if she was serious.

She couldn't be. This was the alcohol talking.

She was serious. She told him why.

She had married a man who was decades older than her, old enough to be her father (older, in fact, than her actual father, a loser she had lost contact with long ago. Her mother was dead). Before that, she had been married and divorced young, no children from that marriage, and for the next ten years she had pulled herself up by her bootstraps, made a life for herself, by herself. No family behind her, no partner, just her. She became a successful florist. Her clients were among the wealthiest and most prestigious people in Los Angeles. She had been in a few serious relationships, but felt no need to be married again, so inevitably, those relationships ended. She was fine being on her own, in charge of her life.

Then the man who became her second husband

came into the picture. He was rich, worldly, dynamic, and married for forty years. His marriage had been stale for a long time; a marriage in name only. But until he met her he had not considered leaving it. He would soldier on, filling his life with work, children, grand-children. But after he met her, he knew that wasn't enough.

What dreary, pathetic bullshit, Wycliff thought as he listened. Women like her had been singing this same sad song since Eve bit into the apple. Why had he agreed to stay? Because he was a sucker for a crying woman who happened to have terrific breasts? Probably, what other reason could there be? Now he was stuck. He would have to wait until she finished her tale of woe.

'Can I get some coffee?' he called to the bartender. 'Make it two,' he added. 'Black.'

He brought the mugs back to the table and put one in front of her. He sipped from his cup. Too acidic, it had been sitting in the pot all morning. She moved hers to the side without trying it. She didn't need coffee. Talking was sobering her up.

She continued her story. The man was relent-less in his attentiveness, persistence, and gener-osity. He showered her with expensive gifts. Took her to New York, Vegas, Europe, in the guise of business trips, introducing her as his personal assistant, although they didn't take separate rooms, so that cover was pretty trans-parent. She knew getting involved with a married man was wrong, hurtful to others, potentially hurtful to herself. She kept trying to break it off, but he wouldn't let her. He had accumulated his wealth, his power, by never giving up when he wanted something. More than anything, he wanted her. In the end, he wore her down. And she did love him. That was the problem. If she hadn't loved him she would have been able to resist.

The usual horror show ensued. His family was shattered. They blamed her, of course, not him. The conniving bitch who had preyed on an old man's desire to turn back the clock, leaving his spurned wife on her own, wandering the divorce wilderness.

'She got a thirty-million-dollar cash settlement and the house, boo hoo hoo, but oh, the grief! She kept bitching and moaning that she was too old and tarnished to attract another man, but somehow she began a new relationship less than a year later and is very happy now. Still unmarried, though, which is shrewd. Marrying again doesn't make financial sense. As long as she stays single, she collects alimony, even after his death.'

All three adult children turned against their father; but eventually, two of them, his sons, came to accept her. She was good for the old man, she lifted his spirits, doted on him, wasn't a prima donna.

So you say, Wycliff thought. He wondered what the real feelings were. Not that he would ever find out, God forbid.

The problem, the woman explained, was the man's daughter. She never budged in her hatred and anger towards the new wife, and by extension, her father. The relationship between father and daughter was shattered beyond repair. It had broken the man's heart.

She and her husband had a good life together anyway, and then he died. A heart attack out of the blue, right on the tennis court after two sets of doubles. No history of heart problems. He was scrupulous in taking care of his health. Ate properly, drank sparingly, no drugs or tobacco, saw his doctors on schedule. His number had come up. One day here, the next day gone.

There was no pre-nuptial agreement. She didn't feel it was necessary, and she knew he would do the right thing by her. Besides, California is a community-property state. Half of his estate was hers, by law. Except it turned out it wasn't, because he had made all his money and accumulated all his physical property – houses, cars, art, everything – before she married him. He had been so happy hooking up with her that he had sold his company before their marriage and put it all in a trust, to be shared by his children. And her, she thought. But that's not how it happened. He had never changed his will; nothing malicious, simple carelessness. His kids got everything. She got the shitty end of the stick.

'I had a home of my own,' she told Wycliff. She had discarded the swizzle stick and was shredding a napkin. 'I sold it. I had a prosperous business. I sold that, too. That was seven years ago, before the market crashed. I don't have the money to buy a new house now or start a business from scratch. I don't want their money. I just want what I deserve, what I know he wanted me to have. God knows there's more than enough for everyone.'

Despite his resolve not to get involved, Wycliff felt a pang of pity for the woman. Wasn't he in the same situation, sort of? Trying to weasel his way into a piece of a relative's inheritance? If this woman's story was legit, and by now he had decided it probably was, she had a stronger claim to some of her late husband's money than he had for his brother's.

Who ever said life was fair? Not him.

The sons knew she had been screwed and wanted to cut her in. Not an equal share, but what was fair. The daughter, though, was an impenetrable wall. Zero, nothing, *nada*. And without unanimous consent, nothing could be done.

'So that's who you want killed? The daughter?'

The woman nodded. 'For obvious reasons, it should look like an accident.'

Wycliff barked a laugh. 'Sorry,' he said, 'I know this is serious to you, but that's nuts. You would never get away with it.'

'I know,' she answered. 'That's why I have to find someone who will do it for me. Someone completely unconnected to me.'

The coffee was cold now. He didn't want it anyway, didn't need it. He was stone-cold sober, and looking across the table from her, he knew she was, too. 'It won't be me,' he told her. 'If you're smart, it won't be anyone.' He got out of the booth. 'Do yourself a favor. Figure something else out.'

'I've tried, believe me. At this point, there is nothing else.'

'Guess I'll see you on the news, then. Take care.'

The woman opened her purse, took out a card, and held it out to him. 'In case you change your mind. Or want to talk more about it.'

He hesitated, then took the card from her hand. He would toss it later. He walked out of the bar, resisting the urge to look back.

THIRTEEN

'I'm knitting a sweater for my grandson,' Raquel informed Wycliff as she gathered up her yarn and needles and stowed them in her bag. 'He'll be three next month. Child runs his parents *ragged*.' She washed her coffee cup and placed it in the sideboard. 'Ricardo called. He can't make it tonight. Family conflict.'

Wycliff knew that would happen some time or another, so he wasn't surprised or upset. 'How's my brother?'

'Holding his own. He slept most of the morning. His energy goes fast.'

Wycliff looked into the living room. Billy was sound asleep. His face was smooth, untroubled. As smooth as a baby's ass, Wycliff thought. He had never had a kid, so that particular cliché was second-hand knowledge to him, but he understood the underlying sentiment. Babies and old people look the same: fresh and all wrinkled up at the same time. On the outside. Inside, not the same.

'I'm not going to be able to come tomorrow, either,' Raquel said. 'So it's you and him for awhile.'

'That's why I'm here.' Which was true. Everything else was secondary. The abstraction was now the reality.

He closed the door behind Raquel and locked it, a reflex action from when he suspected everything and everybody and had to be constantly on guard, an old habit too ingrained to let go of. His present circumstances were better now, but they were still far from wine and roses: he had to deal with whatever crazy schemes Charlotte had up her sleeve, and then there was the off-the-wall encounter less than an hour ago with a woman who wanted to hire him to murder her dead husband's daughter. What vibe did he send out that gave people the notion that he was some stranger you could out of the blue ask to commit a crime and his response would be *where and when*?

Only certain people picked that up, like Charlotte and that woman just now. People who carried their own sins and could smell out a kindred soul. Amelia had not seen that in him. He was going to make sure she didn't.

Too much internal commotion. Slow everything down. Sit in this quiet house, watch his brother sleep. Charlotte had plans for them tonight. He needed to call and tell her to cancel them. Not a prospect to look forward to. It was early yet, he could hold that off a while longer.

He made himself a ham-and-cheese sandwich on rye and put on a fresh pot of coffee, Italian Roast he had bought and ground at Trader Joe's, now his default grocery store. He had never been domestic like this before – his life had been a series of unconnected episodes, drifting from place to place, one crummy job to the next, no permanent relationships, no plan. He still didn't have one, really. Whatever scheme he wound up doing with Charlotte was her thing, not his. And the idea that he could actually have any kind of real relationship with Amelia was a fantasy. He had nothing to offer her. They were flawed from the beginning, because he had lied to her from the first words out of his mouth. He would need a time machine to fix that, and what would he replace it with?

He would deal with all that later. He finished his sandwich and washed his dishes. He liked keeping a clean house. And with Billy here, so susceptible to infection, it was an absolute necessity.

He couldn't put off calling Charlotte any longer. This would not be a fun phone call. Now that he had his new iPhone he would learn how to text, so he wouldn't have to actually talk to her when he had bad news to deliver.

Suck it up, he rebuked himself. She'll rant for a minute and then it will be over. He punched in her number.

There was dead silence for about ten seconds

after he gave her the news. Then: 'Did I hear you correctly?'

He told it again. 'The caretaker can't come tonight, so I have to stay here.'

'Get a different one.'

He would learn how to text today. 'It doesn't work that way, Charlotte. It's not like calling a babysitter. These people are specially trained to do this. You can't just find someone in the *Yellow Pages*.'

Another long silence. His hand was sweating, holding the phone. 'I find this unreasonable, Wycliff,' she said, her voice icicle-sharp. 'I'm sure you can work something out.'

Her narcissism was infuriating. 'I wish I could, but it isn't possible. Look, this isn't something we should be arguing about over the phone. Come over here and we'll discuss it face to face. You need to see what it's like here, so you'll understand.'

'I can't do that.'

'Why not?'

'I'll explain when I see you, but not there. Not at your brother's house.'

This is weird, he thought, not for the first time. Was there something between her and Billy that she didn't want to confront? Maybe they'd had a falling out. Or maybe, like so many others who knew his brother, she couldn't take seeing him as he was now.

'I'm sorry you feel that way,' he told her, hanging firm, 'but I'm stuck here tonight. I'll do my best to work something out for tomorrow. Sorry to have messed up your plans.'

He hung up. He waited, prepared for a verbal reaming, but she didn't call back.

On impulse, he called Amelia. She didn't answer – he figured she was working – but he left a message. He couldn't see her tonight, either, but he wanted to hear a friendly voice, and he knew she wouldn't bust his balls over the phone.

What would it be like to be in a relationship with a woman who was just herself, who had no agenda? He could deal with schemers, he was a schemer himself. But someone who wasn't shady, who in the world he'd always lived in would be thought of as a patsy, a mark to be played, how do you relate to someone like that? Lies came easier to Wycliff than the truth and always had, from the time he had learned that if he told the truth he would most likely get the snot kicked out of him.

Anyway, there was no future for him with Amelia. Some fun, some laughs, hopefully some good sex. But no legs. She would eventually figure him out and that would be the end of it. He could fool all of the people some of the time, but not forever.

And there was something else, square in his face. Billy was going to die soon. Maybe he could eke out a few more months, but it was deep in the fourth quarter and the clock was running out. Once his brother died, there would be nothing here for him. This house would go to whomever Billy had left it to in his will, ditto his money, and the older brother would be on his own again, out on his ass.

144

One hundred thousand dollars would go a long way to solving all his problems. He wished he hadn't met that woman in the iPhone store. Life is simpler when you don't have to make choices.

'Wycliff? Are you here?'

His brother was awake.

'Yeah, Billy, I'm right here. What do you need?'

Wycliff bathed his brother, powdered him dry, changed him into fresh clothes, and made him comfortable in the special chair in the living room. Billy's complexion was sallow yellow. His liver was failing, Wycliff knew. Pretty soon everything would shut down, and then it would be days, not weeks.

Billy's body was decaying from the inside, but his style was intact. Looking at himself in the mirror, he commented dryly, 'I'll need the make-up artist in my trailer, please. The genius who worked such miracles on Michael Jackson. He's so good around the eyes. And while you're up, would you pour me a glass of champagne? Have one for yourself as well. Imbibing by oneself is so uncivilized.'

Wycliff rummaged around the back of the refrigerator and found a bottle of Bollinger Reserve. Dusty champagne flutes (he knew what they were now) were in the breakfront. He rinsed two in the sink, popped the cork and poured two glasses. Handing one to his brother, he raised his glass in toast.

'To a life worth living,' he proposed.

Billy held his glass high. 'That's pretty heavy, Wycliff. I didn't know you were such a deep thinker.'

'I stole the quote off the back of a Wheaties box,' Wycliff said. 'The one that had the secret decoder ring inside.'

Billy smiled and sipped champagne. 'Scrumptious. What do you think I should have for my last meal? Besides more champagne.'

They had been avoiding talking about Billy's actually dying. Wycliff still didn't want to. 'We'll worry about that when the time comes,' he said, sounding more gruff than he meant. He had come here to watch his brother die and try to scope out a piece of the estate. Now he didn't want Billy to go. Billy was prepared, but he, Wycliff, wasn't.

'The time has come,' Billy answered. 'We both know that. We're just waiting for that hooded figure with the scythe to knock on the door.'

'I don't hear any knocking,' Wycliff said. 'So let's leave it alone.'

Billy stared at him with sunken eyes. 'You can do that. I can't.'

'Fair enough,' Wycliff conceded. What goes through a dying person's mind? Fear, relief, anxiety, wondering if there could actually be an afterlife after all? He didn't have a clue. Just thinking about it paralyzed him.

'But today, you're alive. So let's deal with today.'

They played Hollywood-style gin rummy, a penny a point. Billy kept score. Wycliff was rusty; he hadn't played in ages. Texas Hold 'Em and stud poker were his card games. Before he knew it he was shut out in the first game, about to be in the second, and was down ten dollars.

'You need to concentrate,' Billy advised him. 'If I'm picking up fives don't throw me another five.'

'I didn't know you were picking up fives.'

'That's because you weren't paying attention. You're so rich you can afford to lose money?'

Wycliff, who was basically broke when he hit town, now had a couple thousand dollars from the Lexus-BMW swap in his pocket (not his actual pocket, the money was hidden in his underwear and sock drawers), but he understood what Billy was talking about. Money doesn't come easy and you don't know when you're going to see any more, so you have to be careful about what you do with it. Like not losing at gambling. Not gambling, period. Their father's mantra, drummed into them like a tom-tom whenever they had approached him for school clothes or lunch money, had been *money doesn't grow on trees, you little assholes*, usually followed by a dose of the strap. But this was penny-ante stuff with his brother. He was happy to lose a few bucks if it kept Billy from thinking about how little time he had left.

'You know what I'd like for dinner?' Billy said. It was late in the afternoon, coming on evening. They had been playing cards for hours. Wycliff was down over thirty dollars.

'More champagne?' He threw an eight of clubs and immediately remembered his brother has already picked up an eight. Pay attention, he admonished himself.

Billy scooped up the eight and threw a jack. Wycliff wasn't collecting jacks. 'Pizza. Thin crust, with mushrooms and peppers and extra cheese. From a real pizza parlor, not a chain.'

'Is that on your diet?' Wycliff was being careful to make sure Billy didn't eat anything that could upset his system more than it already was.

'Who cares? What's it going to do, kill me?' Billy laughed his throat-rattle laugh. He coughed up a wad of phlegm into a tissue. 'I want to enjoy what time I have left, not hoard it like a miser counting his nickels and dimes.'

'You're right,' Wycliff agreed. The man was at death's door, why deny him a simple pleasure like that? 'Where do you like it from? Some place not too far that delivers, it has to be.'

'Pizza Royale on Sunset is good. Tell them it's for me and they'll deliver. What time is it?'

Wycliff checked the time on his new cell phone. 'Ten after five.'

'We'll call at six and we can eat by seven. On me,' he added.

Wycliff's cell phone rang. He clutched – Charlotte dropping another shoe. She had a full wardrobe of them she could pile on him. 'I'll take this outside,' he said, getting up from the table.

'Got a honey on the line?' Billy teased.

Wycliff didn't answer. He went out onto the back patio. The phone was still ringing. He looked at the ID. It wasn't Charlotte.

He answered it. 'Hello?'

'You called me,' Amelia said. 'What's up?'

She would pick up the pizza and a bottle of wine

148

along the way. 'I want to meet your brother. You upended your life to be here for him, he must be special.'

'He is. But you don't have to do this. Driving across town at this time of day is brutal. Why not wait when it's easier? He isn't going anywhere.'

'It's never easy in LA, and I've got a hankering for pizza. Unless you don't want me to come.'

'Of course I do,' he answered, maybe too hastily, but he wasn't going to play it cool with her. 'I think Billy will like meeting you.'

'I'll be my most charming. And I'm bringing pizza. He's going to adore me.'

He will, Wycliff agreed silently. He'll be surprised that a woman of her character would want to be with Wycliff, but he would certainly like her.

He went back inside. 'Who was it?' Billy asked out of idle curiosity.

'The person who's going to deliver the pizza.'

Billy was confused. 'What are you talking about? Why would they call?'

'It's a mystery,' Wycliff agreed. He couldn't help but smile. 'Which will explain itself, in its own time.'

It was love at first sight. Billy fell head over heels for Amelia. 'Why haven't you brought her here before?' he cried out to Wycliff.

'We just met, bro.'

'You're lucky, man.' To Amelia: 'He's lucky.'

'Of course he is,' she answered, softly stroking Billy's arm.

Wycliff, dazed, watched the two of them

149

banter like they had been best friends forever. In his wildest dreams he couldn't have imagined it this good. He had wanted her to come and he hadn't. His life was compartmentalized. No two people that he knew knew each other. He had always lived that way. That was how he protected himself. Now he was naked.

Amelia plumped up Billy's pillows. 'Better?' she asked.

'Much.'

The pizza was excellent, as Billy had promised. They washed it down with a nice Santa Barbara County syrah. 'The wine country up there is as beautiful as Napa,' Amelia told Wycliff. 'Have you ever been?'

'No,' he said. 'I just got here,' he reminded her.

'It would be a nice day-trip. The three of us,' she said, making sure Billy was included. 'We could rent a minivan, fix up the back like a bed, you would be as comfortable as you are here,' she told Billy.

'I'm up for it,' Billy enthused.

'Sounds like a plan,' Wycliff said. Charlotte had talked about taking the same trip, but without Billy. Going with Amelia and Billy would be much more fun.

As Wycliff knew would happen, his brother's energy didn't last. He faded as soon as dinner was over. Wycliff took him into the bathroom to wash him up before putting him to bed.

Billy suddenly convulsed, a forceful spasm. He leaned over the toilet and threw up most of his dinner. Wycliff held him steady over the rim

150

until he was finished, then washed his face clean, brushed his teeth, and gave him a cup of mouthwash to gargle.

'Don't tell Amelia,' Billy implored him.

'What happens in Vegas stays in Vegas.'

'Thanks.' Billy's smile was a grimace of embarrassment. Wycliff stripped him, washed him, changed his diaper, put fresh pajamas on, and helped him to bed. He was asleep within seconds.

They retreated into the kitchen so they wouldn't disturb Billy, who could be a fragile sleeper. 'You're wonderful with him,' Amelia said, keeping her voice low.

'I don't have a choice, so I might as well do it the best I can.'

'Not everyone would.'

Not everyone had a shot at a million-dollar house and a substantial estate. Wycliff kept that thought to himself, even though he knew it wasn't going to happen, and by now wasn't the reason he was taking care of Billy anyway. 'Thanks,' he said, feeling embarrassed. 'Coming from you, that means a lot.'

They went into his bedroom and started making out. Amelia came on strong, giving herself to him, no inhibitions this time. They stripped out of their clothes and made love. It wasn't volcanic like with Charlotte, but it felt better. As her orgasm crescendoed she bit his shoulder to keep from crying out and waking Billy. Wycliff flashed that he would have a bodacious hickey tomorrow, which was probably the next time he would be having sex with Charlotte. She would demand to know who gave it to him. That would be a bitch to explain.

What a tangled web he was weaving.

Charlotte called at two thirty, long after Amelia, whose shift started at seven in the morning, had kissed him goodbye and left. Wycliff didn't know what his schedule was going to be for the next few days, so he and she would play it by ear. Get together again as soon as possible, for sure. He had fallen asleep in a state of bliss. Charlotte's phone call brought him crashing back to reality.

'Don't you ever sleep?' he complained, groggy from being awakened.

'The early bird gets the worm. Where were you tonight?'

'I told you. Here. With my brother.'

'Just the two of you?'

She had to be spying on him. Not personally, she wouldn't stoop to do the physical legwork. She would have hired a detective to track him and report back to her. He should have thought of that and taken steps to cover his tracks.

He got out of bed, padded into the dark living room, and peeked out through the drawn blinds. The street was empty, no traffic, a puddle of light from a single street lamp halfway down the block, otherwise dark. No one was out there that he could see, but that meant nothing. A decent detective wouldn't be in the open. His paranoia was coming on stronger. But paranoia doesn't come out of nowhere, he reminded himself. There has to be a basis in reality.

Her focus was like a laser. 'Was there someone else there?'

Stop being afraid of your shadow, he cursed at himself. 'Yes,' he answered.

'I knew it!' Her voice was triumphant. 'Who was it? Don't lie to me.'

'A nurse.' Not a lie.

'A nurse?' That threw her. 'Has something happened to your brother? Has he gotten worse?'

'He gets worse every day.'

'I know that.' She sounded subdued, suddenly passive rather than aggressive. 'I meant something specific.'

'He was having trouble breathing.' Again, not a complete lie. Billy was continuously having trouble breathing. He was on the oxygen tank part of every day, some days more than others. Today, actually, he hadn't needed it as much. But Charlotte didn't have to know that.

'Emphysema,' Charlotte said, as if she knew.

'It's everything.' Awake now, the cobwebs cleared from his brain, he played a trump card. 'If you actually saw him, you'd understand.'

'I've already told you. I can't do that.'

He had guessed right, she wouldn't come here, no matter what. In the past, her refusal hadn't mattered to him, one way or the other. He had attributed it to queasiness, being around a dying man who was physically repellent. But now he wasn't sure if that was the reason. 'Why not?' he asked, pushing her.

'I just can't,' she said testily. 'Please do not bring the subject up again.'

153

'Fine, I won't. But then don't be bugging me about not being able to be with you whenever you want. It isn't always possible.'

'I understand. So will I see you tonight?' She seemed to be almost pleading, while trying not to.

'It's after two in the morning, Charlotte. I'll find out what's going on later.'

'And you'll call and let me know?'

This time he hung up without answering.

FOURTEEN

'Wear your suit. The dark shoes that go with it, a fresh white shirt, and a tie, of course. Make sure the suit is pressed and the shoes are polished. Pick me up at seven.'

There she was again, this time instructing him on how to dress, like he was ten years old. *I'm not the same man I was when you met me*, he contemplated reminding her; but that impulse only lasted for a second. He didn't sweat small stuff like this anymore. He told her he understood the drill, and let the bile pass out of his system.

Earlier, Amelia had called. She had to work an emergency double shift, so she wasn't free tonight, and Ricardo was back on the job, so he was available to be with Charlotte after all. He thought about lying, using Billy as an excuse,

154

but he decided not to. Charlotte would find out in the end and there would be more hell to pay. He had bought his ticket to ride, and she would decide when it was time for him to get off.

Besides, he had a different perspective on their relationship now, so he could be with her and not feel like he was falling down a rabbit hole. She was a fascinating woman. She was helping him broaden his horizons, and would continue to do so. And, of course, she was insane in bed. That still counted for a lot. Yes, she was using him, how and why, he still didn't know. But he could use her, too. There was some rough balance in their relationship now, and that gave him a feeling of security.

'You would be on time.' Charlotte was wearing a robe, stockings, no shoes. Her makeup was only partially done – he could see age lines and blotches where she hadn't put on foundation yet. She scampered back into her bedroom. 'Fix yourself a drink. You know where everything is.' The bedroom door closed behind her.

He would pass on imbibing. Wherever she was taking him would be serving alcohol. He was going light on the booze tonight. Stay sharp, keep his wits about him. He didn't want Charlotte to have an edge.

He crossed the room and opened the side table drawer where he had put the gun. He didn't want it, but he was curious to know if it was still there. It was. He picked it up and hefted it in his hand. Heavy, solid. Beautiful, in its lethal way. He cracked the cylinder. It was loaded, the same as the last time he'd handled it.

Why did he want to know if the gun was there, he wondered. The security of feeling you're in control if there's a weapon at hand? He didn't want a gun on his person. He couldn't afford the risk. But he felt a sense of security that it was here. He put it back where he had found it and closed the drawer. He walked back into the living room, picked up a recent issue of *Vogue* from the coffee table, and leafed through it blankly.

Charlotte, now in heels and full makeup, came out of her bedroom. 'Zip me up, darling.' She turned her back to him. He slid the zipper up her back, the tips of his fingers tickling her spine, leaning forward and inhaling the perfume on the back of her neck. She smelled good. She always smelled good.

'Later,' she said, reading his mind as she squeezed his hand. 'We don't have time now.'

He would have fun tonight, he thought, as they rode the elevator down to his car in the garage. He would meet some of whoever *they* are. The big deals of society, presumably, movie moguls, kings of real estate, financial wizards, celebrities whose pictures were plastered in *People*. Maybe some of the Kardashian girls would be there, like the one married to the basketball player. That would be cool, meeting an actual star athlete.

No Kardashians. No celebrities at all that he recognized. Most of the guests milling around were middle aged and older, the men dressed like him (they looked at ease in their expensive suits, which he didn't), the women in fashionable cocktail dresses.

Charlotte, comfortable in this milieu, air-kissed like a pro. The greetings were generic: *sweetheart, darling.* It seemed to Wycliff that no one here really knew each other but were acting as if they were best friends forever. If there were any actual actors in the bunch they weren't people Wycliff knew of or had seen.

Aside from the suits, a small minority of the crowd were his age or younger. Artists of various kinds: painters, musicians, writers, according to Charlotte, who was giving him a whispered running commentary as this and that face passed in front of them. The younger men were not in suits. They had on T-shirts and torn jeans; a different kind of uniform, but still a uniform. The women wore mini-skirts that barely covered their behinds. There was an excellent representation of tattoos and body piercings on both men and women. No one from this crowd of either sex gave him a second look. He was on the other side of the border.

The event, an art-opening benefit for some charity Wycliff had never heard of, was being held in a gallery in West Los Angeles, near the Design Center. Wait staff circulated the large space, bearing trays of wine and unappetizing hors d'oeuvres. Paintings by the featured artist hung on the walls. The paintings were massive nudes of both sexes, showing huge asses and tits and thighs and cocks in contorted sexual postures. Kind of cool, Wycliff thought as he looked them over, although he couldn't imagine having one in his house on an everyday basis. It was like porn: you look at that stuff too much, it doesn't turn you on anymore.

'Do you think he's stolen more from Francis Bacon or Lucien Freud?'

Wycliff turned to face the man standing behind him who had asked the question. Mid-to-late forties, thin, hair slicked back in a Fred Astaire Brylcreem comb-over, in his double-breasted Versace suit looking like he had just stepped out of the pages of *GQ*. As to the man's question, he didn't have a clue.

'Freud, of course,' Charlotte answered for him, her arm entwining with his. 'Don't be a show-off, John, it confirms your lack of breeding.'

'I'm only a coal-miner's son, what do you expect from me, finesse?' the man bantered back. 'It's good to see you, darling.'

They air-kissed. Wycliff kept his distance. He didn't want some guy kissing him, even if no skin touched.

The man held Charlotte's hand in his fingers. 'Are you keeping busy?' he asked, looking from her to Wycliff, who was beginning to feel like a butterfly ensnared in a collector's net.

'Busy enough. You know me, I have a Mexican jumping bean in my DNA.'

The man turned to Wycliff. 'John Cummings,' he said, extending his hand.

'How rude of me,' Charlotte interjected. 'John, say hello to Wycliff.'

The men shook hands. 'Good to meet you,' Cummings said. 'What brings you out on this dark and stormy night? Aside from the company of this charming lady?'

Charlotte answered for Wycliff again. 'He is a friend, from out of town.'

'Whereabouts?' Cummings asked in a tone that implied he couldn't care less about where Wycliff was from or anything else about him. He was making cocktail party small talk, nothing more.

This time Charlotte didn't speak up, so Wycliff answered the question himself. 'Arizona. Tucson.'

'I like Tucson,' Cummings said, as if he actually meant it. 'Clean air, great golf, still livable, unlike here.' He opened his arms wide, embracing Los Angeles, California, the entire west coast.

'So move there,' Charlotte chided him. 'You can play golf to your heart's content.'

'Maybe when I retire,' Cummings answered. 'My work here is not yet done.'

'John manages a hedge fund,' Charlotte explained to Wycliff. 'He's very successful.'

'I keep my head above water,' Cummings said. He lifted a glass of white wine from a passing waiter's tray. 'What's your racket, my friend?'

Again, Charlotte stepped in. 'Wycliff is a contractor.'

Cummings raised an inquisitive eyebrow. Charlotte nudged Wycliff in the ribs. 'Housing,' he said, responding to his cue. 'Mostly remodels, these days.'

'Are you any good?'

'He's excellent,' Charlotte said forcefully.

Cummings breathed out a long *hmmm.* 'Nice to know there's someone decent in that business. I can't tell you how badly I was ripped off by my last contractor.' He shuddered.

'It's a crapshoot,' Charlotte said with seeming expertise.

'True that. But if I am gambling, I prefer to do it in Vegas, not with my *home.*' He clapped a hand on Wycliff's shoulder. 'Perhaps I could prevail on you to come take a look. It's still a mess.'

Wycliff was out of his league here. Charlotte knew that, of course, but she wasn't going to bust him. Just the opposite: she was puffing him up. To make her look good, so he wouldn't be just a boy-toy on her arm. Still, ten minutes at the guy's house and it would be clear he was a bullshit artist.

Fortunately, he had an out, one he had used before. 'I'd like to help you,' he told Cummings, 'but I'm not licensed in California.'

'Too bad,' Cummings said. 'I pay top dollar.' He took a sip of wine, wrinkled his nose. 'So what is your business here, if you're not working?'

Wycliff could knock that one out of the park with his eyes closed. 'My brother's dying. He doesn't have much time left. There's no other family, just the two of us.'

Cummings seemed genuinely mortified. 'My God. I'm sorry.'

'Wycliff walked away from everything to take care of his brother in his final days,' Charlotte told Cummings. She gave Wycliff an adoring

160

look.

'That's damn noble of you, man.' This time Cummings' hand on Wycliff's arm was for real. 'No one in my life would do that for me.'

'No one in most peoples' lives,' Charlotte chimed in. 'The older we get the more cynical we become, but this gesture moved me tremendously. It's one of the reasons I've become so fond of Wycliff.'

There might not be any movie stars here, Wycliff thought, but there was one damn good actress, the lady whose arm was in his. He felt like he was a character inside a video game. Everything was a close facsimile of the real world, but it was all make-believe. Nothing was how things are in real life, like what was happening to his brother or how he felt when he was with Amelia.

He helped himself to a glass of wine from a passing serving tray. The trick was to not give a damn. He had been scamming his entire life, just on a lower level. Now he was raising his sights, thanks to Charlotte. He could skate through this without breaking a sweat.

'If you two lovely men will excuse me for a moment,' Charlotte said, breaking into his thoughts, 'I'm going to powder my nose.'

She made her way through the crowded room, exchanging greetings along her way. Wycliff and Cummings, thrown together without ballast, awkwardly stood next to each other. 'How about them Dodgers,' Cummings cracked.

'They're getting it together.' Wycliff had been in Los Angeles long enough by now to have learned about the pathetic saga of their former owner and the hopes raised by the new ones.

'I have season tickets, but I rarely go. You're welcome to use them, if you'd like,' Cummings offered. 'Good seats, field boxes at first base.'

Amelia might like that. He'd check with her.

'Let me ask you a personal question,' Cummings said. 'You don't have to answer if you don't want to. What is your brother dying from?'

'AIDS. He's in the final stages. Everything's shutting down.'

Cummings shuddered. 'That's brutal. I feel for you.'

'I'm doing okay. He's the one to feel for.'

'I'll pray for him.' Cummings changed the subject to a safer one. 'Your business that Charlotte mentioned, contracting. That's a cash business, isn't it? Cash and checks. That's how I paid my contractor. Almost all transactions all over the world now use credit cards, but yours seems to have sidestepped that. Or am I wrong? Do you take credit cards?'

Wycliff didn't have a credit card, let alone a business that took them. His last Visa card had been confiscated by a geek store employee when it was refused on a sixty-dollar charge for socks and underwear. Day-laboring and temp jobs, the only straight work he had done the past several years, were strictly cash and carry.

'Some of my vendors do,' he lied smoothly. 'I don't. The surcharge they tack on would put me out of business. I prefer to pass the savings on to my clients.'

Cummings leaned in close, as if they were

conspirators. 'I know exactly what you mean! All those government regulations. They're killing the American dream. If someone in power had the guts to pass a law abolishing the federal government, I'd be the first one to sign up.' He laughed. 'Don't take me seriously. But entrepreneurs are way over-regulated. That's why the economy's still in a mess.'

Wycliff nodded. He didn't give a shit about politics, they were all jackals. He'd never voted in his life, a perverse distinction he took pride in.

'So without getting personal,' Cummings continued; then he laughed. 'I already said that, didn't I? Sorry.'

'It's okay.' This man was uncomfortable with silence. He didn't have to answer any question he didn't want to.

'Thanks.' Cummings paused. 'What do you do with your money? Are you in the market?'

It was time to end this charade before he said something stupid and blew his cover. 'Like you said, that's personal.'

Cummings took a step back. 'You're right. It's none of my business. You seem like a really good guy, taking care of your brother, putting your business on hold.'

He took out his billfold from his inside coat pocket and pulled out a business card, which he handed to Wycliff. 'Helping people manage their money is what I do. I'm good at it. Charlotte will attest to that. If I can ever help you, give me a call. No strings.' He looked around the crowded room. 'You're doing something worthwhile. Most of the people in this room wouldn't know

163

what the right thing was if it kicked them in the balls,' he said bitterly. 'Hang in there.'

'I don't know about you, but I'm famished,' Charlotte declared. 'Those were the most insipid hors d'oeuvres I've ever eaten. Who hired that caterer?'

Wycliff smiled. Charlotte was being real, a regular person. She could be fun when she wasn't pushing his buttons.

They were on Melrose, driving towards her apartment. It was slow going, normal LA evening traffic. 'We could try Dan Tana's, but they'll be mobbed,' she said, thinking out loud. 'Why don't we just pick up burgers and fries? We'll wash it down with a good red wine, it'll be like eating in a funky bistro in Paris. Native food and decent plonk.'

They detoured to the In-N-Out on Sunset (his choice, Charlotte would never set foot in a place like that by herself, she wouldn't even know it existed) and picked up burgers and fries, which they nibbled on as he drove to her place. 'These are *good*,' Charlotte exclaimed with delighted surprise.

As soon as they got to her apartment they made love right away. Charlotte was her usual insatiable self, but there was an undercurrent of tenderness and maybe anxiety he hadn't seen in her before. If she noticed the bite mark on his shoulder she didn't comment on it. Her bedroom was dark, there were no lights on, and they had gone to it right away without foreplay, so maybe it hadn't been visible to her. Or else she had decided tonight was not a good time to get in his face.

They reheated their food in the microwave. Wycliff had put his pants and shirt back on; Charlotte was comfortable in one of her silk dressing gowns. When they finished eating she boiled water for instant coffee which they laced with Kahlua and took outside. Traffic hum drifted up from the street. A warm fog was rolling in. The view was shrouded, as if covered with a watery veil.

Charlotte put her feet in Wycliff's lap and purred as he began to massage her arches. 'What did you think of the auction?' she asked, as she lit a cigarette and exhaled through her nostrils. 'Could you believe the prices those paintings were selling for?'

What Wycliff thought was that the whole shooting match was bullshit ego-stroking. It was about showing off. I'm rich and I want everyone to know it. I'm so rich I can spend thousands of dollars on a painting that's no better than something I can download off the Internet for free.

'Rich folks tossing their money around,' he responded. 'I notice you didn't bid on anything.'

'There was nothing I wanted.'

His coffee was getting cold but he drank it anyway and fired up a cigarette. 'Then why did we go?'

'For the usual reasons people go out, Wycliff. To get out of yourself, have fun. I enjoy being among people. And to show you off. You're a desirable man. Being with you makes me desirable, too.'

'You already are. You don't need me to prove that.'

'That's nice of you to say. And I don't disagree, I know men find me attractive. But at my age I need reassurance.' She stubbed out her cigarette. 'There, I've said it.'

'Said what?'

'That I'm getting old.'

'We all are.'

Charlotte shook her head. 'That's not what I said. Of course we're all getting older, every person on the planet gets older every day. Getting older and getting old are two very different things. One is benign and natural, the other is...' She put her coffee cup down. 'Tragic. And comic. And pathetic. All of the above. Especially pathetic.'

Christ, he thought, how did talking about a bunch of lame paintings and the jerks who buy them turn into a dialogue about the meaning of life?

'You're not pathetic, Charlotte.'

She gave him a penetrating look. 'You're right, I'm not. But I am getting old. Older.' She sat up. 'I'm being selfish. Here you are, living with a dying man who is half my age and I'm complaining about crow's feet around my eyes. Now that is pathetic. Can you forgive me for being selfish and shallow?'

He didn't need this conversation. Charlotte was a living, breathing force of nature: sexy, fascinating, chock-full of surprises. She wasn't close to the end of her life. When he was away from his brother he wanted relief from death and dying. He sure as hell didn't want to be talking or thinking about it. Especially not with her.

'I forgive you.'

'Thank you.' She stood and wrapped her arms around herself. 'I'm getting cold. Let's go inside.'

He followed her back into the apartment. 'I'm having a cognac,' she said. 'Do you want one?'

'No thanks. I need to get home and relieve the caretaker.' He sat on the sofa and started to put his socks and shoes back on.

She kissed him on the cheek. 'Thanks for being a good sport. I know events like tonight's are boring to you.'

'It was okay. I liked talking to your friend. He seems like a sharp guy.'

'He liked you, too. He was really impressed by what you're doing.'

Wycliff shrugged off the compliment. No one knew the real reason he was taking care of Billy. No one had to.

'John's brilliant.' She crossed to her portable bar and poured two fingers of Hennessy into a snifter. "He's made a lot of people very wealthy, even in this turbulent economy.' She tasted her cognac. 'I'm sure he would like to help you.'

Wycliff stared at her uncomprehendingly. 'Like how?'

'By investing your money.'

He guffawed. 'You mean my millions?'

'He doesn't require that much to get started.'

'That's good, because I don't have that kind of money. Nothing like it. Which you know.'

'Your brother does.'

He shook his head. 'Money doesn't matter to Billy anymore. Not where he's going.'

'But it matters to you, doesn't it?'

'So what if it does?'

'Couldn't he loan you the money? You're going to inherit his estate. Why couldn't you ask him for some of it in advance? You've thrown him a lifeline, Wycliff. He'd be alone and dying in a hospital bed if you weren't so big-hearted. Don't you think he'd like to return your kindness?'

Wycliff felt like puking. 'Who says he's leaving his money to me?'

'You're his only living relative. Who else would he leave it to?'

Anyone else, he thought. Anyone but me. 'I don't want to talk about it,' he told her roughly.

She stepped back, jolted by his strong reaction. 'I've touched a raw nerve. I'm sorry. I didn't mean to upset you, darling. I'm trying to help. Really.'

He needed to get out of here and breathe some fresh air. 'I'll see you.'

'It wouldn't require that much to get started,' she persisted. 'You need to think about your future.'

Christ, let it go. But now there was an itch in his brain that needed to be scratched. 'How much?'

'It doesn't matter. I shouldn't have brought it up. It was insensitive of me.'

'But you did.'

She nodded. 'Yes, I did.' She was silent for a moment, then told him. 'Five hundred thousand.'

He gawked at her.

'That's the normal minimum to open an account with John's firm. But I think he would let you in for less,' she said in a rush. 'I think he'd accept a hundred thousand dollars. I'm sure he would.'

He should have taken her up on that offer for a drink. He didn't keep a flask in his car because he didn't want to give a cop any reason to run a check on him. He wished he had one in his glove box now, though. He'd pound a stiff bourbon as soon as he got back to the house. 'That's not only out of my league, it's out of my world.'

She blushed. 'I shouldn't have said anything. It was rude of me. I'm sorry.'

'I have to go, Charlotte.'

'You'll call me?' There was more than a hint of desperation in her voice.

Just get out. 'Yes. I'll call you.'

FIFTEEN

The coughing was loud and harsh. For a few seconds, discombobulated from being awakened unexpectedly, Wycliff didn't know where he was; then he remembered with a jolt. He rolled over and looked at the numbers on the digital clock next to his bed: 3:35. The coughing grew louder, a gasping death rattle. He lurched out of

169

bed and staggered into the living room.

There was enough moonlight streaming through the windows to see that Billy was turning blue. Wycliff had a checklist for emergencies he thought he had memorized, but now, almost paralyzed with panic, his mind had gone completely blank. The physical list was in the kitchen, but Billy was dying right in front of him. He couldn't take the time to leave him, go to the kitchen, find the list, and then read it to figure out what was going wrong.

He forced himself to think. First thing: make sure the oxygen mask was securely in place. Billy could use the nasal inhaler on and off during the day as he needed it, but at night he had to be masked, to insure that he kept breathing while he was asleep.

Wycliff looked at the mask. It was on tight, the way it was supposed to be, but nothing seemed to be flowing through. Was there a crimp in the air line?

It was too dark to see clearly. He turned a light on at the side of Billy's bed and stared at the gauge on top of the oxygen canister. *The needle was all the way down to zero*! Really panicking now, he tapped the side of the canister. It rang hollow. Oh my God, he realized, it's empty.

He had checked it last night before he went to bed. He was positive he had.

It was empty.

He disconnected the empty tube, grabbed one of the spares, and attached it, his hands shaking, fingers fumbling with the threads, making sure it was connected. He turned it on.

Immediately, the gauge shot up. He could hear the flow moving through the tubes into the breathing mask. Hang on, Billy, he prayed. He held the mask tight against his brother's face to make sure none of the precious oxygen was leaking out.

For a few seconds, there was no change in Billy's complexion. He was chalk-white, his body rigid, as if rigor mortis was already starting to set in. Wycliff put his hands on Billy's chest and started pumping, in, out, in, out, trying to force the air into his brother's lungs.

With another cough and a gasp, Billy started taking the oxygen in. Almost immediately, the color began returning to his face and body. In a few more seconds he was breathing normally again.

Wycliff sagged into the chair next to the bed, his body drenched in fear-sweat. My God, he thought, I almost killed him. He reached over and took his brother's hand. Forgive me, he begged silently. I'll never do anything like that again.

Billy's eyes popped open. He turned and stared at Wycliff. 'What's going on?' he asked.

Sadie arrived at nine in the morning for a normal checkup. Billy was asleep, so she took what vital signs she could without disturbing him. 'He seems to be holding his own,' she told Wycliff, as they retreated into the kitchen so their conversation wouldn't wake Billy up. 'Have you noticed any changes?'

Wycliff was exhausted. He hadn't slept a

second since he had brought his brother back to life. The weight of his irresponsibility was crushing. He had hovered at Billy's bedside until Billy, breathing normally, went back to sleep. But the fear of another incident had wired him as if he were on meth. He made himself a pot of coffee and drank it watching all-night movies, the sound muted so the noise wouldn't wake his brother.

Sadie appraised his haggard condition with professional understanding. 'This is hell on everyone,' she commiserated. 'It's as hard on the caregivers as the patient, even more when it's family. You need to take care of yourself, Wycliff. You won't be able to help your brother if you aren't sharp.'

He told her about the oxygen canister running out. 'He could have died last night. I know he's going to die pretty soon, but I don't want my screwing up to be the reason.'

'We all make mistakes,' she said sympathetically. 'Anyway, it's not on you. Ricardo should have checked before he left for the night. He's been trained to do this, you haven't.' She took a sip of the coffee he offered her. 'Ricardo's having problems at home. His wife has left him,' she confided. 'I see it all the time. The stress from doing this work is debilitating. It can mess up your mind, make you forgetful. I'll talk to him about paying closer attention.'

'Thanks,' Wycliff said gratefully. He looked at her, sitting across from him, drinking her coffee. 'You live this day in and day out. How do you maintain?'

'The best I can. It's messed up more than one relationship for me, that's for sure.'

'Then why do you do it?'

'Because it's my job. Because my patients need me. It feels good to be needed, even if it hurts like hell sometimes.'

There really are good people in this world, Wycliff thought, as he looked at her kind face. He wouldn't switch places with this woman for all the money in the world, but he admired people like her. Amelia fit into that category, too. It had been less than two days since they had last been together, but he missed her. He would find a way to see her as soon as possible, even if it meant driving across the city to her hospital so they could be together while she was on a break.

'Well, thank you,' he said. 'I really appreciate everything you're doing.'

'You are paying me,' she reminded him, deflecting his praise.

'It isn't enough.'

'So give me a raise.' She smiled. 'The doctor will be here this afternoon. I'll try to make it back so we're all in synch.' She picked up her bag. 'Don't beat yourself up over what happened. No one's perfect.'

If only you knew.

The doctor, an ER resident wearing a Grateful Dead T-shirt who volunteered for the hospice, showed up at four, an hour past the appointed time, hassled and frazzled. 'Sorry I'm late. My last patient went into full-on cardiac arrest. We had to call 911. It was touch and go, for real.'

'What happened to him?' Wycliff asked anxiously. He had a fear of something like that occurring to Billy, especially after last night's near-disaster.

'It was a woman, and I don't know,' the doctor answered, taking his instruments out of his bag. 'Once they take them away they're out of my hands. Let's have a look at this puppy.'

Sadie, who had been waiting patiently with Wycliff for over an hour, helped the doctor prop Billy up. Ricardo wasn't there; he had taken a pass again, pleading more family problems. 'I'll have a replacement tomorrow,' Sadie told Wycliff, clearly annoyed. 'I understand why he's bailing out, but he can't leave you in the lurch. I'll get someone good, even if I have to do it myself.'

'It's okay,' Wycliff reassured her. 'I'm fine, being here.'

Billy sat vertically against his pillows, his pajama top open, exposing his emaciated torso. His ribs were protruding. You could play the xylophone on them, Wycliff thought, they were so prominent in his withered, blotchy chest. The doctor poked and prodded, listened to Billy's insides with his stethoscope, and checked all his vital signs.

'How's he eating?' he asked Wycliff, as if Billy wasn't there. To Billy, he said, 'I can't ask you, soldier, you'll bullshit me. You're too damn tough for your own good.'

Billy mustered a smile. 'That's why I'm still alive, sawbones.'

'Stay that way. So about his eating?'

174

'He's doing pretty good,' Wycliff told him. 'He had pizza the other night.' He didn't tell the doctor that Billy had thrown it up afterwards.

'Perfect,' the doctor deadpanned. 'Nothing better for clogging the arteries.'

'It was one time,' Wycliff said defensively. 'He's got to live.' Immediately, he regretted his phrasing.

'That's the point,' the doctor said. 'Which is why eating that garbage is not advisable.'

'We won't do it again. Right, Billy?' He looked at his brother for confirmation.

Billy's breathing was fast and shallow. 'Wrong,' he gasped. 'Pizza and wine every night. And ice cream. With hot fudge.'

'It's your life,' the doctor replied matter-of-factly. 'Do what you want with it, I'm not going to stop you. But if you do want to live longer, and you can, be sensible.'

Billy slumped back into his pillows. 'I know.'

The doctor patted him on the shoulder. 'Hang in there, man. You're doing good.' He gave Wycliff an eye roll indicating that he wanted to talk to him outside of Billy's hearing.

'I'll walk you out,' Wycliff told the doctor for Billy's benefit. Leaving Sadie at his brother's bedside, he followed the doctor out of the room, into the kitchen.

'There's fluid building up in his lungs,' the doctor told Wycliff, keeping his voice low so he wouldn't be overheard. 'He's lost significant breathing capacity since I last saw him. I'm worried about pneumonia. If he gets that, we're going to lose him sooner than expected.'

175

Wycliff felt the shame of his neglect course through his body, even though he knew that no matter what, Billy wasn't going to hang on much longer. Hearing the doctor say it out loud, though, jolted him. 'How much time does he have?'

'If his condition doesn't get any worse, a month or two. Three is probably the outside limit.' He sighed, a groan from the gut. 'We're heading for the finish line, my friend. You have to come to grips with that.'

Wycliff started shaking. 'Shit,' he cursed.

'Is he in pain?' the doctor asked.

'On and off.'

'I'll increase his pain medication dosage. That's the last thing we want, for him to be in pain.'

'Good,' Wycliff said dully.

The doctor stood up. 'It's always harder on the ones who are left behind.'

Wycliff, pinned to his chair by emotional paralysis, shrugged. 'I wouldn't know.'

'It's true,' the doctor said emphatically. He laid a compassionate hand on Wycliff's shoulder. 'You have each other. That's huge. It's lousy to die alone. Your brother isn't going to. You can both take strength from that.'

He wasn't going anywhere tonight. Even if Ricardo had shown up, which he hadn't, he needed to be here, close to his brother, making sure there weren't any more screw-ups. He left messages for Charlotte and Amelia, to let them know. He instructed Charlotte not to return the call, that he was too busy taking care of his brother and would call her when he had some breathing room. He didn't leave that message for Amelia. He hoped she would call him back.

Two weeks, three months, any time between: his brother was going to die, and when he did, the life he, Wycliff, was living, was going to come crashing to an end. What would he do, where would he go? For the past few weeks, since he had forced his way into Billy's life, he had been in high cotton. Nice pad (free of charge), cool car, not one but two lovers, money in his pocket from his car-theft exploit. Not to mention his personal rebirth, both physically, courtesy of Charlotte, and emotionally, because of how his relationship with Billy had changed. With Amelia, too. He was a different, nicer person when he was with her. Taking care of Billy had forced him to change his harsh ways for the better, and it was rubbing off on how he was with other people, especially her. It felt good to be nice to her. He sure as hell didn't want to hurt her. Of course, he was living a complete lie: who he was, what he did, his background, basically everything. Sooner or later the truth of who he was would rise to the surface. You can fake the past for a while, but you can't hide it forever. He had tried to do that at various times in his life, and it had always blown up in his face. Especially nowadays, with the Internet and all the other high-tech ways of searching people out, you couldn't kill an old life and start a new one from scratch. Even people in the government's witness-protection programs left trails now. You can run, but you can't hide, an old con had once warned him. The con told him Joe Louis, the famous boxer, had said that. It was true. He couldn't hide.

He could hear Billy in his hospital bed in the living room, breathing through his oxygen mask. Even breathing, the most fundamental act of life, was almost too hard for the poor bastard now.

That reality jerked him back to the here and now. He had a dying man on his hands. That was plenty to deal with.

He filled a tumbler with Maker's Mark and ice and went outside to the back patio, leaving the door open so he could hear if there were any changes in his brother's breathing. It was so pleasant here, so peaceful. He sipped his bourbon. *There's nothing permanent in life. But it sure would be nice if the temporary of now could go on longer.*

SIXTEEN

Gus Levine, Billy's lawyer, arrived at nine thirty. Levine was a portly man in his fifties, dressed in a double-breasted suit and a bow tie. He was accompanied by his assistant, a tall, horse-faced woman with a sour expression. Billy had called Levine without telling Wycliff. Wycliff was miffed that he hadn't been notified, because as

178

Billy's legal caretaker (for medical reasons, but not financial) he felt he should be in on everything. But he had to acknowledge that Billy had the right to handle his affairs himself as long as he was mentally sharp, which he was, that wasn't in dispute. So after he and Levine exchanged awkward introductions, and Levine started taking documents out of his briefcase and laying them out at the side of Billy's bed, he excused himself and took his coffee outside.

The lawyer showing up was a shot in the gut. One thing Wycliff had learned about his brother: the man did not bullshit himself. He knew the end was near and he was making sure his bases were covered, that all the legal stuff was nailed down and squared away. Who got the house, who got his money, all of it. How long did he have here after Billy died, he wondered? Weeks? Days? Twenty-four hours and don't let the door hit you on the ass on your way out?

The daydreaming was over. It was time to face reality.

'Can we talk?'

Wycliff, startled, turned around. Levine was standing in the doorway.

'Sure.' He pushed up from his deck chair and followed the lawyer inside.

They sat across from each other at the kitchen table. The assistant wasn't present; she was waiting outside, in the passenger seat of Levine's Mercedes.

'Your brother is very grateful for everything you've done for him,' Levine told Wycliff. 'He wouldn't be here if it wasn't for you.' He paused,

179

then added somberly, 'He might not even be alive. You've helped raise his spirits.'

That was a heavy load to contemplate. 'I did what had to be done,' Wycliff replied. 'I'm not looking for brownie points.'

'Even so, you didn't have to. You two were estranged your entire adult lives. What you are doing is an exceptional act of kindness. That it was unexpected makes it even more meaningful to your brother.'

Wycliff had no answer for that. When he thought about it, which he had been doing more frequently, he still didn't understand why he had done what he'd done. Okay, he had a warm bed and a roof over his head. That counted for something. But he could have figured out another way to achieve that. He had money on him, and if he needed more he could get it (although his current MO of stealing cars was a risk he hoped he wouldn't have to take again). He could have rented a short-term place where he would not have to worry about whether the oxygen was flowing, wipe the shit off a grown man's ass, lie awake at night with worry, trying to hear if Billy was still breathing. He could even have hit up Charlotte for money. She probably would have said yes, but the conditions that would have been attached to doing that would have made his life even more complicated than it already was. Amelia wouldn't be in the picture, that was for damn sure. Reason enough to maintain whatever distance from Charlotte that he could.

'Somebody had to do it,' he told the lawyer. 'Otherwise...' He didn't finish the thought. It wasn't necessary.

Levine stood up. 'Your brother appreciates what you've done. He wants you to know that.'

That and three twenty-five buys me a latte at Starbucks, Wycliff thought, as Levine turned to let himself out. 'How long do I have?' he asked.

Levine turned back to him, a puzzled look on his face.

'To stay here. After Billy dies.'

The lawyer's eyes widened behind his bifocals. 'I can't say. There is a provision in his will for caretaking until the property is disposed of, according to his instructions. I can't tell you what that is.'

'You mean you won't.'

'I'm bound by confidentiality. Please try to understand.'

Wycliff felt weary. Like always, he was fighting against the machine, and like always, the machine was winning. 'Oh, yeah,' he answered. 'I understand.'

'You won't be asked to leave immediately,' Levine said, throwing Wycliff a crumb of hope. 'At the least, you won't have to move out until your brother's will is finalized.'

Not much, but something. 'How long will that take?' Wycliff pressed.

'Not long,' the lawyer conceded. He seemed flustered at being interrogated, rather than being the one who did the questioning. 'You will be notified in advance. One more thing: as your brother's principal caretaker, it will probably be you who is with him when he dies. When that happens, God forbid, but sadly, it's going to be

181

soon, you must inform me immediately. To with-hold that information could cause severe legal consequences. Now if you will excuse me...' He turned and let himself out, casting a nervous look over his shoulder as he shut the front door behind him.

Wycliff walked into the living room. Billy was awake, staring blankly at the television screen. 'Everything good?' Wycliff asked.

Billy turned to him. His face contorted. Even the slightest movement caused him pain. 'Every-thing's perfect.'

'Then let's play gin. Loser takes out the trash.' He picked up the deck, sat down at the side of his brother's bed, and shuffled the cards.

Amelia had the evening off. She would pick up dinner on the way over. 'No pizza,' Wycliff cautioned her. 'His doctor reamed me out over that.'

She shopped at Gelson's and cooked a stellar gourmet vegetarian meal. Wycliff cut Billy's food into small, bite-sized pieces, to make sure he didn't choke on a hunk of asparagus. After dinner was over and Amelia had loaded up the dishwasher (she insisted), they sat around Billy's bed and played hearts. Billy dumped the Queen of Spades on Wycliff three hands in a row, which got him to cackling like a witch.

'Careful there,' Wycliff said, 'I don't want you laughing to death on me.'

'There's worse ways to go,' Billy rejoined gleefully. His nails-on-the-blackboard laughter turned to guttural coughing, painful rasps which became desperate gasps for air. Before Amelia could spring into action, Wycliff, who dealt with his brother's abrupt reversals every day and was accustomed to this by now, sat him up and stuck his fingers down his throat until he coughed up a glob of yellow phlegm. He wiped the goop from Billy's mouth and held up a glass of water, which his brother swallowed in thirsty gulps.

'Let's call it a night,' Wycliff declared, 'you've taken all my matchsticks anyway.'

Billy nodded glumly. 'Sorry about that,' he apologized to Amelia, for being sick.

'There's nothing to be sorry about,' she assured him. 'I'm a nurse, I see much worse all the time.'

'I don't envy you,' Billy told her. 'It must be exhausting.' His chest rose and fell from the effort of sucking air into his lungs.

'Sometimes,' she admitted. 'Sometimes it's rewarding. Most of the time it just is.' She washed Billy's flushed face with a damp washcloth. Smiling wanly with appreciation, he lay back against the pillow, eyes closed, his breathing returning to a semblance of normality. In less than a minute, he had fallen asleep.

After Wycliff fitted the oxygen mask securely over his brother's face, he and Amelia went into the kitchen. 'You'd make a good nurse,' she told him. 'You're calm, you're competent, you care without letting your feelings interfere.'

He shook his head. 'Thanks, but that's not my thing.'

'Don't be stuck in the past. Nursing isn't only a woman's profession anymore. There are lots of male nurses now. There's nothing unmasculine about it.' She reached over and stroked him through his jeans. 'That's one thing you don't have to worry about.'

Her caress got him going, like it had from the first time he had touched her. He pulled her to her feet and kissed her on the mouth. They stumbled their way into the bedroom, trying not to make a ruckus so Billy wouldn't wake up, and fell onto the bed, fumbling their clothes off, coming together with hot strong kissing. He pushed into her and they pounded each other, trying to get into each other's skin, body. She grabbed his hair with both hands and he pulled her ass tight to him and came right after she did, and he pushed up on his elbows, panting, staring into her eyes, and she was looking at him and laughing silently, burying her face into his neck.

She would stay the night. She'd brought an over-night bag with her essentials. 'It's been quite a while since I spent the night in a man's bed,' she told Wycliff. 'I hope you don't snore.'

The situation was the same for him. He couldn't remember the last time a woman had shared his bed for more than sex. He couldn't bring himself to tell her that, she had more guts than he did. 'Wake me up if I do. How long has it been?'

'That doesn't matter. I'm doing it with you, that's what counts.'

'I'm flattered,' he told her.

'You should be. I'm very picky.'

'Okay, then I'm honored.'

Which he was, both flattered and honored. It

was one thing for Charlotte to lay the bullshit on thick. She had cards up her sleeve she was holding back. Amelia had no ulterior motives, as far as he could tell. She just liked him.

What he really was, more than anything, was scared. His inner devil reared his head yet again: what the hell did he have to offer her?

There was nothing he could do about that now, so he tried to force himself to put those thoughts out of his mind and enjoy the moment. He knew that wouldn't be easy.

She was the one who brought his circumstances up, after they had brushed their teeth and climbed into bed for the night. After setting her cell phone alarm for six a.m., she propped herself up on an elbow and stared him in the face.

'I work with dying patients every day, Wycliff. You learn early in your training that it happens and you can't stop it. You do your best, but you can't let it tear you apart.'

He winced, hearing it put this directly. 'I know.'

'What's going to happen after Billy dies? He isn't going to live much longer, even under the best of circumstances. I live with life and death every day. I've seen more than enough of my share of dying people to know that his time is about up. What's going to happen to *you* when that happens? Are you going to stay here? Are you going to live here?'

He forced himself not to look away. 'I don't know how to answer those questions. I've been thinking about them, but I don't know about any of it yet.' He stared up at the ceiling. 'I don't

185

know how I'm going to feel. I've never been in this position. I'll find out when it happens, I guess.'

'Don't close yourself off. That's vital.'

'Another lesson they teach you in nursing school?' He didn't want to talk about this, not now, not while they were lying in each other's arms. He didn't want to talk about it ever.

She wasn't going to let him put her off. 'No, it's what I've learned in real life,' she replied calmly. 'Watching people die and seeing how those who survive cope with it.' She kissed his neck. 'I'll be right back. Don't go away.'

She got up and softly padded naked into the kitchen, returning with two glasses of wine. They sat against the headboard, their glasses cradled on their bellies. With a pang like a fist to his chest Wycliff realized he had not felt so vulnerable since he was a kid, if even then.

'So if it's just you and him, does that mean you inherit his estate?' she asked. She wasn't going to let him duck this. 'Have you talked about that?'

'No, we haven't talked about it,' he answered tightly.

'But you're going to. Aren't you?'

Wycliff shook his head. 'I don't know.'

'Why not?' she asked, puzzled but still insistent.

He groaned. 'Do we have to talk about this now?'

'Not if you don't want to. But I do think you need to. What are you afraid of?'

'Everything. Shit, babe, it's so fucking compli-

186

cated. I feel like a dog chasing his tail.'

She stroked his chest. 'Tell me,' she coaxed him. 'You can trust me.'

It all came gushing out, a verbal tsunami. Two half-brothers, a couple of years apart in age, both abandoned by their different mothers virtually at birth, raised by an abusive, insensitive father, each finding his own damaged way to deal with their shitty young lives. The older one – him – became physically strong and emotionally shut down, a street-smart ass-kicker, little interest in school, no interest in anything society considers proper, right, moral. Drifting from place to place, lame jobs, no emotional attachments of any duration, because if you don't get attached to anyone you can't get hurt. Without embellishment or self-pity he told her about his time in jail, his petty crimes, his lack of focus or long-range planning. Almost everything – not all the details, he didn't remember some of them any-more – but the broad strokes.

What he didn't tell her about was his recent history. The past was the past, he could rational-ize it away, buried under layers of denial. But his current situation couldn't be excused as youthful immaturity and callousness. It was right now, a set of circumstances he was not only indulging in, but embracing. Charlotte, for all her crazi-ness, was exciting to be with, and the danger that was an essential part of her was too alluring to turn away from. But she was way too risky to count on. He had to come up with anther way to make money, on his own.

'Then I found out he was dying and I thought

this could be my pot of gold at the end of the rainbow. So what if we hated each other like forever, I'm his only blood, at the end of the day he can't deny me. Right?'

Wrong. Billy could. There was going to be nothing left to him. He would be shut out, another dead end. Any delusions he'd had about getting a piece of the action had been stopped cold by Billy's lawyer's chilly attitude.

'So why have you stayed on?' she asked. 'Why have you become his caretaker? Even more, his lifeline.'

Wycliff shook his head in bafflement. 'That's the million-dollar question, isn't it? I've been asking it myself, but I haven't come up with an answer.'

'Maybe it's because...' She hesitated.

'What?'

'You're not such a bad guy after all. What you've told me about your past is upsetting, but that's not the man I know.'

There were dreams, and then there was the real world. 'Thanks, but how well do you really know me, Amelia?'

She sat up and faced him. 'Not as well as I want to, but good enough to know that you are a decent and kind man. Anyone who would do what you've done, knowing there's no reward in it, is not a bad person, he's a good person.'

That's what she wants to believe, dude, because she's falling for you. Like you are for her.

He could never cop to that in a million years. 'Maybe it's an act,' he said instead. 'Maybe I'm pulling the wool over everybody's eyes.'

She laughed. 'Then you've landed in the right town, because you're giving an Academy Award performance.'

Amelia slept easily, but he couldn't. His internal clock woke him up every two hours so he could check on Billy to make sure he was breathing easily, that the humidifier he needed to keep his lungs and throat clear was running smoothly, that everything was working as it was supposed to. Normally when he was alone he would go outside and have a cigarette, but with Amelia here, he couldn't. She thought he had quit, and he wasn't going to let on that he hadn't. He slipped back into bed, trying not to disturb her, but she was awake, enfolding him to her body.

In the morning she was up before him, showering and dressing, turning the coffee machine on, setting the breakfast table. He woke up to the smell of bacon frying. He shuffled into the kitchen. A cup of hot coffee was on the table, a glass of fresh orange juice next to it. Silverware laid out, a cloth napkin. They ate breakfast comfortably, not feeling the need to talk, just enjoying being with each other.

'I have to work tomorrow night,' she reminded him, 'so I won't see you. I'll call.'

Billy woke up as she was about to leave. They watched the *Today* show for a few minutes. Billy took Amelia's hand and squeezed it. He didn't have much strength in his grip, it was like holding a baby's hand, all softness, no muscle. She kissed him goodbye and promised to come back soon.

Wycliff walked her outside to her car. 'Have a good one,' he told her.

'You, too.' She buried her head in his chest. 'I miss you already.'

'Me, too.'

He watched until she drove away, then went back inside.

SEVENTEEN

There was chump change, and then there was real money. Chump change came from boosting cars or stealing television sets from the back of a truck, like he had had done in his wild and crazy youth and was too old for now. Real money was what Charlotte and her friends had, like that financial guy he'd met at the party. Not a thousand here and a thousand there, but hundreds of thousands, millions. He had seen the movie about the guy who invented Facebook. The scene that had really struck him was the one where Justin Timberlake said *a million isn't cool, what's cool is a billion.* A billion dollars was ludicrous, so out of his orbit it would be like flying into the sun. But a million, that sounded sweet. You could buy a cherry house for a million, with plenty left over in the bank to live on very nicely for the rest of your life.

Too damn soon he was going to be back on the street, closer to the gutter than the sidewalk.

That was a reality he couldn't sweep under the rug like last night's dinner crumbs. He had a few thousand dollars in his pocket. Chump change. If he was going to have the life he'd always wanted, he needed real money.

After Raquel arrived to start her shift, Wycliff drove to Beverly Hills and made a call from a pay phone. He didn't know whether cell phone calls could be traced, but he wasn't taking any chances.

If the woman was surprised to hear from him, she didn't let on. She suggested they meet for lunch at a restaurant in Marina Del Ray, where the odds were good no one would know them.

The restaurant was an updated knockoff of the old Trader Vic's franchise – classic surfboards and fishing nets festooned the walls, along with boat accessories – old-fashioned life-preservers, wooden tillers, large nautical compasses. Outside, seen through the floor-to-ceiling windows, boats bobbed on the water in the harbor. The woman was already there, waiting in a booth in the back. A deliberate calculation on her part, Wycliff assumed, to make sure no prying eyes or ears would eavesdrop on them. A smart move. He slid in across from her.

The woman looked better than when he had met her. No smeared mascara around her eyes, and the rest of the package was also more attractive, more age appropriate. Her attire, blouse and skirt, was modestly conservative, and her hairdo was stylishly casual. A tropical drink with a little paper umbrella perched on top nestled on her placemat.

'It's nice to see you again,' she said, her smile dazzlingly white. 'Even after you called, I wasn't sure you would come.'

A waiter in a Jimmy Buffet-style shirt glided over and handed Wycliff a laminated menu embossed with pictures of 60s' era beach movie starlets in bikinis. 'Virgin Mary,' Wycliff ordered. 'Easy on the heat.' He was here on serious business, he wanted his head to be clear: no booze.

'You're not drinking?' the woman asked, leaning forward and sipping her own concoction from a straw.

'Maybe later,' he answered. 'After we've talked.'

She glanced at her own menu and put it aside. 'You've been thinking about our last conversation.'

'Yes.'

Her eyes widened. 'Good!'

'Thinking,' he repeated. 'Not deciding, not yet. There are basic things I need to know. For openers, who you are. Name, address, phone number, etc. The business card you gave me doesn't count, anyone can make a business card. I mean real physical proof.'

'Like what? A driver's license?'

'If it's legit.'

She grimaced. 'It is. I promise.' She took her wallet out of her purse, removed her license, and handed it to him. California, current. Expiration date two years down the road. The same name as on her business card. So that part, at least, was real.

'The address is in Bel Air,' she pointed out. 'Off Stone Canyon, if you know the area.'

He knew where Bel Air was. The air up there was way too rarified for peons like him. Only serious money need apply.

The woman winced as Wycliff read over her license. 'I don't live at that address anymore. They kicked me out. I have a small apartment in Beverly Hills. Below Wilshire,' she added, as if to emphasize how far she had fallen. Her laugh was harsh, self-mocking. 'I can barely make the rent.'

Wycliff looked at her more carefully. Her license listed her age as forty-three, a few years older than he had guessed. Par for the course for women like her. Rich women in LA work hard to stay young. They pay good money to help make that happen.

He flicked at the license with a fingernail. 'The last time I saw you, you asked me if I was a cop. I told you I wasn't, which is true. I need to know the same thing about you. I don't want to walk out of here and find the police waiting to slap the cuffs on me because a pretty cop entrapped me.'

'I am not a cop in any way.' She smiled. 'No one has ever asked me that one before.'

'You never propositioned anyone like you did me before, have you?'

'No,' she answered, quickly serious. 'Definitely not.'

'If I do this,' he continued, 'that's *if*, not *will*, I'm going to need solid information about the target. There's nothing more serious than what you're asking me to do. I have to make sure I'm protected in every way I can think of.'

She nodded. 'I understand.'

'You'd damn well better,' he warned her. He palmed her license as the waiter arrived with his drink.

'I do, absolutely.' To the waiter, she said, 'I think we can order. Are you ready?' she asked Wycliff.

'You decide.'

She ordered a large appetizer platter for two. The waiter freshened their water glasses and left. 'Tell me whatever you need to know, and I'll do my best to find it for you,' she told Wycliff.

'I'll make a list. *If* I do it. We're still on *if*.' He leaned back, looking at her eyes, not blinking. 'First things first,' he said. 'Let's firm up the price.'

The woman looked confused. 'A hundred thousand dollars. Don't you remember?'

'That was *your* number. I never agreed to it.'

She sat back. 'I don't like hearing that. That sounds like...'

'Blackmail?' He waggled her driver's license in front of her face. 'Anyone who lived in a Bel Air mansion and drives a Porsche isn't scrounging in dumpsters for tonight's dinner. That rock on your finger is worth a fortune and there's got to be plenty more swag where it came from.' He palmed her license again. 'Two hundred thousand.'

She started to say something in rebuttal, exhaled heavily. 'I don't have that kind of money. I'm scraping the bottom of the barrel for a hundred

194

thousand.'

'Scrape deeper.'

She started shaking, visibly. 'I'll try. I don't know if I can.'

'You'll find a way,' he told her. 'You've got too much to lose not to.'

She buried her face in her hands. When she looked at him again, she said, 'All right. Two hundred thousand. You have to promise me you won't hold me up for more.'

'I won't. You have my word.'

She almost choked. 'Your *word*? Do you know how ridiculous that sounds?'

'It's the best you're going to get.'

'Honor among thieves. There is none, right?'

'Sometimes. You never know till it's over.'

The waiter set their lunch platter on the table. 'Looks good,' Wycliff said, forking an egg roll and some ribs onto his plate. 'Didn't realize I was so hungry.'

'A hundred up front, the rest when the job is finished.'

The woman wasn't eating. She seemed to have lost her appetite. 'That's going to be difficult,' she said, toying with her cocktail umbrella. 'I don't know if I can get my hands on that much cash at short notice. Can we work out a payment schedule?'

'You're not buying a dress on layaway,' he told her. 'When you have the money, let me know. In the meantime, you can start collecting the information I'll need.'

'I can do that,' she said, 'but the money, I don't

know when I'll be able to.'

He licked his fingers from a greasy rib. 'You should have figured out how to get it before you hit on me back then. This isn't a walk in the park, this is serious.'

'I know.'

'I'll get it.'

'All of it. All two hundred.'

'Wait a second!' She reared up, then looked around to see if anyone was listening in. They were out of earshot of the other customers, so she continued, her voice lowered, 'You just gave me your word you wouldn't change the rules, and now you are.'

'No,' he corrected her. 'Not changing, just protecting. You give me the first hundred up front and hold onto the rest. I need to be sure it'll be there. You have to look at this deal from my side of the table. You could pull the rug out from under me and I'd be standing in the corner with my thumb up my ass.'

'I wouldn't do that,' she vowed, 'I promise.'

'So there is honor among thieves after all?' he mocked her. He shook his head *no*. 'The only way this can work is for neither of us to trust the other. I perform a service, you pay me. Strictly business.'

She ran her fingers through her hair. 'I guess I have to. You leave me no choice.'

'Not true.' He sucked on a rib bone. 'You could find someone else.'

She couldn't. They both knew that.

She paid the bill in cash. She was being exceedingly cautious; she wasn't going to leave a paper trail. Like Charlotte. Birds of a feather.

The young parking valet brought her car to the curb, giving her the once-over as he handed her the keys. Like I would have done not long ago, Wycliff thought. How times had changed.

'I'll call when I have some information for you,' she told Wycliff.

'Okay,' he answered. 'But don't lag coming up with the money, I don't want to be putting in time and effort and then find out you can't raise it.'

'I'll get your damn money,' she said, tight lipped. She stuck out her hand palm up, the one with the big diamond on the third finger. 'You forgot to give me my license back.'

'I didn't forget to give it back. I'm hanging on to it.'

The woman looked like she was going to have a panic attack right there. *'Why?'*

'Insurance, against you. If this blows up, you could claim deniability. Who would believe a working stiff against a rich society dame? Think of your license as my *get out of jail free* card. When it's all over and we've settled up, I'll give it back. And that's a promise I will keep.'

Whether she believed that or not, he didn't know and didn't care.

EIGHTEEN

Wycliff had been cool and collected in the restaurant, but now, in his car, he began shaking. Had he actually agreed to kill someone he didn't know, had no grudge towards, had never even laid eyes on? He had lived on the low-down for most of his life, and, not withstanding present events, probably would for the rest of it. He was too old and too cynical (and too beaten down) to con himself.

To make the situation ever more difficult, the killing must not look like a premeditated hit. Laurie Abramowitz (the name on the crazy bitch's driver's license), had hammered that point home. A contract murder would lead to her. The killing had to appear to be the product of a fucked-up car jacking, botched home burglary, random holdup on the street gone wrong.

He lit a cigarette, feeling the nicotine rush bang his lungs. What are you thinking, he railed at himself. You're going to commit murder? Who the hell are you kidding? You have as much business trying to pull this off as you do performing brain surgery. Stick to what you know: highjacking cars, stealing from widows and orphans. Penny ante shit. Because you're a penny ante guy.

Except he wasn't, not anymore. He wasn't ready for the big leagues yet, not by a long shot, but he was not the small time grifter he had been the day before yesterday, before he had landed here, taken charge of his brother's life, met Charlotte, met Amelia, gotten a taste of the high life.

There are a few defining moments in a man's life. What he did with this opportunity would be one of them, because that's what it was: covered in blood, yes, but still, a chance. To be someone, instead of what he was and always had been, a nobody. The opportunity had been handed to him. All he needed was the balls to take advantage of it.

Of course, Laurie had to come up with the money, or the scheme was all smoke. Until she did, he didn't have to make a decision.

His cell phone rang. He checked caller ID and answered. 'Call the doctor and Sadie!' he screamed at the caller on the other end of the line. 'I'll be there as fast as I can.'

By the time he arrived back at the house Billy's condition had been stabilized, as much as was possible now. His organs were failing; he was essentially poisoning himself from the inside out. The doctor had given him medications to counter that, and they were working, but only temporarily. He was sleeping now, his frail body trying as hard as it could to suck in air and push it out.

'It's never been *if*, it's always been *when*,' the doctor told Wycliff wearily. 'Until *when* actually happens, it's an abstraction.' He rubbed the bridge of his nose with thumb and forefinger. 'When is now.'

Wycliff's stomach was in knots. 'How long?'

'A week to ten days, give or take. But it could be tonight or tomorrow. His system is completely shot. He has nothing left to fight with. We could put him on a respirator and maybe squeeze a little more time out, but his living will stipulates no heroic measures. My intervention this time was walking right up to the line. I don't think we should go beyond that. I know I can't.'

'No, we're not going to,' Wycliff agreed.

The doctor grabbed Wycliff's shoulder and squeezed tight. 'I'm really sorry. You can know it's coming, but you're never ready.'

The sun went down but the moon was full and it was pleasant outside, the kind of dry, balmy evening that makes Los Angeles so enjoyable to live in at night. Billy hadn't awakened, but he was breathing regularly. Wycliff, a nervous mother hen, finally stopped checking on him every two minutes and went out back to catch a smoke.

Earlier, he had phoned Charlotte and given her the news, which meant they were not going to see each other tonight and maybe not tomorrow, either. She told him that she would pray for Billy. He thought about probing her more about Cummings, the financial planner she had introduced him to who had become the catalyst for what could be his plunge into the abyss, but he held his tongue. Under the circumstances it felt callous, and he didn't want her thinking

about his money, either from his brother or anywhere else. She didn't know there was an anywhere else, and he needed to make sure she
wouldn't.

Amelia was a much harder call. She was a
nurse who lived with life and death on a daily
basis, but this was personal. She had bonded
with Billy, and Wycliff knew this bleak information would be devastating to her.

It was. She started crying over the phone. He
wanted to hold her, comfort her, but they were
fifteen miles apart and that distance couldn't be
breached. Adding to her upset, she had to pull an
extra shift this afternoon and tonight. Three of
the nurses had called in sick. A powerful flu was
going around the wards, so all healthy hands had
to be on deck.

They talked for a few minutes, inconsequential
chatter, nothing from the heart, that would be too
painful. Tomorrow, after she was relieved and
grabbed a few hours of sleep, she would come
over. No pizza, but chicken soup from Nate 'n
Al's, better than any miracle drug.

'This man has more lives than a bushel basket of
cats,' the doctor declared when he arrived in the
morning to examine Billy, who was awake and
cleaned up, courtesy of his brother's morning
ministrations. 'You're definitely better than you
were yesterday. The big fella upstairs must be
looking after you.'

Billy shook his head against divine intervention. 'Him,' he whispered, fluttering a hand
in Wycliff's direction. The hand looked like a

201

dry leaf: veinous, mottled, the flesh taut and fragile. A mummy's hand, Wycliff thought as he looked at it, dug up after centuries of its burial. Except Billy was still alive.

'How are you with the pain?' the doctor asked. 'Worse?'

Billy answered *yes* by blinking his eyes. He tried to speak, but couldn't. Wycliff leaned over and fed him water through a straw.

'I'll increase your meds,' the doctor said. 'Keeping you comfortable and pain-free is what's important now.'

Billy nodded his thanks, then closed his eyes. In a moment, he had fallen asleep again.

'How are you doing?' Sadie asked Wycliff anxiously, after the doctor had left. 'You must be exhausted.'

'I'm running on fumes,' he admitted, 'but I'm okay. Can I ask you a favor?'

'Sure.'

'Can you stay with him for a couple of hours? There's something urgent I have to do. If I could put it off I would, but I can't.'

'Of course. Don't beat yourself up, Wycliff,' she counseled him.

'Thanks. I'll be back as soon as I can.'

If Charlotte was surprised to hear from him, she didn't let on. 'Of course I want to see you. You know where to find me.'

He showered and shaved and dressed in one of the outfits she had bought him and was at her condo in less than an hour. She was ready this time, dressed smartly in a white silk blouse and black skirt, makeup and hair perfectly in place. 'How are you?' she asked. 'You look very nice,' she complimented him, running a finger along his shirt collar. Then she turned serious. 'It must be awful, what's going on.'

'It's been the shits, and it's getting worse.'

He looked at her. Then he cupped the back of her neck and roughly pulled her to him. He lifted her off her feet and carried her into the bedroom. They made love quickly and violently, finding a harsh, needy rhythm.

They lay on top of the covers, sharing a cigarette. 'What can I do for you?' she asked him.

'You just did.'

'Besides that.'

'Be there when I need you.'

'I try to be, as much as I can. I hope you know that.'

'Thanks. I'm sorry.' He slumped back against the pillows.

She propped herself up on an elbow to look at him. 'You don't have any reason to be sorry.'

'I can't help it. I know feeling sorry isn't going to change anything, but I still do. For him, not for me.' He tried to force a smile, but couldn't. 'Thanks for letting me use you.'

She kissed him tenderly. 'I've used you, too.'

'Don't get up. I'll let myself out.'

He was dressed again, sitting on the edge of the bed, tying his shoelaces. She was still lying on her side, watching him. 'I'm glad you came,' she said. 'I know how hard it must be to get away.'

'I needed to.' He leaned over and kissed her. 'I'll call when I can.'

He closed the bedroom door behind him and walked across the living room to the front door, pausing long enough before leaving to open the side table drawer and take out the gun.

NINETEEN

Billy drifted in and out of consciousness all afternoon and into the evening. Wycliff hovered at his bedside. The house was dark, the shades closed against the glare of the fading sun, the only sounds the hums of the air-conditioner and Billy's ventilator. Amelia, bringing wine and groceries, came over after her shift ended. Even though Billy was asleep she talked to him while she prepared dinner, as if they were having a normal conversation. Wycliff sat by quietly.

They went out back after dinner, bringing their glasses of wine. 'Smoke 'em if you've got 'em,' she said, grinning at his surprised, you-got-me look. 'I know you're still smoking. You can't be expected to quit under this emotional pressure. Just make sure you brush your teeth before you kiss me.'

He mumbled thanks, went inside, and came back out with a crumpled pack of Camel filters and a vintage Zippo lighter he'd bought in a

204

head shop on Hollywood Boulevard. He fired up and sucked in a lungful of smoke. The nicotine hit felt good. It was a crying shame smoking was bad for you.

'I really am trying to stop,' he told her sheepishly. 'I'm going to, I promise.'

'The least of your worries. My heart is so sad, for both of you.'

'I'm really glad you're here. He is, too. He'd tell you if he could.'

'He doesn't have to say any words. I can feel it.'

He pulled her to her feet and kissed her and she didn't push him away even with his cigarette breath, kissing him back with equal passion. 'Goddamn,' he whispered into her neck, 'thank you.'

They drank some more wine. He had felt bottled up all day, from being with Charlotte and why he had gone to see her, feeling guilty about using her, and now using Amelia, too. 'All I think about is what's going to happen after he dies. It'll be merciful when he goes, he's paid more dues than he needs to. But still...'

She nodded and listened, knowing this was not the time for her to speak, he didn't want conversation, he needed to spew out the emotional bile that was festering inside of him, poisoning him.

'Mostly I think about me, which is selfish as hell, but I can't help it.'

She wanted to tell him it wasn't selfish, it was natural, but she remained silent.

'What will I do, where will I go?' He took in

their surroundings with a wave of his arm. 'I've cut all my ties in Arizona. This is the only home I've got.'

'Maybe you'll be able to stay here.'

He shook his head like an old dog trying to escape a swarm of fleas. 'That's not going to happen.'

He told her about the deathbed meeting between the lawyer and Billy from which he had been excluded. 'I thought maybe...' He threw his hands up in surrender. 'It's not going to happen.'

'You don't know that,' she argued half-heartedly.

'Yeah, I do. I came here for a reason and Billy knows it, and my last-minute good Samaritan dog-and-pony act couldn't make up for a lifetime of anger and distrust. He saw right through me the minute I showed up. You could have read my intentions in Braille.'

He drank some wine and inhaled again and blew the smoke out his nostrils. 'But that doesn't matter, 'cause you know why? It changed me, coming here and taking care of him. It made me a better person. I'm not coming to Jesus or anything, but it changed something in me.' He made a face at the sound of the words coming out. 'That sounds stupid. I'm rambling, I'm sorry.'

'It doesn't sound stupid,' she retorted. 'You can't be stupid if you're real, Wycliff. Doing what you're doing didn't make you a better person. It was always there. You can't manufacture that, it had to have been there already. You just didn't know it or couldn't feel it or didn't believe it in yourself. Whatever the reason, it's real.'

'Thanks,' he muttered, not looking at her, knowing that if she looked into his eyes she would see through to the cheating soul hiding behind them. Then he did look up at her. 'You know what, though, either way? I did learn one thing. I learned that I actually love him. And that some part of him loves me, too, even if it's just a tiny part. We hated each other all our lives, and now we don't. That has to count for something, doesn't it?'

They went to bed and made love and he felt like a total hypocrite. Charlotte before, now Amelia, using them both, he castigated himself to himself, lying there beside her, her body snuggled up against his, knowing that she loved and trusted him, which made everything worse, more rotten. She could praise him to the heavens, but he knew the truth. His future was bleak. Billy would die and she would learn his true nature and whatever scheme Charlotte was hatching would come crashing down on him. All that was coming, and there was nothing he could do to stop any of it.

In the morning Amelia showered and dressed and put the coffee on while Wycliff checked on Billy, who was sleeping easily. The sunshine on his face through the kitchen window as they drank coffee and ate toasted bagels made him feel better, not much but enough that he could keep moving on, that his emotions wouldn't paralyze him.

Billy woke up and Amelia said goodbye to

him, promising she would come back later. Wycliff walked her to her car.

'I didn't want to say it in front of him, but I can't come tonight and probably not tomorrow,' she said. 'Nights are my shift this week. I got covered last night, but I can't again, unless it really turns worse. If it does, promise me you'll call. If I have to walk out, I will. I've got too much seniority for them to mess with me.'

They kissed goodbye and she drove off. He watched her go for a moment, then went back inside and took care of his brother's needs and sat with him and they watched *Regis and Kelly*, until Sadie came to relieve him.

'I won't be long,' he apologized. 'You'll call if anything—'

'Of course.' She had her knitting, she was all set.

'I really appreciate this.'

'Don't worry,' she assured him. 'I've got it covered.'

TWENTY

Laurie had already arrived at the Westfield Shopping Mall in Century City when Wycliff came out of the underground parking garage, checking the surroundings for suspicious activity from force of habit. Satisfied he wasn't being spied on, he sat next to her on one of the benches outside the movie complex. She was visibly jumpy, one jiggling leg crossed over the other.

'You need to calm down,' Wycliff warned her. 'You start acting weird, people are going to know something's screwed up.'

She took a deep breath. 'I'll be okay.'

'You'd better be.' When he spoke again, he didn't look at her. 'The money has to be in cash. No bills bigger than fifties. Checks or wire transfers can be traced.' He had been thinking this part through. It worried him. 'How are you going to come up with that amount of money without raising a red flag?'

'I've been preparing this for months,' she said, following his lead of not looking at him as she talked. 'I've lived the high life. My having an ample amount of cash on hand isn't unusual.' She held up her left hand, now ringless. 'I've cashed in other resources, too.'

That felt better, knowing she wasn't flying by the seat of her pants. 'Where is the money now?' he asked.

'At my apartment. I wasn't going to carry it around with me. It's practically a whole suitcase full.'

'Is it there now?'

'Yes.'

'All right, then. We're on.'

'Great.' She took a file folder out of her purse. 'I brought the information you wanted,' she said, handing it to him.

'When can I get the first payment?' he asked her.

'Anytime you want to come over.' Her leg was

209

dancing overtime.

Her nervousness was contagious and he fought his own urge to shake. 'I'll try for later today,' he told her. He tapped the folder. 'I need to get started on this. Figure out how I'm going to do it.'

He stood up and looked around, old force of habit. No one was paying them any attention. 'When you leave, go in the opposite direction. I'll call you, you don't call me.'

He walked away, resisting the impulse to look back and check to see if she was doing what he had told her to.

Sadie assured him that Billy was holding steady, that he didn't have to hurry back. He wanted to anyway, but that would have meant driving clear across town and then coming back over to the Westside, so he again promised her he would do what he had to do as quickly as possible.

The prey was easy to find. Laurie's dossier informed him that the victim was a creature of routine. He waited in his car across the street from the yoga studio in Brentwood where the woman took instruction, and sure enough, out she came at five after one, wearing designer workout sweats, a rolled-up exercise mat under one arm, Gucci purse adorning the other. She walked with the aid of a cane, which threw him off – Laurie hadn't mentioned that. It gave him a pang, that he was going to kill a cripple, but that meant she wouldn't be able to offer as much resistance as a healthy woman could when he made his move. On his way over he had paid cash for a camera with a zoom lens at Samy's Camera in Culver City, and he used it as a telescope to check the woman out more closely. According to her bio she was Laurie's age, but she looked older: short, heavy in the hips, curly hair dyed copper-red with gold highlights. Thank God she wasn't a doll, it would be harder to kill a pretty woman. Hard to kill any woman. He forced himself not to think about that.

The woman's car, a jaunty eggshell-blue topdown Audi convertible, was parked in front of the studio. She got in and pulled away from the curb. Wycliff waited for a break in the sparse traffic, made a casual U-turn, and followed.

She led him on an unhurried chase. Her first stop was for groceries, mostly frozen and premade, from the Whole Foods in Westwood. Then she dropped off laundry and dry-cleaning at a cleaners on Barrington and bought two bouquets of cut flowers from a florist off San Vicente.

He checked in with Sadie again. Billy had been awake briefly and had been able to keep down some broth. Nothing else to report. Nothing else was good news.

The customers at the Louis Vuitton store on Rodeo Drive were mostly women, but there were enough men that he didn't stand out. Knowing he was going to be tailing a rich woman, Wycliff had dressed up-scale in one of the ensembles Charlotte had bought him, so he wasn't conspicuous. Still, he wore his Dodgers hat low, a precaution against the security cameras.

After trying on several shoes, the woman bought a pair of ankle-high calf-skin boots. When Laurie had told him the basics about the woman – that she was unmarried and unattached (and straight) – he had thought a way to do the job would be to hit on her, get her in a private situation, and kill her in her bed or some other compromising situation. But now that he knew what she looked like, that wasn't an option. He couldn't fake it with a woman who looked like her, he wasn't that good an actor. Plus she would know he was conning her, and would avoid him like the plague. However he wound up killing her, it wouldn't involve sex.

Before he followed her out of the store, he checked the price of her new shoes. Over a thousand dollars. One pair of skimpy boots you couldn't walk three blocks in without your feet killing you. He had been with Charlotte on enough occasions by now to know this was how some people spent their money, but it was still hard for him to get his head around stuff like this. I guess if you have that kind of money, he thought as he followed her on foot down Rodeo Drive to the lot where they had both parked their cars, you can buy anything you want. Burn a hundred dollar bill to light your cigarette if that floats your boat.

He was going to have real money soon, but he would not blow it on frivolous shit. He had waited too long for the big payoff, he wasn't going to squander it.

The woman lived in one of the expensive high-rise condos that line Wilshire between Beverly

Hills and Westwood, fortresses that come with a twenty-four-hour doorman, underground parking, and tight security. The killing wouldn't be done here. Even if he could get in there would be cameras and other alarms. This woman seemed to be alone most of the day. He would find a time and place where there was no one around.

He wondered if she would be wearing her new boots when her time was up.

The three-story Spanish-style apartment building off Charleville in Beverly Hills was ordinary, compared to the one his prey lived in. No doorman or lobby, just a hallway with mailboxes and a security door you could open in five seconds with a screwdriver. He might look into what the rent went for in a place like this. Billy's house was primo and he could be happy living there forever, but since that wasn't going to happen, he needed to start thinking about new digs. A Beverly Hills address had class. It was closer to where Amelia worked, too. Someday, he hoped, that would matter.

Laurie lived on the top floor. He rode up on the elevator, which smelled of take-out Chinese food, walked down the hallway to her number, and rang the doorbell.

She opened the door immediately. 'Did you see her?' she asked fretfully, moving aside so he could come in.

'Yes,' he replied. 'You didn't tell me she was a gimp.'

'What difference would that make?' Laurie asked, immediately on-guard.

213

'It feels weird. Like picking on a wounded bird.'

'She has MS,' Laurie said defensively. 'Having a bad leg doesn't change the fact that she's a bitch. Are you growing a conscience now?' she sneered. 'It's a little late for that, isn't it?'

She was right. It was too late to make any moral distinctions. 'I'm just saying ... you're right, it doesn't change anything.'

'Good,' she said, relieved that he hadn't lost heart. 'Eyes on the prize.'

To take his mind off the victim, Wycliff checked out Laurie's digs. Bland to the point of anonymity. You couldn't tell anything about the person who lived here. Probably came furnished. A place to hunker down and lick your wounds until you were ready to move on with your life. Two months ago, if he had been presented with a pad like this, he would have thought he was on top of the world. Not anymore.

'Do you want something to drink?' she asked. 'I have white wine open. Or there's beer, and whiskey.'

'No, thanks.'

Along with the camera, he had bought a North Face daypack at a sports store. Half the population of LA carried them, no one would give it a second look. He took it off his shoulder and set it on the floor.

'Where's the money?' he asked her.

'In the bedroom.' She turned and walked down a short hallway. He followed her.

Her bedroom was of a piece with the rest of the place: featureless, no personality. We could be in a Hilton in Omaha, Nebraska, Wycliff thought. Billy's house, his framework for living now, was special and unique. Time and thought had gone into everything in it, whether it was a chair, a sketch on the wall, a plate, rug, towel. His surroundings had never mattered to him before. Now they did. He was changing in ways he didn't know about. But he could feel how they affected him.

'There,' she said, pointing into the closet. 'You take it out. It freaks me out, handling that much money.'

The suitcase was a gray Samsonite hard-shell, a bland-looking, secure bag you would normally check in at the airport. But you wouldn't check this one, not with a ton of cash inside. They opened suitcases now, for security checks. A minimum-wage airport security drone would crap his drawers if he opened this bag.

He took the suitcase out and set it on her queen-sized bed. Wordlessly, hand shaking, Laurie handed him a key. He opened the suitcase.

Forty stacks of fifty-dollar bills, fifty bills to a stack, neatly arranged and bundled.

Wycliff had never seen this much money in his life, except on the *Texas Hold 'Em* show on ESPN. But this wasn't television. This was real.

'A hundred thousand dollars,' Laurie said, looking over his shoulder. 'It's all there, but you can count it if you don't trust me.'

He stifled a laugh. Trust her? He didn't trust her as far than he could throw her, and she was not a petite woman.

He picked up a bundle and riffed it like in a gangster movie, trying to look like he knew what he was doing. It looked legitimate, as legitimate as a deal this filthy could be.

'I'll count it later,' he told her. 'If you're short, I'll let you know.'

'What if there's too much?'

'Is there?'

'No. It's exact, to the penny. I triple-checked it.'

He put his backpack on the bed next to the suitcase and started transferring the money. 'Where's the rest of it?' he asked.

'Nearby.'

He kept stuffing the bundles into his pack. 'Show me.'

She shook her head. 'No.'

He turned to her, wads of cash in each hand. 'What do you mean, no?'

She took a nervous step back from him. 'I'm not going to show the rest of it to you now. You're going to have to take my word about it.'

More bullshit about trust. 'We had an agreement.'

'Which I'm keeping. Half now, half when it's done.'

'I'm not going to take it,' he said, trying to sound reasonable, so he wouldn't scare her. 'But I need to know that it's there.'

'It is.'

This was turning into a Mexican standoff. 'I don't know that.'

She held her ground. 'I'm not going to.'

'Why not?'

'Because you could take it now and screw me,' she answered. 'Keeping half back is the only insurance I have.'

She had a point, not that he wanted to concede it. 'I could take what's here and screw you. Half a loaf is sometimes better than the whole thing.'

She gave him a slit-eyed stare, like a rattlesnake ready to strike. She's tough, he realized. Tougher than I expected. 'But you won't,' she answered, confirming his intuition. 'You want it all.'

He carried his pack, now stuffed with cash, into the living room. 'No more contact until this is over,' he warned her. 'One wrong move and everything could blow up in our faces.'

'You're running the show.' She twisted a tendril of hair around her finger. 'When are you going to do it?'

'I don't know yet. The sooner the better.'

'Amen to that,' Laurie answered.

He slung the pack over his shoulder and walked to the front door. He could feel her eyes burning a hole in his back as he left and shut the door behind him.

TWENTY-ONE

The daypack full of bills was in the bedroom closet, hidden under his laundry bag. Wycliff was nervous as hell about leaving it there, but he couldn't think of anywhere safer to put it. He couldn't open an account at a bank with it; he'd be arrested before he walked out the door. He could stash it in a safe deposit box, and maybe that's where it would end up, but before he did he wanted to talk to Charlotte's friend to find out if what she had told him about the guy lowering the amount it would take to get on board was real or bullshit.

He double-checked Billy. His brother was sleeping. Satisfied that he had some time for himself, he dialed Charlotte's number.

'I want to get together with your money man,' he told her.

'Why? Do you have money to invest?' she asked, sounding skeptical.

'Yes.'

'How much?' He could hear the surprise in her voice.

'I'm not going to talk about it on the phone. I can be a player, if what you told me is true about him bending his rules because of you and him being good friends.'

Be a player. Damn, that sounded good.

'I'm pretty sure he will.' Charlotte sounded excited, but then he heard her gasp. 'Did your brother die?' she asked him. 'Is that why you...?'

'No,' he cut her off. 'He hasn't died yet. He's going to, real soon, but for now, he's still alive.'

'I'm glad,' she said, sounding relieved. 'I know it's inevitable, but as long as he's alive, there's hope.'

There was something in the way she expressed her sympathy that sounded wrong, like she was faking it because it was the right thing to do instead of actually feeling it, but that was probably his own projection. He was the last person on earth to judge anyone else, especially now.

'Yes,' he said. 'There's still hope.'

There was a moment's pause, then she asked again, 'But you have money anyway?'

'Yes. I have some money.'

'An advance on his will?'

Jesus, she could be pushy. What business was it of hers how he had it? But he wasn't going to call her on it. She was his connection to the big time. He wasn't going to jeopardize that. If she wanted to believe that his brother had fronted him some money, all the better. In fact, he realized, her thinking his money was an advance on Billy's estate was the perfect cover-up for the real reason. That the money was in bundles of cash, rather than in a bank account, would be hard to explain, but he'd come up with some excuse.

'I have money,' he told her again. 'That's all I can say for now.'

219

'Fine,' she answered, her voice now brisk and neutral. 'When do you want to meet with John?'

'As soon as it's convenient for him.' He looked across the room to his brother in his drug-induced sleep, his chest barely rising and falling. 'And when I can get someone from the hospice to watch over Billy while I'm gone.'

'Of course,' she said, coming on sincere again. 'Do you want him to come there? I wouldn't come with him, I couldn't take seeing your brother like he is now, but John doesn't know him. His condition wouldn't affect him like it would me.'

That was the last thing in the world he wanted, some stranger coming in, sizing up the lay of the land as it actually was, and upsetting his tidy little applecart. The hundred large in small, used bills was enough of a red flag, he didn't need to throw more oil on the fire.

'Not a good idea,' he told her firmly. 'We're keeping everyone out who isn't essential.'

'I understand. All right, then. I'll get in touch with John and let him know you want to meet, and you two can work out the details.'

'Thanks, Charlotte. I owe you one.'

'You'll find a way to pay me back.' He could almost hear her purring over the phone. 'I'm glad you're finally going to have some serious money, Wycliff. But I'm saddened by how you're getting it.'

It was late, after midnight, but he couldn't sleep. The lethal combination of the money in the closet, which was throwing off psychological heat like molten lava from a volcano, the senseless murder he was going to commit, and his brother's imminent death, combined to fry his emotions. He had already gotten up twice to go outside for a cigarette and a drink, hoping to calm his nerves, but it hadn't worked. He lay wide awake in bed, staring at the ceiling. What in God's name had he been thinking?

He kept replaying what might have been, over and over in his head. He could have backed out the first time Laurie propositioned him. He didn't have to call her. He could have walked away from her at the mall, yet again when he went to her apartment. But he hadn't. At every step where he had faced temptation, temptation had won. He had been a coward, a pathetic loser afraid to say no.

Too late to back out.

Leaving Billy alone was a huge risk, but he had to take it. He had to kill the woman and put it behind him. Before the fear ate him alive, before he lost his nerve and chickened out.

A last-minute check of Billy's condition. His breathing was shallow, but regular. He was almost in a coma now, but he could stay in that state for an indefinite amount of time. The doctor didn't think he was going to last much any longer, but there were no certainties. Wycliff had done some research about it online. People sometimes lasted like this for weeks, even months.

He placed a palm on his brother's forehead. It was cool and dry. I'll be back as fast as I can, he promised. Don't die on me while I'm gone, he prayed silently to his sleeping brother.

It was dark out. Sunup wasn't due for another hour. The freeway traffic was sparse. Wycliff made the drive to the victim's apartment in less than half an hour.

He still didn't know how he was going to kill the woman. He had read her dossier again, but it hadn't given him a specific enough schedule that he could make a move on her with absolute certainty that he would be successful. The only thing he could think of was to wait until she came out today, stalk her, and see if there was someplace where he could jump her when she was alone.

He tucked into a parking spot across from her building, sipping a McDonald's take-out coffee. To the east, shards of sunlight were starting to spackle the roadway and highlight the palm trees towering above the sidewalks. The traffic was picking up, at this early hour mostly commercial vehicles. Pre-dawn joggers floated by. Wycliff was dressed for movement himself: running shoes, comfortable jeans, a white T-shirt with no logo, and his Dodgers hat. Nothing that would draw attention. He didn't want anyone to give him a first look, let alone a second.

Cars began emerging from the victim's underground garage. Sporadic at first, then a gathering stream. He studied the drivers through his camera's zoom lens. They were prosperous looking in their German and Japanese and Swedish vehicles. The sun had risen. The flow of traffic was picking up. The fullness of the day had begun.

The little blue convertible, top up this time, popped out of the shadows and turned right, heading east. Wycliff, startled by its sudden emergence, laid rubber as he pulled out into traffic, hung an illegal U-turn across four lanes of traffic (still not heavy, fortunately) and began to follow her. Adrenaline pumping, he checked his rear-view mirror for cops; there weren't any.

He spotted the Audi a block ahead, puttering along in the slow lane. Sit chilly, he admonished himself as he tailed her. Let the action come to you. He had to be clear-headed and alert when he made his move. And fast. It had to work the first time. There wouldn't be a second.

The woman turned south onto South Beverly Drive and pulled into a city parking lot. Wycliff parked on the street in a loading-zone space and watched as she got out of her car and entered a Starbucks. He opened the information folder and checked her schedule again. She had an appointment with her psychiatrist in twenty minutes. The shrink's office was a few blocks away. He pulled back into traffic and headed for it.

The therapist's office was in a modest two-story Spanish-style building on a quiet, tree-lined street, flanked on either side by small apartment houses. Wycliff parked down the block, got out of his car, nonchalantly crossed the street, and entered the lobby. No security doors. No guards. He looked up at the ceiling. No cameras.

There was a directory on the wall next to the

mailboxes. Dr Lovitz's office was on the first floor. The other tenants were all psychiatrists and psychologists. He opened the unlocked inner door and walked down the long corridor. He located Lovitz's office, the last one in the back.

Years ago, he had seen a head doctor for a couple of months, as a condition of his parole. He hadn't learned a thing from the guy, except that talking about yourself and analyzing your feelings was bullshit. One thing he remembered was the layout of the doc's office. You came in one door and left from a different one. For a lot of people, seeing a shrink is embarrassing. A patient doesn't want to encounter another patient, especially one you might know.

He walked outside and went around to the back. An alley ran parallel to the street. There was a small parking lot in back of the doctor's building. A sign in front of the lot declared *For Visitors Only*. You parked here, you went in and saw your shrink, you came back here and you left, your anonymity protected. Not a bird's nest on the ground, but as good as he was going to get on short notice. He needed to do this before his nerves or circumstances froze him.

The victim's car turned into the alley and approached the lot. He stepped away to the other side of the roadway, hiding behind a large city trash container. The little convertible pulled into one of the available parking spots. The driver got out, Starbucks cup in hand. She went in the back door. Wycliff checked the time on his cell phone. Ten minutes before the hour. A couple of minutes later, a middle-aged man came out. He got into a Jaguar that was parked a few slots from the Audi and drove away down the alley.

Another thing Wycliff remembered: a normal therapy session was fifty minutes long. This allowed a patient to leave before the next one's session. Hopefully, the following patient would arrive and go in before his quarry came out. If that didn't happen, he'd abort and wait for another chance. Nothing he could do about that except wait and see.

He walked back to the street and moved his car around the block. He didn't want anyone seeing it in front of the therapist's building and being able to describe it to the cops. A thousand to one shot, but he was going to take every precaution he could think of. He took a short stroll around the neighborhood to calm his nerves. Not much pedestrian traffic. He didn't present anything special that would single him out. A man on foot, wearing a short-sleeved shirt, jeans, sunglasses, and a baseball hat. Hundreds of guys would fit that description.

It was time to get the show on the road. The alley was quiet. He checked the time. Almost ten before the hour. He hovered behind the trash dumps, using them for cover. Sweat was forming in his armpits again. The front of his shirt was wet, too, along with his hair under his hat. He wiped his hands on his pants.

A Lexus SUV drove down the alley and pulled into the lot. The driver was a small woman dressed in a business suit and slacks. She stood outside her car for a moment, checking her makeup in her compact mirror. Satisfied that she passed muster, she went inside.

Everything was going according to plan. He had brought a pair of construction worker's gloves with him. He took them out of his back pocket and pulled them on. He didn't want his hands touching the victim's flesh. He was going to walk up behind her, grab her by the neck, and snap it. She was a pudgy, middle-aged woman, and he was a large, strong man. It would be like breaking a chicken's neck. Then he'd grab her purse and take off. To the cops it would appear like another LA robbery that went off the rails, like the one of that famous publicist who had been accidentally murdered during a botched car-jacking.

The gun, tucked behind his belt at the back of his pants, felt like a tumor. It was a mistake to have brought it. He should have left it in the car. Too late now – by the time he went to his car and returned, the woman would be gone.

The back door opened. He tensed up, watching.

The woman was on her cell phone, blabbing away a mile a minute. Son of a bitch! he cursed silently. He couldn't go for her while she was talking. Even if he broke her neck instantly, the party on the other end would hear the impact, her last gasp or cry before her lights went out.

'I'll call you later,' she said into the phone. 'I have to go.' She hung up and rummaged around in her purse for her car keys.

He had let his guard down, so now he wasn't ready.

He would never be ready.

He crossed the alley, walking towards her. The woman glanced up as he approached. He continued on past her, as if he was going into the building, and she looked away from him. She found her car keys and buzzed the remote.

Two steps and he was behind her, his hands on her neck, squeezing violently. He felt flesh and muscle tense, then start to spasm. He bent her neck back, trying to snap it. But immediately he realized, with a surge of panic, that this was not going to be the piece of cake he had assumed it would be. The woman was stronger than he had expected. She started bucking wildly, kicking her legs like windmills, her long fingernails clawing at his hands. He tightened his grip on her throat. Hardly the chicken's neck he'd expected, it was thick and muscular. He lifted her off her feet so her legs couldn't get a purchase to push back against him.

'Sofia! You left your coat in the office.'

Still clutching his victim in a death grip, Wycliff jerked around in the direction of the voice. A man was trotting towards them, brandishing a suede jacket. 'You don't want to...' He stopped in his tracks as he realized what was happening.

The psychiatrist was middle aged, balding, sporting a graying, neatly trimmed Van Dyke. For a moment, he and Wycliff stared at each other, both frozen. Then he turned and ran back towards the building.

Wycliff let go of his victim, who thudded to the ground. He ran after the therapist, who was reaching for the handle to open the back door. Wycliff pulled the gun out and fired. The therapist went down in a heap. The back of his jacket was red with blood, spreading fast.

Wycliff rushed to him. He hovered over him for a second, looking down in disbelief. Bile rose in his throat. He swallowed hard to keep it down.

The woman.

She was on her knees, coughing, her face crimson, veins pulsing in her temples. She started crawling away from Wycliff, fumbling in her purse for her cell phone.

He kicked the phone out of her hand. It skittered across the asphalt. Her look to Wycliff was primordial venom. 'That bitch Laurie,' she spat out, still trying to crawl away, like a broken-legged dog.

He shot her in the back of her head.

He was shaking uncontrollably. 'Oh God,' he whimpered. 'Oh God.' Then he was running down the alley in the other direction, sprinting, his lungs on fire, still grasping the gun, the murder weapon, as if it was welded to his hand.

The driver of the SUV had rushed outside when she heard the gunshots. She hovered over the therapist, then whirled and looked in Wycliff's direction and screamed. 'Stop!' she cried out, from forty yards away. 'Help! Police! Stop!'

Wycliff burst out of the alley onto the side street where he had stashed his car. He shoved the gun into his pants pocket and managed to unlock the car. He dove inside, fumbling the key into the ignition. The car roared to life. He tore away down the street, running a stop sign and turning onto a larger street, driving blind, then another turn, then he was crossing Wilshire heading north, lucking out by catching a green light, and he was on one of the leafy residential streets between Wilshire and Sunset in Beverly Hills and he slowed down to the speed limit, but he didn't stop.

TWENTY-TWO

The house was quiet. Wycliff let himself back in and tiptoed across the living room to where his brother was sleeping. He touched a hand to Billy's wrist. He was still alive, sleeping. He checked the machines. Nothing had changed.

He grabbed a Corona out of the refrigerator, drank half of it in one swallow, and collapsed into the chair at the side of his brother's bed. He had murdered two people he didn't know. Shot them in cold blood without mercy. For what? Not revenge, not passion, not from the heart. For money. What a weak, stupid reason. He had wanted to be a player. He sure as hell was one now.

He drained his beer and checked on his brother again. No changes. He stripped off his clothes and took a long, scalding shower, trying to wash his sins and fear away. He couldn't. They were inside of him, unreachable.

He dressed in fresh, clean clothes, bundled up everything he had worn, including his hat and shoes, and stuffed it all in a trash bag. When he could get away again he'd find a dumpster far from here, one used by a commercial establishment, so he could bury it under dozens of other bags. He hid the gun under his mattress until he could return it to Charlotte's apartment. It was the property of a woman who had probably never fired it. There would be no reason to link it to the murders.

Not yet noon, but he went outside with a stiff bourbon and his cigarettes to calm his nerves. He was still shaking uncontrollably. He had to stop that, he had to force himself to appear calm. Pretty damn soon, if not already, the killings would be all over television and the Internet. This would be a media circus, of which he was the unknown star. He had to make sure it stayed that way.

He smoked two cigarettes and downed his drink and went back inside. His brother was stirring, slowly coming to. He took Billy's hand in his and held it like he would hold an injured bird, softly, a caress. Billy's eyes opened. He looked at Wycliff.

'Where have you been?' he asked, his voice so thin it was like a faint wind blowing on a reed. 'I woke up earlier. You weren't here.'

'That must have been when I was taking a walk,' Wycliff lied.

Billy's voice was so faint the words were

almost inaudible. 'I was worried about you. That something had happened to you.'

'Nothing happened to me,' Wycliff told him, fighting to keep his emotions in check. 'I'm right here. I'm always going to be right here.'

By noon the murders were the leading story on every TV station in Los Angeles, the Internet, the newspaper web sites. While Billy slept, Wycliff watched the story unfold on television, switching from one station to another. The woman who had seen him fleeing the scene couldn't offer much useful information, since she had only seen him from the back, at a distance. Still, she was able to state without any doubt that he was a tall white man. That narrowed the field, but as yet not enough to matter, the police spokespeople dealing with the media crush explained. They were terse regarding releasing information, but they did let slip that an autopsy would be done on the victims, to find out if the murderer had left any traces of his DNA on them.

Wycliff shuddered when he heard that. The woman had clawed at his arms like a mountain lion. The police might find scrapings under her fingernails. Would they be able to trace them to a crime committed over a decade ago, for which he had gone to a county jail, but not a state or federal prison? Despite all the hype on *CSI*, he knew that most local police forces were woefully behind the times in gathering forensic evidence. So maybe he could dodge that, at least buy some time.

The best thing to do was hunker down. He had a mountain of money hidden away. Worst came to worst, he could run, like he had so many times before. He didn't want to this time, he was hoping he could have a future here, but if it came down to staying or surviving, there would be no choice.

His cell phone rang. He clutched when he saw the caller ID. He got up from Billy's bedside and went out to the back yard.

'What are you doing, calling me?' he raged at Laurie.

She sounded hysterical over the phone. 'Do you know what's going on? The media is covering this wall to wall. My in-laws are out of their minds. His son has already been here. He came to console me. I thought I was going to lose it. I'm petrified.'

His worst fears about her were being confirmed. 'Calm down,' he told her. 'You have to stay cool. There's nothing that can involve you.'

'You can involve me!'

'And incriminate myself? Don't be ridiculous. I'm the last person you have to worry about. Now listen,' he continued, fighting not to lose control, 'do not call me again. The police might put a trace on your phone.' He thought for a moment, his brain racing. 'Go to Radio Shack and buy some pre-paid phones. I'll get some, too. We'll use them to communicate. You use it one time and dump it, go on to the next one. That way, our calls can't be traced.'

He didn't know if that was true, but he had to

settle her down. She was a loose cannon, firing blindly.

'All right,' she groaned. 'When am I going to see you?'

'Not for a few days. We have to let this cool down. You go about your normal routine, don't change anything. I'll get word to you about how to get in touch with me. Until then, we do not communicate, do you understand that? That is absolutely crucial.'

'Yes,' she told him. She sounded scared out of her mind. 'I understand.'

An hour later, Charlotte called. He panicked when he saw who it was. Had she somehow connected him to the murders? She had wormed herself inside his mind. Had he sent some brainwave signal to her?

She didn't have a clue about that. She was calling to find out when he could meet with John Cummings. She had talked to John, and he was excited about helping Wycliff.

'Isn't that wonderful, darling?' she cooed. 'I'm so happy this is going to happen.'

'Me, too,' he replied, almost choking on his words. 'Listen, though. I've got to be here. I can't be leaving, not even for an hour.'

He could hear an intake of breath. 'Is he...?'

'It could be any time now.'

'I'm so sorry.' She sounded sincere.

'Thanks. I can't talk now. But I do want to see you.'

'I'm glad to hear that.'

'I'll call you when I can.'

'I'll be here. I'll be praying for him. And you.'

Amelia showed up late in the afternoon. 'What happened?' she exclaimed in alarm when she saw the scratches on his arms.

The lies kept coming. 'This goes under the heading of no good deed goes unpunished. Some lady's cat was up in a tree and I volunteered to get it down for her. The cat didn't want to come down.'

She laughed. 'That's why you call the fire department, dummy. Does it hurt?'

'It stung like hell when I put alcohol on, but it's okay now.'

'Good. I don't want anything to hurt you.'

He didn't know whether to shit or go blind. *Oh, baby, if you only knew.*

The doctor came by at dinner-time. He was downcast after he examined Billy, who by now was barely breathing. 'Nothing more I can do now,' he told Wycliff mournfully. 'His systems are failing, one after the other. If there are final plans to be made, now's the time.'

Amelia left and the brothers were alone again. Billy didn't wake up. Wycliff watched the murder story unfold on television. It was the only thing the talking heads could talk about. A pack of vultures.

Before he went to bed he cleaned Billy up, changed his pajamas, shaved his hollowed-out cheeks. Billy knew none of this; he was unconscious, asleep, drifting further and further away.

He was so thin now every bone in his body showed through, as if his skin was nothing more than a covering of his skeleton. They shoot horses, don't they? Animals are shown more mercy when it's their time to die than is given to humans. What was the point of his brother living any longer? Thank God for pain medication; otherwise, this would be unbearable. Let go, he begged his brother silently, just let it go.

He had already been involved in two deaths today. Two horrible, brutal, unnecessary deaths, a role he should not have been allowed to take on. But this one, the one he desperately wanted to do, he couldn't.

He went to bed, but he couldn't sleep. He was up all night, checking on Billy, going outside for a drink and a smoke, coming back to bed and writhing in emotional agony over what he had done. Even if he wound up pulling it off, getting away scot-free, he would never escape it. He would carry what he had done to his grave and maybe beyond, if there really was a god.

A few of Billy's old friends, including Stanley the loser, dropped by in the morning to say their last good-byes. Wycliff, physically exhausted and emotionally strung-out, stayed in the background. They didn't want him there, especially Stanley, who shook with indignation and fear when he and Wycliff locked eyes. *Fuck you all*, Wycliff thought with powerful bitterness. Where have you been these past weeks, when his brother could have used some company to cheer him up? He doesn't even know you're here now.

I've been the one to keep him going. Me and me alone. If I wasn't here, Billy wouldn't be, either. He'd be rotting away in a hospital bed. Probably dead already. Coming home had raised his brother's spirits and given him an extension on his life. He had nothing to apologize for on that score.

The friends left, and the house was quiet again.

They sat together all day long. Billy was barely conscious, and when he was, it was only for a few minutes at a time. Wycliff made sure his brother knew he was there. When Billy was asleep, he watched the news. No breaks in the case so far. The police were pursuing leads. When they had something more definitive, they would say so. What that meant was, so far they didn't know shit. Fingers crossed that they never would.

Three things to worry about. First, that someone had gotten a better look at him fleeing the scene than the woman in the alley. He had been running blind, he didn't remember anything about his flight, it had all been a blur. The hat and shades should have been decent camouflage, but it was a possibility. It was amazing how good a picture you could take from a cell phone.

Nothing he could do about that.

Second complication: the possibility of scrapings from his arms under the woman's fingernails. That was his main concern. He couldn't do anything about it, either the cops would tie them to him or they wouldn't. If the police were able to connect the dots he would deal with it, by taking off and starting a new life.

The third potential problem, Laurie, was of a much higher level. She could fry him, but then she'd be jumping in the pan, too. It was a delicate situation, but if he played it smart, he could control her. Time was their ally. The longer they were able to sit chilly and hold on, the better their chance of beating it. They had one last critical piece of business to take care of, and then it would be over between them. She would want to stay away from him as much as he did from her.

But who was he kidding? It would never be over between them. They were tied together forever. Even when he got the rest of his money and never saw her again they were two bastard twins from the same malignant womb.

Night fell. He cooked himself bacon and eggs for dinner, washed down with shots of Jack Daniels and several Coronas. He and Billy watched *How I Met Your Mother, Law and Order*, the local news. Billy slept through it all. The murder story still led off, but the coverage wasn't as hysterical as it had been. Life, as always, was moving on.

It was past midnight. He went outside. Another drink, another cigarette. He felt numb. Not calm, rather no feeling at all. At least that was better than feeling he was about to jump out of his skin.

He was in over his head, way over. He needed an escape hatch, but he had no idea what it could be. Beat the rap? If he did, what then? Would he actually be able to live like a civilian, obey the rules, be quote *productive* unquote? Have an ongoing relationship? Make a living beyond the day to day?

He'd had a simple plan. Blow into town, con his sick brother out of some money, get the fuck out of Dodge. He had pulled off the first part: he was here. The rest had not gone the way he had planned, not remotely. Up was down, right was left, in some ways he felt more connected to the world than he ever had, in others he was totally out to sea.

One step at a time. Be present for his brother until the end. Get the money from Laurie. He would see about the rest later. Right now, those two things were all he could handle.

He finished his cigarette and whiskey and stood, stretching, looking up at the sky. Too many streetlights to see any stars. The moon was hidden behind a cloud. He went back inside.

The house was dark except for a solitary night light, glowing like a lightning bug, which was plugged into a socket near Billy's bed. Wycliff gently lifted his brother's arm and felt his wrist for a pulse, as he did a dozen times a day.

There was none.

He leaned over and put his ear near Billy's mouth. No breath.

Softly: 'Billy.' Again: 'Billy.'

No answer.

He could call the paramedics like he had done before, but his brother had made the decision: no heroic gestures. Do not keep me alive artificially.

He went into the bathroom, found a small hand mirror, and held it up to Billy's mouth. The mirror remained clear, not a trace of fog.

One more time, he checked for a pulse. Neck, heart.

He kissed his brother on the forehead and called Sadie.

TWENTY-THREE

The funeral, at Forest Lawn, was held at sunrise, per Billy's instructions. It was not private, but it was sparsely attended nonetheless. The lack of mourners pissed Wycliff off. His brother had enriched people's lives. Why weren't more of them here to pay their last respects? They couldn't haul their sorry asses out of bed to say goodbye to a friend?

As the sun broke through, the minister, a functionary provided by the mortuary, droned out a laundry list of homilies. He didn't recite anything about who Billy actually was, what his unique achievements were, his bold struggle against the scourge. Wycliff stood silent as he listened. The minister had asked if he had anything to say; Wycliff had declined. What was the point? He and his brother had been estranged all their lives, now one was alive and one was dead. For some, life moves on. For others, it doesn't.

Amelia was supportive, as usual. She rubbed

Wycliff's back as the minister sputtered to his conclusion. The ceremony was over and done with in less than fifteen minutes. After Wycliff threw the first clog of earth on the coffin, Amelia picked up a handful and threw it on top of his. By the time the cemetery workers had half shoveled the dirt over his coffin, the crowd had dispersed.

They walked to his car. Stanley came over to them. He seemed nervous as he approached. Wycliff stopped and waited for him to catch up.

'I'm sorry,' Stanley began. His voice was quivering.

'Thanks,' Wycliff answered. The man had shown up. Reason enough to treat him civilly. 'Me, too.'

'I just wanted to say...' Stanley flushed. He wiped his forehead with a handkerchief. His eyes were red; he had been crying. 'What you did made a lot of difference for him. His friends really appreciate that. I appreciate that.'

Wycliff was surprised and touched. 'Thank you,' he mumbled.

'Whatever I feel about you,' Stanley continued, 'it doesn't matter. You were there for him in the end.'

He stuck out his hand. Wycliff took it. The hand was sweaty. He had been sweaty when Wycliff had first encountered him. He hadn't changed. Wycliff had.

'Thank you,' Wycliff told him. 'He really valued your friendship. He spoke of you often.'

The man's eyes lit up behind his Coke-bottle lenses. 'He did?'

'Yes. He said you were a great friend. Someone who had been there for him when the going got tough.'

Stanley blushed. 'I loved him. Others did, too.'

'I know,' Wycliff said. 'He was well loved.'

Stanley turned and trotted away towards a couple of other men who were watching with wary eyes. Wycliff watched them get into their cars and drive off. Amelia took his hand. 'He's the man who was house-sitting for your brother before you came?'

Wycliff nodded. 'I treated him like shit. I feel like an asshole now.'

'Don't.' She took his hand. 'It's time to go.'

Wycliff had sprung for a nice deli spread, plus wine, beer, and sodas, but only a handful of mourners showed up at the house. The few who came had a quick drink and a bite to eat and left. Wycliff surveyed the untouched trays of food with annoyance: what a waste of money. He went outside and had a smoke.

Amelia came out to join him. 'No one's left,' she said. 'I'll wrap the food up and put it in the refrigerator.'

'I'm not going to eat it. Take it to a food bank.'

'You sure?'

He nodded.

She rubbed his back. 'I have to go to work, honey. I'm sorry. I wish I didn't.'

'I know. Thanks for being here.'

'Of course I would be here,' she told him. 'You know that.'

He kissed her. They held onto each other for a

moment.

'I'm going to miss him,' she said. 'He had real soul.'

'That he did.' Wycliff dropped his butt and stubbed it out with his foot. 'Tomorrow I'll start packing up. It won't take long. I don't have much. Just my personal stuff.'

'You can stay with me,' she offered.

He cupped her neck and drew her to him. 'Thanks. I may take you up on that temporarily, but I nccd to find my own place.'

'You can't stay here?'

'Not for long. Once the will is settled...' He shrugged.

She nodded in understanding. 'I'll call you later.'

They kissed again and she left. The house was empty. He poured himself a drink and had another cigarette to go with it.

Laurie opened her door almost before he knocked. She pulled him inside and slammed the door behind him, double-locking it.

'I've been jumping out of my skin waiting to see you,' she scolded him. 'Why didn't you come earlier?' She wasn't holding it together very well. 'It's been three days!'

'I had other business to take care of.' He wasn't going to tell her what that business was. The less she knew about him, the better. 'And I didn't want to show my face here too soon. I didn't want to run into anybody.'

Wycliff had checked her building out thoroughly before entering it. He couldn't see that anyone was watching. There was no logical reason for that, but he had to be extra cautious with everything about her. This was a woman on the verge of a nervous breakdown. He had to keep her calm at all costs.

She slumped onto her living room couch. 'My life has been utter hell. My in-laws, the police. Question after question. Everyone's been solicitous of the poor widow, but underneath you can feel the accusations. No one has come straight out and said I had anything to do with killing her, but I can feel the tension. It's no secret we hated each other. Her family knew that, and I'm sure they told the police.'

She laughed, a high nervous laugh, then she coughed harshly. There was a glass of water on the side table next to her. Wycliff picked it up and handed it to her. She gulped it down.

'The cops described you,' she went on. 'Not your face, I don't think they have any idea what you look like, they only have that witness who saw you from the back. They asked if I knew anyone who fit your description. I told them I knew dozens of men who did. From the gym, from where I shop, where I used to work.'

From the way she was telling it, they didn't have a description of any of his features. So there was no other eye-witness, at least not so far. Every day that held up the case grew colder. All to the good.

'I have to get going,' he told her.

'You want your money.'

'That's why I'm here. You know that.'

She struck a pose. 'It's not to see me, too?'

This woman had been trouble from the get-go. Why did he think that was going to change?

'I'm happy to see you, Laurie, but let's take care of business, okay?'

She pouted. It felt phony. 'Whatever you say.' He followed her into her bedroom. The suitcase in her closet was the same Samsonite the first payment had been in. Wycliff picked it up. It was heavy. He laid it on the bed and opened it.

Stacks of bills, like before. She had come through.

He had a second backpack with him, from the same store where he had bought the first one. He started transferring the money.

'Aren't you going to count it?' she asked, hovering behind him.

He didn't look back at her as he kept transferring the stacks. 'I trust you.' *On this. Anything else, no way in hell.*

The transfer didn't take long. He zipped the pack up and turned to her.

She had taken off her blouse and bra. Her naked breasts were cupped in her hands, thrusting up at him. 'We're finished with our business now,' she said tantalizingly.

Wycliff tried to look away, but he couldn't. They were gorgeous. Real or fake, it didn't matter. He felt himself getting hard. He cursed his relentless sexual nature.

'You want me. I know you do.'

It took all the self-control he had, but he managed to force himself not to reach out for her. 'We can't do this, Laurie.'

She took a step towards him. 'Your eyes have been falling out of your head since the first time you saw me,' she mocked him. 'Now you can have these. And everything else.'

Think with your brain for once instead of your cock. 'It's too dangerous for us to be together. I fit the police description.'

'The police don't know shit,' she retorted in anger. 'They want the family to think they're on the case. They pretty much came out and told me that.'

'But they're still going to keep an eye on you. If they see me they'll wonder who I am, start to nose around. That's no good, Laurie. We can't take the chance.'

She paused, looking him over as if trying to see if he was telling her the truth, and if it didn't matter. Her expression became glum as she saw he wasn't going to succumb to her.

'You're right,' she said, sounding deflated. 'I was thinking with my heart, not my head. I was hoping you would, too. But you won't.'

He exhaled. His bones were jelly.

'Obviously, I'm attracted to you,' she said. She tried to force a self-effacing laugh, but it fell flat. 'But you're right. We need to cut this off cleanly, before we do something we'll both regret.' Another sorrowful breath. 'You won't hear from me again.' Wycliff left the apartment before she could change her mind.

A FedEx envelope was on the doorstep when he got back to the house. Inside, a single page legal document, informing him that his brother's estate would be probated the following Wednesday, at his lawyer's office. His presence was requested.

He carried the backpack inside and stashed it in the closet with the first one. One hundred thousand dollars in each. More money than he'd ever thought he would have in his entire life. The backpacks were practically glowing, they were so hot. He needed to get them out of here, to a more secure place.

One detail above all worried him. He had been trying to put the thought out of his mind, but couldn't. How had Laurie been able to come up with two hundred thousand dollars in cash? Maybe she was richer than she said she was. But then why would she be living in a nondescript apartment in the regular-people section of Beverly Hills? Unless her late husband had given her more money than she had let on, and she didn't want his kids to know about it, because it would jeopardize her claim for more. That would make sense, if anything about this fiasco made sense.

He knew nothing of her background. The story she had fed him about her life could be a pack of lies. Hell, he lied about practically everything. Why should he be surprised if others did the same? Everyone wants to reinvent themselves as someone better, more special. He was doing that on the fly, day after day. Why shouldn't others do the same?

What upset him more than anything was him. This was the second woman he didn't know anything about who had seduced him into being

246

her partner in crime. It had been bad enough with Charlotte and her crazy jewelry scam. But his situation with Laurie was on a much different level. Murder for hire, that's life without parole, or the needle. What kind of moron allows himself to be duped like this, over and over again? All he had to do to find out was look in the mirror.

You can't turn back the clock, no matter how much you want to. He had the money, that was the bottom line. How Laurie had gotten it was not his business. He had too much on his own plate to take care of to worry about someone else's problems.

The house felt claustrophobic. He locked up, jumped in his car, and took off.

He had no destination in mind. He took Sunset over to Santa Monica Boulevard, stopping in a convenience store in west Los Angeles for a six-pack of Sierra Nevada out of the cooler, continuing west into Santa Monica, Wilshire to Ocean Avenue, down the incline to Highway 1, north past the Palisades, past Topanga Canyon, the ocean on his left, shimmering in the sunlight. He drove through Malibu, past Trancas, past Zuma Beach, until he got to Leo Carrillo State Beach, almost to the Ventura County line. He parked in the public lot on the beach side and got out of his car. He cracked one of his cold brews and drank it with a cigarette, sitting on the hood of his car, staring out to the water, the horizon where the ocean meets the sky.

He had arrived in Los Angeles driving a stolen car, a thousand dollars in his pocket, eight hundred of that also stolen, and the clothes on his back. Now he had a wardrobe full of fancy threads, a car clean enough to fool the cops, and two hundred thousand dollars stashed away in his dead brother's closet. In his wildest dreams he could never have imagined having two hundred thousand dollars. By any standard he had ever set for himself he had it made.

He could stay or he could go. If he left, he could put his worries behind him. Two hundred thousand dollars would last him a long, long time. He could settle down in some out of the way town and buy himself a little business. You see these ads for low-rent franchises: laundromats, car washes, hardware stores. He could take a community college class in how to run a business, learn basic bookkeeping. If he did it right and stayed under the radar, he could be set for life. Lots of people did. He could, too.

If he stayed, what? He could still start a business. LA was a good town, better than most. But that was not enough reason to stay here, particularly with two murders hanging over his head.

If he left, he would be on his own again. Like he had always been, his entire life. If he stayed, he could be with Amelia. They could have a life together. He had never been in love before.

Hard choice, but no choice. He couldn't leave, at least not yet. If the police wound up closing in on him, he'd rethink his position. For now, he had to stay here. He had to give himself a chance.

He had a pair of running shorts and a towel in his trunk from when he had gone to the gym to work out. He shucked his clothes in the back seat of his car. What a lame-ass farmer's body, he thought, looking at his naked torso. Dark as an Arab on the arms, whiter than milk on his body and shoulders. He needed to be careful or he'd get burnt to shit, he didn't have any lotion. He put on his shorts, got out of the car, and walked across the expanse of sand, past the wind-surfers in their wet suits, the hot college girls in their skimpy two-pieces. At the water's edge he stuck in a foot to feel the temperature – cold but tolerable – and kept going until the surf was at his waist, then he plunged in and swam out past the breakers. He rolled over on his back and floated.

Of course she wanted to see him, Charlotte said when he called her. She sounded angry. He wondered if she was miffed because he hadn't invited her to the funeral. She had been forceful about not having any contact with his brother while he was alive, so he had assumed she wouldn't want to be present when he was laid to rest. Maybe he'd been wrong. But she hadn't asked him about how the funeral had gone, so she couldn't have been too concerned.

'Where in the world have you been?' she exclaimed as she opened her front door. His hair was damp from swimming. He smelled of salt water.

'Swimming in the ocean,' he replied. 'Good for what ails you. You ought to try it.'

She looked horrified at the suggestion. 'At my age, sunlight is poison. You need a bath,' she told him, wrinkling her nose. 'I'll draw one for you. Get out of those clothes. I'll throw them in the washing machine.'

She went into the bathroom. He heard water running. Before he took his clothes off he put the revolver back in the drawer. He got undressed and went into the bathroom.

Charlotte, wearing a terry cloth robe, was waiting for him. 'I'll join you.'

'Are you seeing someone?' They were lying in bed, smoking their customary post-coitus cigarette.

'Yes,' he answered. No more lying. Not about this.

She ran her fingernails along his thigh. 'I knew you would, sooner or later. Is she classy?'

'Very,' he answered. His throat felt constricted.

'Good. I wouldn't want to be sharing you with a floozy.' Her fingers moved further up his leg. 'Will we keep seeing each other?'

I hope not, he prayed. 'Sure we will,' he told her. Sometimes, you have to lie. 'I can't resist you, Charlotte. You know that.' That wasn't a lie.

She shook her head. 'I don't know that. What I know is that nothing is permanent. It's foolish to try and convince yourself otherwise.'

He wished he had her hard-headed objectivity. He'd be a lot better off.

'When do you want me to set up a meeting with John?' she asked, abruptly changing the subject. 'You have the time now.'

He had been too busy to think about that since the murders and Billy's death. Now that the opportunity was concrete, the idea of turning over his money to someone he didn't know was scary. He had earned that money in blood. But he had to do something with it, he couldn't leave the situation as it was.

'In a couple of days,' he parried. 'I have some stuff to take care of first.'

'Whenever you're ready, just let me know.' Her roaming fingers reached his penis. He lay back against the pillows and moaned.

TWENTY-FOUR

There were dozens of contractor's licensing schools in the area advertising on the Internet. They all charged about the same, $700, which included study DVDs, a weekend of class work, and the two-day state exam. Must not be too hard to pass, Wycliff thought, if they offer a money-back guarantee. He had worked construction on and off for years. Framing, drywall, electrical, plumbing. He could practically build a house from scratch. Many was the time when he had done the actual work for the contractor of record, who instead of framing a door or pouring a foundation was boffing the owner's wife or knocking down brewskis in the local bar.

Contracting would be a good career for him. It was more up his alley than starting a business he didn't know anything about, or investing in the stock market, of which he knew even less. You didn't need a college degree to become a contractor, like so many damn jobs required these days. You practically needed a diploma from Harvard to make cappuccinos at Starbucks these days, the competition for jobs was so fierce. He had never done well working for others. With a contractor's license, he could be his own boss. Use some of the backpack money to seed a new business, the rest would be a cushion against hard times. He knew a hell of a lot about hard times. It was the cushioning part that was strange.

He looked up various schools and chose one in Glendale, fifteen minutes away on the freeway. The paperwork was easy. and it didn't take him long to fill out the forms. The young Latina receptionist, who would have been cute if she hadn't had awful acne, asked him to wait while they were checked over, it wouldn't take long.

He hadn't even finished one article in *Guns and Ammo* when he was summoned to meet the supervisor in his office. The office, behind the reception area, was utilitarian: a desk, one chair behind it and one in front, a row of filing cabinets against the back wall. Some photos of youth sports teams the company sponsored. The only window looked out on the back of a Taco Bell dumpster. The supervisor was Mexican, about his age. Wycliff's knowing eye told him ex-service or ex-prison or both. He could have been a relative of Juan in Sunland, the dude he had sold the stolen car to, their faces had a certain reptilian similarity. This guy looked like he was a workout freak; his muscles bulged under his T-shirt. He tapped an approving knuckle on Wycliff's application.

'You're more than qualified,' he told Wycliff. 'Any particular area you're interested in?' He slid a sheet of paper across the desk to Wycliff. It listed all the classifications available.

Wycliff looked them over. 'I could go different ways,' he hedged. 'Where's the steady work these days?'

'The standards,' the supervisor answered. 'Drywall, framing, plumbing, electrical, tile, painting, welding. You can't go wrong with any of them.'

'If you were starting out, what would you choose?'

'Plumbing, but that's because my brother-in-law already has an up-and-running company. Nepotism has its benefits. You got anyone you could partner up with?'

'No,' Wycliff answered. 'It's just me.' He made his decision. 'Let me go for painting.' He had done that in the past and liked it. It wasn't just grunt work. Mixing and matching colors took real artistry. And you were often outside, not always crouched under a sink or sub-floor. Learn the ropes working under a seasoned painting contractor, then go out on his own.

'Good choice,' the supervisor said. 'The housing market's heating up again, everybody's remodeling. Painting's at the top of the list.' He reached into a filing cabinet and took out a handful of pamphlets, which he passed over. 'General contractors are looking high and low for good painters. You won't have any trouble finding steady work.'

He explained the procedures to Wycliff. Home study, class study, on-the-job training, state exam. If Wycliff hustled, he could be licensed in three months and go to work the following day.

'One thing we do in-house, which you won't get from most other schools, is Live Scan Fingerprinting. We do everything for you here, applications, paperwork, fingerprinting, the whole ball of wax. Saves you the time and aggravation.'

A three-alarm fire bell went off in Wycliff's head. 'You need to be fingerprinted to get a license?' he asked.

'State requirement,' the supervisor answered. 'Going back to 9/11. They want to weed out the deviates and criminals.'

Wycliff drew back. 'That could be a problem.'

The supervisor gave him a knowing look. 'You have a record?'

'Yeah, I do,' Wycliff admitted.

'What, when, and where?'

'Petty larceny. Florida. About fifteen years ago.'

'Prison or jail?'

'Ten months in the county jail. No prison. Nothing after that.'

The supervisor sat back, at ease. 'That shouldn't be a problem. The state's big on rehabilitation. If they disqualified every swinging dick who had done time, there wouldn't be nobody left to do nothing.' He smiled and winked. 'Long as your crime wasn't something heavy, like rape

254

or child molestation or murder.'

Wycliff forced a smile in return. 'None of the above.' He scooped up the pamphlets. 'Let me look these over, and I'll get back to you real fast.'

Make his fingerprints available to the state? He might as well walk into a police station and give himself up for the murders as do that.

He called Charlotte.

Cummings was already seated on a comfortable couch in the lounge of the Beverly Wilshire hotel when Wycliff, cleaned up and dressed in his coolest threads, arrived. The dude has style, Wycliff noticed admiringly. Three in the afternoon and he's drinking champagne. Cummings stood up and gave Wycliff a warm smile and a firm handshake. 'Good to see you again,' he said. He hoisted his glass. 'Care to join me?'

'Sure.'

'The same for my friend, please,' Cummings told a passing waiter. Wycliff lowered himself into an overstuffed easy chair. The waiter returned with a glass of bubbly for Wycliff. He hovered discreetly.

'Care for something to eat?' Cummings offered.

'No,' Wycliff answered. 'I'm not hungry.'

His appetite had gone south the moment he'd put several bullets into two strangers. Eating was torture now. Just the thought of food made him want to puke. He knew he shouldn't be drinking on an empty stomach, but he couldn't turn down such an extravagant gesture. This is how rich

255

people do it. He could learn through imitation. He took a sip of his champagne. Cold and dry, the way he liked it. Charlotte had taught him that. She was a good teacher for this kind of stuff.

Cummings didn't waste time. 'How much do you want to invest?'

Wycliff felt his stomach tightening. 'Two hundred thousand dollars.' Merely saying the words freaked him out. 'I know you usually require more to start off, but Charlotte told me...'

Cummings put up a hand to stop him. 'Two hundred thousand is fine. A good beginning.'

That's all there's going to be, Wycliff thought, but he wasn't going to say that. He wanted Cummings to think he was a player. Players don't stop at two hundred thousand.

'When do you want to do it?'

Wycliff thought of the backpacks. They were like landmines, ready to explode at the slightest provocation. 'As soon as possible,' he said.

Cummings nodded as if Wycliff had given the correct answer. 'That's good to hear, because I'm about to jump into a new investment that's going to be one of the best deals I've ever done. It has all the elements I require: it's short-term, liquid, meaning we can get in and out anytime we want, and it's ready to take off like a rocket. You know what Google is, of course.'

Wycliff nodded. Everyone knew what Google was. With Facebook, it ruled the universe.

'Do you know how fast the price rose after their initial public offering?'

Wycliff didn't know shit about stocks. He had

never owned one in his life. 'Not really,' he said, hoping Cummings wouldn't see him for the ignorant hick he was.

'It doubled in less than six months,' Cummings said. 'Even after the worst recession any of us has ever seen and knock wood ever will see it's worth almost ten times what it was when it began.' He leaned forward, as if about to tell Wycliff a secret. 'Let's say you had put your two hundred thousand dollars into Google when it opened. It was a no-brainer, everyone knew the stock would go up. In six months, you would have doubled your money. Four hundred thousand. Tidy profit, no?'

'Yes,' Wycliff concurred. Even a nincompoop could figure that out.

'So would we wait and see if it'll do better?' Cummings continued. 'Make even more money? Really fatten up the hog?'

Wycliff stared at him, tongue-tied. Was he expecting an answer to that question, too? He didn't have one.

'No,' Cummings said, answering his own question. 'We do not. We get out, we pocket our profits, we move on. That's the secret in gambling, which the market is, a gamble. But unlike Las Vegas or your local Indian casino, the bettor has information. He has the odds in his favor if he does his homework. And believe me, I do my homework.' He sipped more champagne. 'So what do you think, my friend? Are you ready to give this a shot?'

Here it was, the moment of truth. 'Yes.'

Cummings beamed. 'Excellent. You have the

money in your bank account, I assume.' His face went serious. 'I heard about your brother's untimely death. I'm very sorry.' He paused for a moment of commiseration. 'I'll draw up an agreement between us for you to sign and we'll arrange for a wire transfer of the funds. It shouldn't take more than a day or two. We do this whenever a new investor joins the team.'

'It's in cash.'

Cummings looked up. 'Excuse me?'

'The two hundred thousand is in cash. Not in a bank.'

Cummings sat up straight. 'Oh,' he said.

So much for being a player. Legit people don't deal with backpacks stuffed with small bills. Maybe Vegas actually was the way to go.

'That won't be a problem,' Cummings said.

Expecting the opposite answer, Wycliff was surprised. 'It won't?'

'No. Plenty of my clients squirrel some of their money away in cash. With all the problems the banks have been having with the government, who can blame them? Can you bring the money to my office?'

The sooner the better, Wycliff thought. 'Yes.'

'Good.' Cummings took some documents out of his briefcase and laid them out on the table. 'Information that will get you started,' he explained. 'Some of our ongoing accounts, to give you an idea of our diversity. We'll be starting a new account geared specifically for you, because every client is treated individually.' He tapped a finger on the documents. 'Look these over. If you have any questions, jot them down and we'll go over everything. I'll call you when I have your paperwork ready.' He stood up. 'I'm looking forward to this. You come highly recommended.'

Wycliff stood with him. 'Thanks. So do you.'

'See you soon.' Cummings dropped a hundred dollar bill on the table. 'That should cover our drinks.' He picked up his briefcase and walked away.

Wycliff sat back down, sagging into the comfortable cushions. Here we go, he thought. Here we go.

The waiter materialized. 'Did you want change, sir?' he asked.

'Yeah, I do,' Wycliff said.

He waited for the waiter to return with the change. Two glasses of champagne, fifty bucks. The champagne wasn't even that good; Charlotte's was better. He left a ten-dollar tip and pocketed the rest.

TWENTY-FIVE

Amelia swapped shifts with a co-worker so she could take the weekend off, starting Friday night. She and Wycliff spent every minute of their two and a half days together, a lot of it in bed. Wycliff was jittery and uptight, especially at the beginning, which she assumed was due to his brother's death. He didn't correct her misunderstanding.

Besides making love, they talked. Wycliff had already unloaded about himself – now it was her turn. Her history was unremarkable. Third of four children, working-class parents: father a postal worker, mother a stay-at-home mom when the kids were younger, later worked part-time for a local woman's clothing store. One brother was career Army, the other brother a long-haul trucker. Her younger sister was a schoolteacher, married to a barber who owned his own shop. All her siblings were or had been married, all except her had children.

'I can't conceive,' she told him. 'I had ovarian cancer shortly after I completed nursing school. My ovaries were removed. It's been fifteen years and no recurrence, so I'm officially cured, knock wood.'

They were in bed, drinking wine. She had cooked dinner and they had gotten into bed right after, leaving the dishes in the sink for later. They had made love, and now they were enjoying the after-sex glow. 'I was married then,' she went on, 'but he wanted kids and didn't want to adopt, so we divorced.'

'I'm sorry you had cancer,' Wycliff replied. 'And I'm glad you don't anymore.'

'How do you feel about children?' she asked him directly. 'You don't have any, do you?' More a statement than a question. From everything she knew about him, she assumed he didn't.

'No kids,' he confirmed. 'I've never been
260

married, so I've never thought much about it.'

The idea of having kids was ludicrous. His childhood had been an unmitigated disaster. He had no good models for being a parent; it was the reverse, all negative. The thought of being responsible for children scared the shit out of him. He could barely handle taking responsibility for himself. The horrendous events of the past several days presented stark confirmation of that.

What she was really asking him, he knew, was if her inability to have children was a deal-breaker. It wasn't. If anything, it was a positive. He wasn't going to tell her that, though; not yet, anyway. That would imply a level of commitment he didn't know if he wanted to make, or could make.

He had never enjoyed being with a woman this much. His relationships had always been shallow, mostly about sex, not the deeper stuff that makes for a real relationship. He had never been in a real relationship. He didn't know if he was capable of being in one. But he sure felt good being with her.

They drank wine, slept, woke up, made love, drank more wine, and slept until morning. She wanted to make breakfast but he insisted it was his turn to serve her. He brought her coffee in bed and made French toast, another thing he had learned to do in the joint, when he was able to pull kitchen duty. They took their food outside and ate on the back porch. Then they went back inside and got into bed again. In the afternoon they watched the Dodgers play the Giants on the

Fox game of the week, followed by the local news (no mention of the murders) and a CD, *Out Of The Past*, from Billy's extensive collection of classic films. Dinner was take-out Mexican. Then more sex, and sleep.

By Sunday afternoon, he was hooked. He had been hooked earlier, but he wouldn't cop to it emotionally. Now he had to. He couldn't keep his feelings bottled up any longer.

She felt the same way about him. She had worried about that. Her marriage falling apart the way it did had soured her on relationships for a long time. Wycliff was the first man she had slept with since her husband (that surprised and flattered him). Why she had spoken to him in the Minimart that first time they met, she couldn't say. Why she had agreed to have coffee with him was still a mystery to her. But she was happy that she had, even though he was unlike any man she had been attracted to before. Maybe that was why she had fallen for him, because he was so different. Break the mould, start life afresh.

He would have to move out once his brother's estate was settled, which would be soon. Her apartment was too small for the both of them, but she was on a month to month, so moving wouldn't be a problem. Maybe they could find a place together on the west side. He had come to like this neighborhood and she did, too, but her daily commute to Santa Monica would be too long from here. He had no roots and no job yet, so he could live anywhere. It was a big decision, moving in together after knowing each other for such a short time, but it felt right, for both of them.

Monday morning they woke up early, had a quick fuck, showered together, drank coffee, and she was on her way to work. He lingered over a second cup, finished getting dressed, threw the backpacks in the trunk of his car, and drove to west Los Angeles.

Cummings' office was in a small building west of Century City, near the Mormon Temple. Wycliff parked, lifted the money-crammed backpacks out of the trunk of his car, hefted one on each shoulder, and rode the elevator to the third floor.

The reception area was sparsely furnished, as if the occupant had recently moved in. No one was present. He dropped the backpacks on the empty desk. They landed with a thud. 'Hello,' he called out. 'Anyone home?'

The door to the inner office opened. Cummings' head popped out. 'Hey,' he greeted Wycliff. 'Didn't hear you come in.' He was dressed in a sharp single-breasted suit, his crisp white shirt fastened at the wrists by gold doubloon cufflinks. 'Excuse the mess.' He grinned. 'Or rather, the lack thereof. I just moved in here last week. I was operating the business out of my house, but it's gotten too big. So now I'm one of the commuter ants.' He threw up his arms in mock surrender. 'We all make compromises in life to get what we want. In the end, we're all whores. The only distinction is that some of us smell better than others.'

Wycliff liked this man's frankness, his willingness to poke fun at himself. His head isn't too big for his hat, he thought. A point in his favor.

Cummings indicated the backpacks. 'Is that what I think it is?'

Wycliff nodded. 'Yes.'

'Come on into my office. My assistant is out running errands, but I can get you something to drink. Coffee, a Coke?'

'I'm fine,' Wycliff said. He picked up one of the packs. Cummings took the other. 'Damn, that feels good,' he said. 'You just print it?'

'Recently,' Wycliff deadpanned.

'A man after my own heart.'

Wycliff followed Cummings into his office, which was as sparingly furnished as his reception space. A desk, a chair behind it, one in front, a row of filing cabinets against the back wall. The desk was dominated by a battery of laptops, all turned on. Figures and graphs played across the screens. One was streaming CNBC. The figures were as decipherable to Wycliff as Egyptian hieroglyphics. He looked at them, though, as if he was interested and knew what he was watching.

'Noise,' Cumming said, indicating the screens. 'Ninety-nine percent bullshit. I have to watch, in case something unexpected jumps up. In this business, microseconds can mean the difference between life and death.'

You're wrong about that, Wycliff thought. I know the real difference between life and death. It ain't this.

'May I?' Cummings asked, taking hold of one of the backpack zippers.

'It's why I'm here.'

Cummings opened the backpack. He stared at the piles of fresh, crisp, bundled bills. Then he leaned over and inhaled, as if breathing in the aroma of a freshly poured glass of wine. 'I love the smell of money,' he said. 'Best smell in the world.'

He zipped the pack up. 'Sit down,' he said, indicating the visitor's chair. 'Before I take this wonderful lucre off your hands, we have paperwork to fill out.' He opened a desk drawer and took out some documents, which he laid out on an uncluttered area of his desk. 'You can sit here and read these over cover to cover,' Cummings said. 'It's your money, I want you to know what you're signing.'

'What are they?' Wycliff asked. He didn't want to read this gobbledygook, it would take forever and wouldn't mean shit to him anyway.

'We're opening an account for you at Schwab. I will invest your money to the best of my fiduciary ability. I'll have limited power of attorney to buy and sell stocks and other financial commodities for you without having to ask your permission every time I make a transaction. If I'm going to do something big, I'm going to call you first and tell you, explain what I'm doing, and why. Sometimes, though, you have to jump, right now. A ten-second lag can mean the difference between making a fortune and losing one.'

'I get that,' Wycliff said. 'That's fine. You're the expert, not me.'

'Good.' Cummings picked up a second form.

'This explains my fee structure. I take one percent of your gross investment, plus ten percent of profits. That's a good deal,' he said, selling himself a little. 'Most hedge funds take twenty percent of profits. I think that's too much. I'm happy with ten percent. Makes me work harder.'

Wycliff was swimming in quicksand. 'Sounds fair to me,' he responded.

'Let's see, what else? Basic stuff for tax purposes. Social, date of birth, the usual. You can fill them out here, it'll only take you a few minutes.' He leafed through the other forms. The last page of each one was tagged for signature and date. 'If you sign and date these, I can put this money to work today.'

In less than five minutes, Wycliff was finished signing and dating. His hand was shaking slightly as he handed the documents to Cummings.

'Thanks,' Cummings said. 'You won't regret this.' He put the documents into a folder. 'Before you go. How are you fixed for cash for the next few months? What's your monthly nut?'

Wycliff thought for a moment. He was living rent-free and the rest of his expenses were minimal, but he would be taking an apartment soon with Amelia, buying furniture, whatever else you did when you set up house-keeping. A hundred a day should cover everything, he calculated in his head. 'Four thousand a month,' he said, adding a thousand for reserve.

'You going to need more than that,' Cummings said dubiously. 'Los Angeles is expensive. I want you to feel financially secure for a good six months. Let's say five thousand a month.'

He unzipped one of the packs and took out a dozen bundles, which he placed on the desk. 'Thirty thousand dollars. Put it in various banks. If you open up accounts of less than five thousand in each, no one pays attention. This way, I won't feel pressure to sell before we should because you've run out of money.'

This guy's smart, Wycliff thought. And he isn't greedy. Otherwise he would take it all. Cummings gave him a large accordion folder, and he stuffed the bundles into it.

'We'll be in constant touch,' Cummings told him. 'If you have any questions, call me twenty-four-seven. I mean that.' He chuckled. 'I have clients that call me at three in the morning. It comes with the territory.'

'If I call you at three in the morning,' Wycliff said, 'it's because I'm drunk. So don't pay it any attention. Don't even pick up.'

Cummings walked him to the door. 'I'm here for you. That's what I want you to know. I'm here to make you as much money as I can.' He grinned again. 'Without breaking the law.'

The law offices of Goodwin, O'Shaughnessy, and Levine were in a high-rise office building on Sunset at the west end of the strip, not far from Charlotte's condo. The traffic on the Strip was heavier than usual, so Wycliff arrived a few minutes late. He rode the elevator up to the eleventh floor. A receptionist checked his name off a list and asked him to take a seat.

There were about a dozen other people there besides him. Wycliff assumed they were here for the same reason he was. The only person he recognized was Stanley, the former house-sitter. He gave Wycliff a shy smile and looked away. Wycliff didn't recall seeing any of the others at Billy's funeral. Vultures. Deny the man, covet his possessions.

Everyone seemed uncomfortable. Wondering how big a slice of the pie they were getting, Wycliff figured. Some would be happy, some would be disappointed. He had given up worrying about that. Whatever small taste he got, if any, would be a bonus.

The receptionist picked up her phone and listened. 'You can go in now,' she said. 'Come with me.'

Some of the people, Wycliff included, looked at each other awkwardly, until they realized she meant them as a group. They all got up and followed her down a corridor and into a conference room.

Levine, dressed similarly to when he had come to the house, including the old-fashioned bow tie, was seated at the head of a long mahogany table. A stack of legal-size envelopes was assembled in front of him. Captain's chairs lined the table on either side. Levine's horse-faced assistant sat perched behind him, her back against the wall, the way a seasoned poker player positions himself. Her expression was dour, like before, Wycliff noticed. It probably never changed.

'Thank you for coming,' Levine said cordially. 'Take a seat wherever you like.'

There was an awkward musical-chairs shuffle until each person secured a chair. Wycliff sat at the far end. Lawyers made him nervous, on principle. Everyone turned to Levine in anticipation.

'You have been asked to attend this meeting because you are the beneficiaries of my client's will,' Levine said. 'It is simple, uncomplicated, and unassailable. He was of sound mind and body when he finalized it. I have a statement from his doctor attesting to that. So if any of you have thoughts of contesting it, put them out of your mind.' His tone of voice was bland, but his intent was firm.

Is he looking at me, Wycliff thought? He fidgeted in his chair.

'As I say your name, please acknowledge yourself,' Levine said. Each person, when his or her name was called, replied 'here' or 'yes'. One woman raised her hand like she was back in grade school. Wycliff muttered 'yo' when his name came up. Some of the people, hearing it, looked at him with curiosity and surprise. It was obvious that no one other than Stanley and the lawyer had known Billy had blood kin.

Levine read the basic boiler plate. Then he got down to the details. 'I am not going to announce the bequests that were made to each of you. That information is in the envelopes you will receive. After I give you your packet I would like you to leave without speaking to anyone here. If you have any questions or concerns you can call my office and set up an appointment to discuss them with me later.'

Smart, Wycliff thought. He wants to avoid a cat fight. Nothing pisses people off more than not getting what they don't deserve.

One by one the names were read off, the packets distributed, the designees thanked for coming. Wycliff waited his turn with growing impatience. Let's get it over with, he fumed silently. Give me whatever lame token I'm getting and I'll move on. As he watched each recipient receive their gift he tried to guess which ones were scoring high and which were getting lumps of coal in their stockings.

Stanley was one of the last called. He received his envelope with trembling hands. 'Thank you,' he told Levine, the only one of the beneficiaries to offer thanks. 'I know this came from Billy's heart.' He looked like he was going to break down and cry. Wycliff felt sorry for the poor little guy. His hero is now with the angels or wherever souls go to, a concept he did not believe in. When you're dead, you're dead. Worm food. If, by the most remote of chances, there was something on the other side, he would be consigned to the darkest part of it. He was an angel himself now, an angel of death. Satan would be a better moniker. Murderer, killer, coward.

He forced himself to push those thoughts to the back of his mind.

Then it was just him, Levine, and the horse-faced assistant. Levine turned to her and said something privately. She got up, gave Wycliff a look even more sour than those she had bestowed on him before, and left the room, closing the door behind her.

Levine settled back in his chair. 'I saved you

for last because I wanted to talk to you without the others being present.' He slid the remaining packet across the table to Wycliff. 'Open it.'

Wycliff slit the seal with a fingernail and opened the envelope. It reminded him of the Academy Awards. *And the winner is* ... Meaning: *and all the losers are* ... He had never won anything.

The document was several pages long. More confusing paperwork, like the material he'd gotten from Cummings (which he still had not read). He had never been big on paperwork.

'You don't have to read it through now,' Levine told him. He took off his glasses and stared at Wycliff; then he smiled. 'He left you everything.'

Everything was the house, the furniture, most of Billy's personal stuff (a select group of friends got keepsakes that had special meaning to them), and his money. Three hundred thousand dollars in an old-fashioned savings account.

'As a high-end decorator with important clients your brother lived well, but he was frugal,' Levine explained, while Wycliff tried to recover from his initial and still ongoing shock. 'His medical expenses sapped a significant part of his savings, but he was able to keep a decent amount. He was adamant that he not die a pauper. To coin a phrase, he didn't want to be dependent on the kindness of strangers. He wanted to make sure he had the financial resources to take care of himself until the end. Which he was doing, to the best of his ability.'

They were in Levine's personal office now, seated across the lawyer's desk from each other. Levine steepled his fingers and sighted Wycliff over them. 'And then you came into the picture.'

Wycliff felt as if he had been caught up in a whirlwind, not knowing where he would land, or if he ever would. He recalled the day he had arrived in Los Angeles. It had not been that long ago, but it felt like a lot had happened. For some things, too much had happened.

'It's no secret your brother detested you,' Levine continued. 'For good reason, from what he told me.'

'That's true,' Wycliff agreed. He was awash in shame and remorse. 'He had every right to hate me. I was a prick to him from the day he was born.'

'And yet, in the end, it was you who gave him the chance to die with his pride and dignity intact. Why?'

How many times had he asked himself that same question? How many times had he failed to come up with an honest answer? 'I don't know.'

'Were you hoping to ingratiate yourself with him, so he would change his mind and cut you in? If that was your reason, you succeeded.' Levine paused for a moment. 'Motives don't have to be pure to bring about positive actions. In the end, it's what you did for him that counted, not why.'

Wycliff shook his head. 'I understand why someone would think that. That's who I've always been. But that's not why.'

'Then what is the reason?' the lawyer persisted.

'There is none. Except that he was my brother.'

He spent half an hour filling out the requisite paperwork, the transfer of title for the house and his brother's other financial assets. He hadn't gotten around to opening a local bank account, he told Levine. He would take care of that today, so the money from Billy's account could be properly wire-transferred. (The truth, which he was too embarrassed to admit, was that he didn't have a bank account anywhere. In Arizona and wherever else he had worked for coolie wages he cashed his paychecks at the local liquor store or a check-cashing service.)

Levine walked Wycliff to the door. 'Good luck,' he said. He gave Wycliff a penetrating look. 'I suspect the man you were doesn't exist anymore.'

Wycliff was still dazed when he left the lawyer's office, but by the time he reached the bank of elevators, the bile that had been churning in his stomach rose into his throat. He was barely able to make it into the men's room before he puked his guts out into a toilet bowl.

Two people murdered because he had wanted to be a player. He had rationalized to himself that he had a reason for killing them, no matter how terrible and selfish that reason was. But the whole catastrophe had been pointless. He had killed them for nothing.

TWENTY-SIX

Amelia was vibrating with excitement. 'This changes *everything*!'

They were in bed. It was almost three in the morning. She hadn't gotten off-shift until midnight. She had to be back at the hospital by eight, but they were too wired to sleep. In her heart, she confided, she had known he would be rewarded for his kindness towards Billy, but she had not dared say so, because she didn't want to jinx him. Now his good fortune could be celebrated openly. The money and the house were great, of course, but the best thing was that the two brothers had reconciled before Billy died. You can't put a price on that.

He surprised himself by agreeing with her. Back in the not-so-long-ago old days, he would have mocked such a sentiment.

'You have to stop smoking now. I gave you dispensation, but no longer.'

'Maybe it wasn't worth it, then.'

She punched him on the shoulder, harder than necessary. 'I want you to live a long time.'

Would they live here? A house you didn't have to pay a mortgage or rent on was enticing. Her commute would be a bitch, but everyone in Los Angeles commutes. The real question was, were they ready to move in together? They had talked about it, but that had been abstract chatter. Now they were facing reality.

'We don't have to decide yet,' she said. She knew he needed to decompress from all the pressure he had been under. 'I have to give sixty days' notice on my place, so we have time.'

'It's not that I don't want to,' Wycliff protested, partly because he knew that's what she wanted to hear, but also because he really felt it. He wanted to share himself with another person. He wanted to change his life.

They finally fell asleep, but Amelia was up at six thirty and out the door by seven. Wycliff, still wired, got out of bed and made her a cup of coffee to go. They would talk later and figure out when they could see each other again. She was pulling double shifts the next few days to make up for the weekend she had taken off to be with him.

After Amelia left Wycliff read the newspaper, took a walk, made some lunch. Late in the afternoon, his phone rang. He checked the caller ID. 'Hey, John. What's up?' He listened for a moment. 'Sure. Tomorrow morning.'

Cummings was waiting in a booth in the Beverly Hills Hotel coffee shop when Wycliff showed up at eight thirty. As he walked through the room, he finally saw an honest-to-God celebrity. That had to be George Hamilton, nobody in the world had a tan like that. The voluptuous young girl who was sitting alongside him looked like jail bait. Nice to be a star, even one who's a punch line on *Letterman*. Not that he had any complaints, he was sleeping with two dynamite women, which was one too many. He had to fix that, and soon.

'Have the orange juice,' Cummings suggested, as Wycliff slid into the booth, 'it's freshly squeezed.' He was drinking a glass himself, along with coffee. 'Hungry? The hash and eggs are good.'

Wycliff hadn't eaten in twenty-four hours. He needed to put some food in his stomach. He couldn't afford to get sick, not with all the balls he was juggling. 'I'll have whatever you're having,' he said.

A waitress came over and Cummings put in their orders. 'How's it going?' he asked Wycliff.

Wycliff shrugged. 'It's going.' He wasn't in the mood for small talk, not after all the personal tumult he had gone through the past few days.

The waitress brought him juice and coffee. He creamed his coffee, took a sip, and surveyed the room. Here he was in Beverly Hills, California, eating breakfast across from George Hamilton. Who would have ever thought he would be living like this?

Cumming waited until the waitress put steaming plates in front of them, then seasoned his poached eggs with Tabasco. 'The investment I put you in.' He forked up a heaping of hash and eggs, swallowed, and said, 'It's gone crazy.'

'That's good,' Wycliff replied. He had been afraid Cummings was going to tell him the opposite, that the money had disappeared down a rabbit hole.

'Good?' Cummings exclaimed. 'This is better than good, my friend. This is spectacular.' He took a swallow of coffee, and continued. 'Normally we get in and out of these deals quickly. But this one has turned out to be extraordinary. It's already gone up twenty percent.'

'Great,' Wycliff said. He didn't have to know anything about finances to know that was impressive.

'You know the saying: pigs get fat and hogs get slaughtered. We're already fat. So I'm offering all my clients the option of cashing out.'

Wycliff was thrown off-balance. 'How much would I make?' he asked.

'After broker's fees and my commission, about twenty-five thousand dollars. Not a bad week's work, if I say so myself.'

Wycliff was frozen. He had just made twenty-five thousand dollars by doing nothing. Never in his wildest dreams could he have imagined this. There actually was a pot of gold at the end of the rainbow. Was this a portent that he was going to luck out across the board, that he could skate the bad shit and embrace the good?

If Amelia hadn't come into his life he'd be gone in a cloud of dust and a hearty Hi, ho, Silver. But she had. So here he was. 'Damn,' he said. 'You're good, man. I mean great.'

'I do my homework,' Cummings said. 'And sometimes we get lucky. This is one of those times.' He pointed to Wycliff's plate, which was untouched. 'Eat up, before it gets cold.'

Wycliff was too wired to eat. 'Let me ask you a question.'

'Sure.'

'I can cash out now, but I don't have to. Is that right?'

Cummings took a moment to answer. 'Yes, that's right. You can let it ride, and hope it keeps going.'

'How many of your other clients are doing that?'

'Not cashing out?'

'Yes.'

Cummings drank more coffee before answering. 'All of them.'

'Everyone's staying in?'

'So far,' Cummings answered. 'There are a few investors I haven't contacted yet, but the ones I've talked to want to keep going.'

'Is Charlotte one of them?'

Cummings leaned back. 'I don't discuss clients' business with other clients. I told you that.'

'I'm sorry,' Wycliff apologized. 'I'm not used to this.'

'I understand,' Cumming said. 'You could ask her,' he suggested. 'If she wants to tell you what she's doing, that's her business.'

Wycliff knew asking Charlotte would be pointless. She would stonewall him and would be annoyed to boot.

'You think this is going to keep doing good?' he asked Cummings, moving off the subject of Charlotte.

'I do,' came the confident reply.

'Let me ask you another question, then. If I wanted to put more money into this, could I? Is anyone else doing that?'

'Some are,' Cummings acknowledged. He gave Wycliff a quizzical look. 'Is that what you want to do?'

The question threw Wycliff. Was Cummings trying to talk him out of it? Maybe this investment had been a favor to Charlotte. The favor had been repaid. Was this the end of their trip together? 'You tell me,' Wycliff said. 'Should I stay in this investment?'

Cummings hesitated before answering. 'We've done nicely, but as I told you before, there are no guarantees.'

'But what do you think?' Wycliff persisted.

'What I think is that this year is going to be good for me. And my clients. It's all about the clients.'

'So what about me? Aren't I a client?'

'Yes, you are. So you want to stay in?'

The small man inside Wycliff said *no*. He ignored that voice. That was the past. He was living in the present now, looking to the future. 'I have more to invest,' he told Cummings. 'More than what I have in now.'

Cummings looked surprised. 'How much more?'

Hold back some for a rainy day, he cautioned himself. Don't be a hog. But he couldn't hold back. This was too good a deal not to go all in on. 'Three hundred thousand dollars.'

Cumming whistled. 'Are you serious?'

'Serious as a heart attack.'

Cummings put his fork down. 'Let me think about this,' he said.

'Why?' Wycliff asked.

'I know how you got this money,' Cummings answered. 'It fell out of a tree and hit you on the head. I have no problem with that. Several of my clients inherited their fortunes. But from what Charlotte's told me, you've never had this kind of money. It can play games with your mind. I want to make sure you're thinking this through.'

He thinks the first investment came from money he'd gotten from his brother, Wycliff realized, just as Charlotte had planned it. He wasn't going to set him straight, now that it had actually happened. 'My money's not good enough for you?' he asked, trying not to sound cocky.

'I didn't say that,' Cummings responded.

'Then what's the problem?'

'There is none.'

He shouldn't be with Charlotte. He sure as hell shouldn't be in bed with her. Now that he was in a serious relationship with Amelia it was morally wrong. Not only to Amelia but to Charlotte, too, although he didn't think matters of morality mattered much to Charlotte. But here he was.

He had come over to thank her for setting him up with Cummings, and as it usually did when they were alone together, nature took its course. The last time they had fucked he'd promised himself he wouldn't do it again. Yet here they were in bed, naked, sated.

'This woman you've been seeing,' Charlotte asked. 'Are you still seeing her?'

'Yes.'

'More than seeing her?'

He had come clean with her before. No reason not to now. 'Yes, there's more.'

She got up, put on a robe, and lit a cigarette. 'Do you want one?' she asked, offering him the pack.

'No, thanks. I'm trying to quit.'

'She must be one tough cookie if she can get you to quit smoking.' Charlotte spoke with a twinge of bemusement, but also regret.

'She's strong. She was strong for me when I needed it.'

'Which I wasn't. Touché.'

'I didn't say that.'

'You didn't have to. It's true. I was weak when you needed strength.' She French inhaled. 'Now I'm getting my just rewards.'

'Charlotte...' He swung his legs over the side of the bed.

'You don't have to apologize. You're doing what's right for you.'

'I want to do what's right for you, too. You've done everything for me. I wouldn't be where I was if it wasn't for you.'

She waved a distracted hand. 'I've gotten what I wanted out of our relationship, too. No regrets.'

He started to get dressed. 'I'm glad about that, then. Because you really have helped me. I'm going to be rich because of you.'

'You already are rich. Your brother saw to that.'

'Then richer.' He tucked in his shirt, zipped up his pants, put on his socks and shoes. 'I don't know how I can pay you back for what you've done for me, but I want to.'

She ran her hand along the front of his shirt. 'Don't abandon me, Wycliff. That's what I want from you. We don't have to be romantic. We don't even have to have sex. But I want to stay connected to you.' She stroked his chest with her perfectly manicured fingertips.

He felt a surge of gratitude towards her, mixed with emotion and lust. There was no reason they couldn't have a relationship. Older woman and younger man, mentor and student. There was much more he could learn from her. It would be hard not to keep fucking her, though. They'd have to taper off gradually. The more he was with Amelia, the less he could be with Charlotte. Once he and Amelia moved in together this affair would come to an end. But until that happened, he didn't think he had the strength to withstand Charlotte.

Stop kidding yourself, his inner voice mocked him. *You'll be fucking this woman until your cock falls off.*

That was the old him doing the mocking, the old him being mocked. He was changing. He could do it.

They arranged to get together later in the week on a night when Amelia would be working. A dinner between two friends, for old time's sake. He would wine and dine her royally, a modest payback for all the money she had spent on him, and everything she had done for him.

'Thanks again for the connection to Cummings,' he said as he was leaving. 'He has the magic touch.'

'He does,' Charlotte agreed. 'Take care of yourself, Wycliff. Be careful out there.'

TWENTY-SEVEN

It was a heart-stopper to see his bank balance plummet from three hundred thousand dollars to thirty at the speed of a keystroke.

'Are you sure this was the right thing to do?' Amelia asked with concern. He had waited to tell her until after he did it, because he knew she would react this way. 'Have you really thought this through, Wycliff?' she implored him. 'You-'ve never been in the stock market. And you don't know this man very well.'

He understood her fears. He'd had them, too, that first time he had invested with Cummings. But everything Cummings had told him had happened exactly as he had predicted it would.

There was another reason he was taking this step, besides desiring to get richer. This was found money. He hadn't earned it. It was a gift. If he lost some of it, that's the breaks. He was already ahead of the game. And he knew that Cummings was going to watch this investment like a hawk. At the first sign of anything going south, he would pull out. His clients might lose something, but they wouldn't lose their shirts.

'I understand why you're worried, but I feel

okay about this.' They were having dinner at home, lamb chops, one of her specialties. 'I have the house, I have other savings, I can do this. Trust me.'

'I do trust you,' she told him. 'But I want you to be careful. Look what happened with Madoff. Thousands of people lost everything.'

'That's not going to happen.' Even he knew about Madoff; you would have had to be Rip Van Winkle not to know about Madoff. She was putting him on the defensive, and he didn't like it. It was his money. He could do whatever he wanted with it. He had earned it. With blood, through Laurie, and with time and compassion with his brother.

'It's going to be fine,' he told her. 'I can pull out anytime.' He poured some more wine into her glass. 'After this deal, I'll sit on the sidelines. I'm not going to get greedy. You know the saying: pigs get fat and hogs get slaughtered. I'm not going to be a hog.'

She shook her head. 'That saying is out of a movie, Wycliff. That's not real life.'

'After this one I'll stop,' he said. 'I promise.'

'I'm going to hold you to that.'

The brief three-paragraph story was under the fold on page three of the *LA Times* Metro section. The composite drawing that accompanied it was generic, but it was close enough to raise the hair on the back of Wycliff's neck.

A new witness had surfaced in the Beverly Hills murders. He had seen a man running away from the building where the murders had taken place. This witness, a writer on a television drama, had been on location, which was the reason he had only come forward now. His description was not accurate enough to nail Wycliff, but he did add some features to those given by the first witness that were more specific. Height, about six-two, right on the money. Blond or light brown hair. Most critically, he had seen the perpetrator get into his car, a 3-series BMW, California plates. The witness had been too far away to read the license number before the car took off.

Wycliff could feel the walls closing in. He needed to push them back.

'Look what the wind blew in,' Juan, the chop shop owner, sang out. 'Where you been, man? You got fresh product to lay off on me?'

'Not today,' Wycliff answered. He pointed to the BMW, parked outside in the lot. 'I was wondering if you could take the Beemer off my hands.'

Juan squinted at the car through the midday glare. 'What's wrong, it ain't running good?'

'It's running fine. But I'm starting a business, so I need a truck.'

'I can always use a BMW,' Juan said. 'What kind of truck are you in the market for?'

'I already have one, a used Ford-150.' Wycliff smiled sheepishly. 'I bought it legit.'

Juan laughed. 'You going square on me?'

'I got a good deal.'

'No skin off my ass,' Juan said. 'What did you pay Ricardo for these wheels?'

'Five thou.'

Another laugh. 'He saw you coming, white boy. I can't give you more than three.'

Wycliff shrugged, as if to say *you sharp Latinos got me*. 'I'm down with that.'

Two minutes later he had three thousand dollars in crisp hundreds in his pocket and was waiting for a taxi to pick him up.

'Where's your car?' Amelia asked, as she took groceries and a bottle of zinfandel out of a Whole Foods shopping bag.

Wycliff had rented a Nissan Altima from Enterprise. A nondescript vehicle, the blandest available. 'In the shop. I may sell it. It's a great car, but it's too expensive to maintain.'

She rolled her eyes. 'As if you can't afford to service it. But it's your money, your decision.'

'Every housewife in Santa Monica drives a 3-series BMW.'

'Then you should buy a huge truck with a gun rack behind the seat. You won't find many housewives driving those.'

'No guns,' he answered, his tone angry. 'There's nothing a gun can do except get you in trouble.'

She was taken aback by his brusqueness. 'I'm glad to hear you say that. I wouldn't have expected that attitude from you.'

'Because I'm so macho?' He uncorked the wine and poured each of them a glass. 'I'm trying to get in touch with my feminine side.'

Her hands were wet from washing lettuce. She flicked water from her fingers at him. 'If you had a feminine side, which you don't.'

'You're hurting my feelings.'

'Poor dear.' She kissed him on the cheek. 'Better now?'

His response was to tickle her ribs. 'I'm working here,' she squealed as she squirmed away. 'Save the mushy stuff for later. Get out of my face and let me create.'

He went into the living room and turned on the television. The six o'clock news faded in over a newscaster saying *A break in the recent murders in Beverly Hills.* On the screen, a police spokesman faced a bank of microphones in front of the Beverly Hills City Hall.

Wycliff listened intently as the spokesman read a prepared statement. 'This morning, we received results from the FBI regarding evidence we sent to their lab, relating to the person we believe committed the recent murders in this city. We are hopeful we will be able to identify this person within the next few days, and we will be conducting an extensive manhunt to find him.'

Amelia came into the room, wiping her hands on a dish towel. 'Won't that be great,' she said as she watched. She rested a hand on his shoulder, as if by touching him she felt fortified. 'Do you know how frightened I am sometimes, coming home at night by myself?' She shuddered.

Wycliff's gut was twisted in knots. 'I would never let anything bad to happen to you.'

She squeezed his arm. 'I know. That's what makes you special to me.'

* * *

287

Amelia spent the night, then left early in the morning. She wouldn't be able to see him until the next day, her schedule was jammed. Left alone, Wycliff brooded. That police bulletin had to be bullshit, another ploy to smoke him out, entice him to do something stupid. If they really had the goods on him they wouldn't broadcast the news and give him a heads-up. They must think their suspect was a colossal dumbass.

Even so, it would be smart to go to ground for a while. He could tell Amelia (and Charlotte, she was still part of his life) that he had to go out of town. Unfinished business from before he came here, not sure how long it will take to resolve it. He had plenty of money, he could go wherever he wanted. He didn't have a passport, so he'd have to stay in the country, but that was okay, it's a big country, easy to get lost in.

The important item he had to take care of before he left was get back into cash. Amelia was right, he shouldn't be in the stock market. Stick with what you know, and he didn't know squat about that. It was all rigged, anyway. He had plenty of money, he could live forever on what he already had. He wasn't going to be a hog.

He called Cummings. As had been usual in the past few days, there was no answer, so he left a message. 'We need to connect, it's important. Call me as soon as you get this.'

He puttered around the house, becoming increasingly antsy. He called Cummings again same result. Cummings was supposed to be available any time of the day or night, he had made a point of that. That he wasn't returning phone calls felt weird, disconcerting.

He couldn't stay put. He left the house and took off.

Cumming's office was locked. He knocked on the door, but there was no reply. He knocked again, harder. Banged. Nothing. He dialed Cumming's number and put his ear to the door. No ring tone from inside.

Something was wrong here; but what? Charlotte had to know what was going on. She was the one who had turned him onto Cummings. With all the shit going on in his life, he needed reassuring.

Charlotte didn't answer, either. He left word for her to call him back as soon as she got his message, ASAP. Frustrated, he got in his car and drove to the ocean and up the Pacific Coast Highway to Leo Carrillo state beach. He changed into his trunks and swam out through the board surfers and wind-surfers past the first set of breakers, stroking hard so that he wouldn't get sucked towards the rocks. He had swum here before and he knew the riptide was strong.

Then he was into clear, calm water. He swam and floated for a long time, the sun baking his face and back, the wet brine cleansing away the accumulation of bad tastes in his mouth. A school of dolphins cruised by, almost close enough to be touched.

By the time he let the water carry him back to shore, the sun was setting. The remaining beachgoers were packing up. Some college-aged guys changing out of their wetsuits offered him a cold one from their cooler, but he declined. The ocean had cleansed and purified him. He wanted to stay that way, at least until he got home.

It was late by the time he got back to the house. A notice had been taped to the front door. In the darkness, he couldn't make it out. Probably an ad for a new Thai or Indian restaurant opening nearby, the neighborhood was over-run with ethnic places. He pulled it off and took it inside, tossing it onto the kitchen table while he took a beer out of the fridge and carried the can into the bathroom. He stood under the hot water for a long time, the needles beating down on him, washing away the salt, sand, and sweat. He shaved while in the shower, drinking his beer. He felt at peace. It was only a temporary respite, he knew, but while he was in here he could almost forget about the world outside.

He dried off and put on clean cargo shorts and a T-shirt and rummaged in the freezer for dinner. There was a steak, which he could grill with a baked potato, cut up a tomato and cucumber for a salad. A good red wine to go with it, a civilized meal. He poured a healthy shot of Don Julio tequila, knocked it back in one gulp, and put the steak in the microwave to thaw.

Reading the paper had become a daily ritual, a reassurance that he had embraced the civilized world. The world of people who had money and property. The world he was part of, at long last. He had skipped it this morning. He leafed through now, starting with the sports section, then Calendar, and after that the least interesting parts, the actual news.

This story, like the one about the eyewitness description, was also buried inside the news section. Wycliff almost missed it as he cursorily turned the pages. But he didn't, because there were two pictures with it, and unlike the earlier story, these weren't drawings, they were photographs, side by side. One of the images was a Photoshopped publicity still of Laurie Abramowitz. The other, a grainy black and white, was of the woman he had murdered for her, the wicked stepdaughter.

According to this story, the two women were not related by marriage. They weren't related at all. They had been partners in a wholesale flower business. They had also been same-sex partners.

Laurie is a *lesbian*? Wycliff thought, his brain spinning like a centrifuge. That can't be. She was hot to trot for me.

He continued reading the article with a growing sense of dread. Laurie and the murdered woman had been in a committed relationship for a dozen years. They shared a condo in a high-rise building in Westwood.

The building he had tracked the victim from.

The survivor, Laurie, was in deep mourning. She couldn't bear to return to the apartment she had shared with her partner. She was leaving the country to get away from it all. She would return when the police caught her lover's killer and ended the nightmare in which she was living.

The microwave dinged. The steak was ready to be cooked.

Wycliff had no appetite now. He poured another shot of tequila, to the brim. It burned

291

going down.

Something was rotten in the state of California, and the stench was becoming intolerable. What in God's name had he gotten into?

The notice on the door. He had forgotten about it. He saw it now on the kitchen table, where he had carelessly tossed it. He held it to the light and read it.

What the fuck? He read it again, carefully this time.

He walked to the front window, carefully parting the curtains to look outside. From what he could see there was nothing out of the ordinary, just the regular evening street scene. A quiet street in a quiet neighborhood. He sat down and started to shake.

TWENTY-EIGHT

Levine reacted to the notice with alarm. 'This is not good,' he declared, tapping the offending paper with a fingernail. He placed it on his desk, handling it as if it was a bomb that could go off unexpectedly. 'Not good at all.'

'What is it, exactly?' Wycliff asked. 'I mean I know what it says, but what does it mean?' It was nine thirty in the morning. He hadn't slept a lick all night.

'It means you don't own your brother's house anymore,' Levine answered. 'This is an eviction

292

notice. You have a week to clear out, or a county marshal will throw you out.'

Wycliff was reeling. 'How is that possible? You helped me transfer the deed, right?'

'Of course I did,' Levine answered, annoyed that his competence was being called into question, particularly by someone of Wycliff's character. 'Everything was done exactly by the book. But between then and a few weeks ago' – another fingernail tap – 'according to this, you sold it.' He scanned the notice again. 'To some personal corporation, it looks like. A dummy holding, no doubt, to conceal the real name of whoever it is you sold it to.'

Wycliff buried his face in his hands. 'I did not sell the house, I swear.'

'Have you signed any documents recently?'

Wycliff, startled by the question, looked up. 'No,' he answered. 'I mean, except...'

'Except what?' The lawyer leaned forward, his arms braced on his desktop.

'I met this investment counselor,' Wycliff said. He hesitated; how could he explain his involvement with Cummings without sounding like a complete dumb-ass?

'Investment counselor.' Levine pronounced the words like he was saying *wet turd*.

'A guy who invests money for people,' Wycliff continued lamely, instantly knowing how stupid he sounded. Of course Levine would know what an investment counselor did. He, Wycliff, was the one who didn't.

'Right,' Levine said impatiently. 'What about him?'

'Well ... I invested some money with him.'

Levine nodded. 'Some of your inheritance.'

'Yes,' Wycliff replied. He felt ashamed. He shouldn't, it was his money, he could do whatever he wanted with it. But sitting here under Levine's scrutiny he was uncomfortable, like he had done something wrong. The money Billy had left him was a trust to be protected, not dicked around with.

'So this investment counselor...' Levine prodded.

'I've done fine with him,' Wycliff continued, defending himself. 'He's made money for me. He's really good.'

Levine looked perplexed. 'You've already made a return on the inheritance money? You just got it.'

'Before then,' Wycliff corrected him. 'I mean...' *Shut up, dummy. You're digging your own grave.*

Levine leaned in even closer. 'You had money to invest before you got the money from your brother's will?'

Now he was really in the soup. 'A little bit,' he said, back-pedaling as fast as he could. 'Not much.'

Levine leaned back, but his body language was anything but relaxed. 'So this investor made money for you, and you did what? Reinvest it?'

Wycliff nodded slowly. This lawyer was sharp. You don't try to fake out men smarter than you. 'Yes.'

'And you added some of the inheritance money on top of it.'

'Yes.'

Levine sighed. 'Those were the documents you signed? Giving this investment counselor the legal power to invest your money for you?'

Wycliff nodded.

'In a brokerage account?'

Another nod. 'Schwab.'

The disclosure didn't seem to disturb Levine, as Wycliff had been afraid it would. 'That's prudent, actually,' the lawyer said. 'Parking your money in a savings account isn't worth much these days. You have the Schwab papers, I assume. Did you bring them with you? I'd like to take a look at them, to make sure everything's kosher.'

Wycliff winced. 'I don't have them on me. I was too discombobulated this morning to think straight.'

'That's understandable,' Levine said sympathetically. 'I would have been, too.' He tapped the notice again. 'I'll look into this. In the meantime, go home and get those financial papers and bring them back here. If I'm tied up, leave them with Ms Hopkins.'

The horse-faced assistant, who reminded Wycliff of the Wicked Witch of the West from *The Wizard of Oz*. That character still gave him nightmares. He fought back the panic that was threatening to overwhelm him. 'I'll get on that right away.'

They stood and shook hands. 'We'll get to the bottom of this,' Levine promised. 'You're not going to lose that house. Not after everything you and your brother went through to keep it.'

Another call to Cummings, another voice reply that he was unavailable, leave a message. 'I need to see you, man!' Wycliff screamed into the phone. 'Get back to me *now!*'

He drove to the broker's office. It was locked. He banged on the door, practically breaking it down. *What the fuck was going on?* Whatever scheme Cummings was running, he was going to put an end to it, right now.

The closest Schwab office was on Avenue of the Stars in Century City. Wycliff approached the female receptionist. 'How may I help you?' she asked, offering him a professional smile.

'I need information on my account.'

'Certainly, sir. Let me get a broker who can assist you.'

A moment later a young man came out from the back, introduced himself, and led Wycliff to a cubicle. 'Do you have your account number?' he asked Wycliff, his fingers poised over his keyboard.

'I've forgotten it,' Wycliff said, somewhat sheepishly.

'Not a problem. I'll need your social and ID.'

Wycliff recited his social security number and handed over his driver's license. The broker typed the information into his computer. He frowned as he looked at his screen. 'There is no record of an account in your name, sir.'

'What do you mean, no record? There has to be.'

'No, sir.' The broker gave Wycliff a nervous

look. 'You need to talk to whoever handles your investments for you. And maybe the police.'

Again, Charlotte didn't answer her phone. She was probably angry about his relationship with Amelia, and was holding him at arm's length. He should have lied about that. Nothing worse than a woman scorned. Especially a vain, older woman who was fighting like a wolverine to retain whatever shreds of her youth she could.

He couldn't worry about her feelings, and he couldn't wait for her to call him back, either. He had to get to the bottom of what was happening before his entire world came crashing down around his ears.

From the Schwab office to Charlotte's apartment was only a few miles along Santa Monica Boulevard, then up Doheny, and it wasn't yet noon, so the traffic wasn't particularly heavy, but it felt like he was driving through quicksand. Finally arriving, he pulled into the underground parking and rode the elevator up to her floor. If she wasn't there he would wait for her. Camp outside her door until she showed up, if necessary.

Her apartment door was open. She was home. Thank God for small favors. By now he didn't care if she was angry, pissed off, jealous, sad, or anything else. She was going to tell him what was going on, and how he could find Cummings to fix it.

'Charlotte,' he called out, as he crossed the threshold, 'we have to talk.'

There was no answer. He went inside. 'Charlotte?' he called again.

He passed through the empty living room into the bedroom, and almost fell over from the shock of what he saw. Or rather, didn't see. The closet doors were open, but there was not a stick of clothing in any of them. The same with the dressers: all the drawers were bare. He rushed into the bathroom. Nothing. There was no trace of Charlotte anywhere, not even a lingering aroma of cigarette smoke.

Back in the living room, he slumped against a wall.

'Who are you?'

He jerked reflexively. A woman who looked like she was from Iran or one of those countries over there was planted in the front doorway.

'Why do you want to know?' he asked back. He was not about to take any shit from some Arab, not the way he was feeling today.

'Because I'm the building manager, and I like to know who's in my building, especially when I don't know them,' the woman shot back.

'Sorry,' he apologized. He didn't need any more trouble. 'I'm looking for the woman who lives here. Her name is Charlotte.' He paused. 'I think.'

The manager looked like she was going to explode from rage. 'You're not going to find her here, not by Charlotte or any other name. She left two days ago. Snuck out like a thief in the night, with three months back rent due. No notice, no forwarding address, nothing.'

'She didn't own this place?' His head was spinning a thousand miles an hour.

'Own it?' the manager exclaimed with incredulity. 'She was subletting, on the cheap. The owner lives in Paris. She took a hit on the price but she wanted the apartment occupied by a nice older woman, and your friend fit the bill. Or so we both thought.' She grimaced. 'Now she's fifteen thousand dollars out of pocket and she's blaming me for her loss, because I didn't follow up vigorously enough.'

'I'm sorry.' Wycliff was so numb, nothing was really registering.

'Me, too.' The manager, now understanding Wycliff was not a threat, softened her tone. 'Do you have any idea where she might be?' she asked plaintively. 'I need to get my client's money back for her, or I'm going to have to stand for it.'

'No,' he told the distraught woman. 'I have no idea.'

TWENTY-NINE

Amelia was working a double shift and wouldn't have time to come over, which gave him an excuse to avoid her, thankfully. She'd freak out if she knew what was going on. He didn't have the nerve to go back to Levine's office and reveal what a complete idiot and patsy he had been, and he didn't want to return to the house, either. The house was the physical symbol of how badly he had screwed up. His brother had poured his blood, guts, and hard-earned money into it, and now it was as if none of that had ever happened.

He had to keep the house. It was Billy's monument. He couldn't lose it.

He went to a matinée at the Arc Light on Sunset (an action movie with Matt Damon; he was too distracted to remember anything about the plot or even the title), then ate a top sirloin steak at the counter at Musso & Frank's, washed down with two Manhattans and a half bottle of BV cabernet, the house pour.

He couldn't put off staying away any longer. It was time to go back to the house. He needed to sleep. To try and forget everything, if only until tomorrow.

The house was dark. When he had left in the morning he hadn't thought he would be returning this late, so he hadn't left any lights on. He parked his rental car in the driveway, trudged up the walk to the front door, and let himself in.

He couldn't see Charlotte because it was as dark inside as out, but he could smell her, her special, alluring aroma. 'You took your sweet time returning,' she said out of the darkness. 'I've been waiting for hours.'

A lamp clicked on, creating a puddle of low, soft light. Charlotte was sitting in the easy chair on the far side of the room, fashionably dressed as usual, in sling-back heels, sheer stockings, a silk blouse, and a light-weight wool skirt with a side-split. Her legs were crossed, showing some lovely thigh. Her revolver was cradled in her lap.

She stroked the gun as if it was a sleeping kitten.

Wycliff gaped at her. 'How did you get in?'

'The door was unlocked. You should be more careful. This is not the safest of neighborhoods.'

He was sure he had locked up; he always double-checked when he went out. But with all the shit going on in his life, maybe he had forgotten this time. Add that to the list of his recent fuckups.

He pointed to the gun in her lap. 'What the hell is that for?'

'Protection, sweetheart. You never know who's going to come through the door. A woman can't be too careful.' She stroked the gun again. 'You remember this, don't you?'

The sight of the weapon almost made him throw up. 'Yes, I remember.'

She placed the gun on the side table, next to a glass of red wine. 'I didn't know what you had, so I brought this,' she said, picking the glass up with her manicured fingers. 'The bottle is in the kitchen, by the sink,' she told him. 'Join me.'

Fighting his emotions, Wycliff went into the kitchen, poured himself an almost-full glass of wine, came back out, and sat on the sofa across from her. 'Cheers,' he said, raising his glass. 'I don't know what to, but whatever outrageous shit you're involved with, it can't be any good.'

She gave him an enigmatic smile and raised her glass to his. 'I'll take that as a compliment.' She took a ladylike sip. He knocked half his back with one swallow.

'Very tasty,' he said. 'Always the best for you, Charlotte. Or whoever you really are.'

'Always the best,' she agreed. 'Especially as regards my men, Wycliff. And I really am Charlotte. A Charlotte. There's more than one.'

'There's only one you, and back at you for the compliment. Excuse me if I don't believe it.'

'It's true, but I can understand why you wouldn't.'

He stared at her across the room. 'Are you finally going to tell me what's going on? For real?'

'Of course I am. Why would I be here otherwise?'

'Lots of reasons. You're horny. You need a place to spend the night. You want to mock me. There are plenty of others, I'm sure.'

She took another sip of wine. 'Before I explain everything, and I'm going to, I promise, can we have sex first? We've never made love in your bed, it's always been in mine.'

'It's always been in somebody's,' he corrected her. 'Calling it yours is a stretch.'

'You thought it was mine, so it was.' She crossed her legs languidly, revealing more thigh. 'One last time, for Auld Lang Syne?'

'That's a lovely way of putting it. There is poetry in you I never knew existed, Wycliff. I'm sure there are many facets of you I never knew, and never will. That's a pity. But we can never know everything about anyone, can we?'

'No,' he agreed. 'We never can. And we can't have sex. Not now, or ever again. That ship left the harbor. It's gone to sea.'

Her smile was almost endearing. 'Can't hurt a girl for trying.' She pulled her skirt down over her knees.

It was all clear now. 'You're the new owner, aren't you? You're the sonofabitch who gypped me.'

'Yes,' she confessed. There was no shame or remorse in her voice. 'I am.'

'Why?' He stared at her, sitting so calmly across the room from him. There was not a trace of emotion in her face that would indicate that she had just dropped an atomic bomb on his head. 'For God's sakes!' he cried out, 'why?'

'Because it should have been mine. The house, the money, everything should have been mine.'

'If I'm supposed to understand what that means, I don't.'

'Of course you don't. There's no reason in the world that you could. But it's true.' She paused for a moment. 'You are Billy's brother. That's blood.' She paused again, longer this time. 'But I am his mother. That's blood, too, Wycliff. Even closer than yours.'

At least his relationship with Charlotte had not been incestuous, Wycliff thought as his stomach twisted in knots, because she was not his birth mother. They had never had a relationship at all before now, except for the brief time when they had lived under the same roof after Billy was born. Before she picked up stakes and left for parts unknown.

'I'm going to start at the beginning, so you can truly understand where I'm coming from,' Charlotte said, shifting in her chair to make herself comfortable. 'I had to leave that marriage. Your father would have killed me if I had stayed. I was lucky to escape with my body and sanity intact. That bastard beat the daylights out of me, more than once.'

She wasn't going to get an argument from him on that score. He had been on the receiving end of his father's wrath countless times himself. Billy, being younger and less able to stand up to their father, had had it even worse.

'Fair enough,' Wycliff said, staring at his decades-ago stepmother – now his recent lover – across the room. 'You were justified in bailing out. Nobody's saying you were a bad person for doing that. I would have done the same myself, if I had been able to. But what does that have to do with what's going on with me and you now?'

'I'm getting to that. It's my story, I'm going to tell it my way, at my pace.' She took another sip of wine. 'I've wanted to for a long time, to cleanse my soul.' She laughed. 'If I have one. But I was never with the right person to do it.'

'Until now,' he responded caustically.

She shook her head. 'No,' she corrected him. 'You're not the first person I've wanted to tell it to. Billy was.'

Their father was her first husband. She was young and naive when she married him, and although she was still young when she left, the innocence had been burned out of her. She got married again, twice. Neither marriage lasted long. 'I should have learned my lesson the first time,' she said humorlessly. The circumstances weren't the same with the other husbands, they didn't scare her to death. The marriages just hadn't worked out. 'I guess I'm not the marrying type,' she told Wycliff matter-of-factly. By the time she was in her early thirties she had marriage out of her system. She had not had any other children. Billy was the only one. For decades, she had given hardly any thought to the son she had left behind.

'My family was dirt-poor,' she said, toying with her glass as if it were a microphone, a prop to help her recite her narrative. 'I didn't have much education. That's why I gravitated towards low-lifes like your father when I was young and didn't know any better. And because I wasn't well educated, the only jobs I could get were menial, low paying. I wasn't going to settle for that.'

She had always been attractive, so she never lacked for male companionship. 'As I got older, I became more discriminating. No more losers. I chose lovers who were rich and sophisticated. I was like a sponge; I learned how to appear like I was rich and sophisticated, too. I worked hard at that. I earned every dollar those men lavished on me.'

And she was one of those fortunate women whose attractiveness increased as she aged. She was pretty at twenty-five. At forty, she was, to many men, irresistible. (Listening to her, Wycliff could believe that. He was one of them.) But there was a problem. Despite her many charms, she didn't have money. Real money, fuck-you money. She had proximity to wealth through the men in her life, a tantalizing closeness, but she never had a pile of her own. As usually happens to courtesans – which, bottom line, she was – she was eventually left out in the cold.

The grifting started by accident. She was with one of her beaus at a party being thrown at the home of a wealthy society couple, in San Francisco. It was an older crowd. Having recently turned forty, she was one of the youngest people there (her guy that night was thirty years her senior). Most of the women were drowning in expensive jewelry, earrings, necklaces, rings. 'I was wearing a lovely pearl necklace and I felt like an absolute pauper.'

They were robbed by a gang wearing stockings over their faces and brandishing big, scary guns. The men were taken into one room, the women to another. Most of the women were hysterical, not only because they were scared shitless, but because their precious bling was being stolen.

'I wasn't too concerned about my necklace and ring,' she continued. 'They were gifts that could be replaced. What I was scared of was that one of those airheads would do something stupid to panic the robbers. If one gunshot had been fired, it could have been a blood bath.'

Thankfully, that didn't happen. The thieves were professionals, and no one lost their heads. The entire episode was over and done in less then ten minutes. By the time the host called the police and they arrived, the bad guys had vanished into the night.

Everyone had to be individually interviewed and questioned, a tedious process. By the time she and her escort were allowed to leave, it was after midnight. They weren't the last to go;

several of the guests were still being detained until the detectives could get to them. Before she left, she went into one of the guest bathrooms to splash cold water on her face and freshen up her makeup.

And guess what she found when she opened the step wastebasket to discard her fancy paper guest towel? A Gucci purse. A real one, not a knockoff. Her curiosity compelled her to check the contents, and guess what was inside? Not only makeup, tampons, and lipstick. The bag was stuffed with rings, earrings, a Cartier watch, and an emerald-and-diamond necklace.

'What must have happened,' Charlotte explained, 'was that during the initial confusion, when the men and women were being herded into their respective holding rooms and people were freaked out and hysterical, one of the women managed to sneak away for a moment, strip off her jewelry, and dump the purse there, figuring that she would come back later and retrieve it. Obviously, she was one of the guests who had not had her interview with the police yet.'

When opportunity knocks, open the door. She dumped the contents of the woman's purse into her own and dropped the other back into the trash. When the owner came to reclaim it, she would assume the thieves had found her hidden stash.

She came out of the bathroom, linked her arm with that of her date, and waltzed him out the door. They went back to his place, where she screwed his aging brains out. Then she returned to her humble apartment and never saw the man again. She was moving on, and seventy-year-old squares didn't fit into her new plans.

Getting rid of the booty was harder than she had assumed it would be. She couldn't lay it off on a pawn shop or jewelry store, they have everything on their hot lists. And she didn't dare try to sell it through advertising (this was before E-Bay, Craig's List, other such Internet outlets); she would have exposed herself too much. The police are on the lookout for that. You need to unload that kind of merchandise with a fence. And if you are not in that business, you don't know one.

But where there's a strong enough will, there's a way. One of her former paramours had friends in the know. When she discarded her men she did so on good terms, in case she needed something from them, later. The ex-lover was happy to help her. She was able to sell her ill-gotten goods, and put the money in the bank.

'And that was how my new life began.'

Sitting across from Charlotte, Wycliff listened to her story with a mixture of appreciation and anger. This woman was some piece of work. Part of him was enraged with her, but another part couldn't help but admire her, even though she had totally fucked him over.

She was very careful about the jobs she pulled. She never took jewels while in the company of any particular man more than once. She never went back to the same place after she had robbed it. 'Like the store in Beverly Hills,' she reminded him, not that he didn't remember the episode vividly. 'They will never see me again.'

The theft in Beverly Hills had been an anomaly. She usually didn't work that close to home. But in casing it, she had learned that it was such a soft touch it was impossible to pass up, particularly since the owner was in cahoots with her.

'Anyway,' she went on, 'that's all old business. Let's talk about us.'

Finally, he thought. He leaned forward slightly, fighting to keep his nerves under control.

'I kept a low profile,' she said. 'A few jobs a year, sometimes only one. I made out nicely, but I didn't get rich. When you're selling stolen jewelry you make a dime on the dollar. In a good year I might make a couple hundred thousand dollars. In a down year, not as much.'

She held up her empty wine glass. 'Top me up, please. Just a little. I don't want to get tipsy.'

He got up and refilled her wine glass, but not his own. The reverse of their usual drinking behavior. Now he was the one who needed to stay sober.

'You can fake out a lot of things,' she said. 'But not time.' She looked at him across the room, her eyes unwavering. 'I got old.'

'You've got plenty of tread left on your tires.'

She laughed, a real belly-guffaw. 'Oh, God! I thought I'd buffed all the abrasions out of you, Wycliff. It's refreshing that I haven't.' She looked around the room. 'Your brother had exquisite taste. He was a true artist.'

'Which you never knew,' he threw back at her. 'Feng Shui and all that baloney. It was total BS.

You and Billy never crossed paths in that condo, or anywhere else.'

'No,' Charlotte admitted. 'We never did. You-'ve been there recently, I take it.'

'This afternoon. The building manager is on the warpath. You stiffed her for fifteen grand, and she's not happy about it.'

'She's the least of my worries,' Charlotte said, waving her hand dismissively. 'Certainly none of yours.'

He had to give the devil her due: she was right, and it was good she had reminded him of it. He had to get her back on track before she got lost in her dreams and didn't finish her story. A tale, he knew with a sick feeling in his gut, of which he was an important part.

'You got old,' he repeated back to her.

She winced. 'That's rude. But call a spade a spade: I was no longer the desirable companion of men of a certain age, because I was that age myself. Those men want trophies fresh out of the showroom, not last year's model, certainly not last decade's. I had to find a new way to make money. And I needed a nest egg, which I had never been able accumulate.'

She took another sip of wine, this time for fortification. 'And that is when my only child came back into my life.'

She had moved around. California, Nevada, Arizona, places that were warm ('I hate cold weather') and where she could meet and in-gratiate herself with wealthy people. She never stayed more than a couple of years in any one city, so she wouldn't wear out her welcome or become too recognizable.

'But after I hit the age barrier, I had to find a new MO.'

What she hoped would be her chance to finally have her own piece of the rock came about by a fortuitous encounter that was so unexpected that she knew it had to be an omen. 'I met a woman at a party in Santa Fe who was moving from Los Angeles to Paris for a year, and was looking for someone to sublet her penthouse condominium. As an enticement, she boasted that it had been decorated by a hot young LA designer. She told me his name, which was not that uncommon. But I knew. Immediately.'

Then the other shoe dropped. The young man was dying, the woman told Charlotte. He had incurable AIDS. The last time she had seen him was shortly before he went into the hospital. 'I was his final client,' the woman said regretfully.

Charlotte didn't let on that she had any connection to Billy, but her mind was racing. By coincidence, she told the woman, she was moving to Los Angeles, and the penthouse was exactly what she was looking for. They came to an agreement on the spot. A week later Charlotte flew here, moved into the condo, and that same afternoon, she took a taxi to Cedars-Sinai.

'Billy didn't recognize me, of course. He had almost no memory of me at all. How could he? I ran off before he was three years old.' She laughed. 'That first time, he thought I was some woman who had wandered into his room by mistake. But I knew it was him the moment I laid eyes on his sweet, suffering face. He was the

311

spitting image of his father. As are you. How that miserable prick brought forth two such beautiful men is one of nature's stranger miracles.'

You're a miracle yourself, Wycliff thought bitterly. Of guts and survival.

'He didn't believe me when I told him who I was,' Charlotte continued. 'He didn't want to. I couldn't blame him, I would have felt the same way. He had spent a lifetime erasing me from his mind and he didn't want to readjust to something so traumatic, especially since he knew he was going to die soon, and already had more than enough trauma in his life.'

She put her empty wine glass down on the table, next to the gun. 'It wasn't hard to convince him, though. I talked about things only a mother would know. His favorite bed-time story, his favorite toy. That his favorite meal when he was two was oatmeal with bananas and raisins.'

Oatmeal with bananas and raisins. Wycliff hadn't thought about that in what seemed like forever. But it was true. For months, the only food Billy would eat, morning, noon, and night, was oatmeal with bananas and raisins.

'So then what happened?' he asked her. He couldn't help himself, he had to find out what had gone down between them.

'He told me to go fuck myself, in exactly those words. He ordered me to stay away, and never come back.'

That was my baby brother, all right, Wycliff thought fondly. Feisty to the end.

'I didn't give up, of course. I've spent a lifetime armoring myself. I wasn't going to dry up and blow away. My own needs were too important.'

'Getting your hands on his money.'

'Of course. He had to leave it to someone. Who better than his mother, finally reunited with him after these many years?'

Goddamn, he thought, this woman really does have brass balls. 'What was his reaction when you brought that up?' he asked.

'Give me some credit,' she said, annoyed by the question. 'I'm not stupid. I didn't bring up the subject of money at all. I told him I had always regretted leaving him, and I hoped we could bond together now, before he died. Strictly the love of a mother for her child.'

Wycliff laughed in her face. 'How did that go over?'

'Like a lead balloon,' she admitted candidly. 'He was not going to have anything to do with me. Period.' She picked up her glass. 'I'd like more wine. If you'll do the honors, please.'

He got the bottle from the kitchen and poured her a healthy portion. 'You're not going to join me?' she chided him. 'It's uncouth to drink alone.'

'I won't tell on you.'

'Thank you.' She took a swallow from her glass. 'What happened next,' she said, picking up her narrative. 'I did some research, online. It's easy to access anyone's private data, which is not private at all. You don't have to be a computer genius to do it, a trained monkey could have done what I did. I discovered that he owned his house outright, which is worth at least a million dollars, and that he had money in his retirement plan.'

'And you wanted it.'

'Of course I wanted it. It was my ticket to ride.' She heaved a heavy sigh. 'But what I wanted and what I got were entirely different things. What I wanted was what *you* got, his estate. What *I* got was the door slammed in my face.'

She continued. 'The last time I saw him was when we finally talked about money. *He* brought it up. This was a few days before you came into the picture. I planted myself at his bedside and told him I wasn't budging until he talked to me, even if I had to bring a sleeping bag and camp out.'

'So he did talk, finally?'

Her features contorted. 'He blistered me. There were three people in the world he hated. His father, who was a miserable prick. The bastard was dead now, and he hoped he was rotting in hell. His brother, who had always made his life miserable. And his mother, who abandoned him.'

Now she was the one who was shaking. 'I couldn't help myself. I started crying. Forty years of repressed emotion finally boiled over. Billy didn't cry, though. He was a stone wall. "Get the fuck out," he said to me. For someone so frail, he was incredibly harsh and powerful. "Get out and never come back. You don't exist to me." "Why?" I begged him. "I had to leave that marriage. You know what a monster your father was. You can't hold my escaping him

314

against me." And that's when he really unloaded on me. "I don't hate you because you left him," he said. "I hate you because you didn't take me with you. You abandoned me, and I will never forgive you for that."'

Wycliff wanted a drink badly now, but he had to stay strong. His survival depended on that.

'Billy never said a word about you,' he told her. 'Not once.'

'Of course he wouldn't,' Charlotte said. 'He was shutting me out. He might have thought that if you knew I existed you might have reached out to me. He wanted to make sure that never happened.'

Wycliff nodded. That made sense, in a weird, twisted way. 'So what happened after that?' he asked.

Charlotte composed herself. 'He got an injunction against me. I couldn't get within five hundred feet of him. Stay away from Billy or you'll be arrested, his lawyer warned me. He wasn't whistling Dixie, he meant it.'

Damn, Wycliff thought. 'So what did you do?'

'What could I do? Defy the injunction and go to jail? This was my last chance to score, and it was gone, over, done.' She smiled. 'And then, like a miracle, you showed up. Heaven dropped you right into my lap.'

Wycliff felt like she had kicked him in the balls. But only for a second, because he realized she was fucking with his head, yet again. 'You and I met only a couple hours after I first got here, when you picked me up in that bar. There's no way in hell you could have known I had come

315

to LA'

'But I did,' she replied, her voice juicy. 'A little bird whispered into my ear. Actually, it was a good fairy. His name was Stanley.'

Wycliff was dumbstruck. 'That faggot who was living in Billy's house?'

'Yes,' she told him triumphantly. 'That *faggot*, as you so crudely put it. Like the *faggot* who left you this house and all his worldly possessions. The *faggot* who, in the end, embraced you.' Bitterly: 'As he never would me.'

Wycliff winced. 'I didn't mean it like that.'

'Who cares what you meant?' she said derisively. 'What you care about doesn't matter. What matters is I was thrown a lifeline. You.'

She wasn't going to give up. She couldn't, she had no plan B. If she didn't make this score she would be scuffling for the rest of her life, a prospect that at her age terrified her. She went to Billy's house, met Stanley, and industriously cultivated him. She didn't tell him she was Billy's mother. Billy would have warned Stanley about her and he would have called the cops. Instead, she masqueraded as a former client who wanted to do whatever she could to help Billy. She flattered Stanley, telling him how much he meant to Billy, how appreciative of him Billy was, she spread a line of bullshit ten miles long and twice as thick. And Stanley, the poor gullible doofus, swallowed her story completely. He told her everything there was to know about Billy.

'So when you showed up, Stanley, being the protective mother hen, called me in a panic. He was afraid you would harm Billy. He couldn't stop you himself, your very presence scared the poor man to death, but he hoped I could.'

She drove to Billy's house and there was Wycliff, shirt off, mowing the lawn. 'You were an Adonis, darling. Like your brother must have been, before his illness ravaged him.'

She tailed him to the Chateau Marmont. 'I was winging it. You might have rejected me. Not all younger men go for older women, even when they're served up to them on a platter. Fortunately, you weren't one of them.

'I couldn't know how it would play out,' she continued. 'Billy could have turned his back on you, like he did me. It wasn't until you told me the two of you had buried the hatchet that I came up with my plan.' She smiled. 'My masterpiece.'

She reached into the purse at her feet and pulled out a slim document. 'Read this,' she instructed him.

'What is it?' he asked suspiciously.

'Read it. It's not hard to understand.'

He took the papers from her. When he finished reading, he looked at her in disbelief. 'This says I transferred the deed for the house over to you. That's bullshit! I've never seen this.'

'Yes, you have,' she corrected him. 'You saw it, and signed it.' She pointed at the document. 'This is a copy, in case you get some clever idea that you can tear it up and everything will all go away. The original was filed with the county last week. Officially signed, sealed, and delivered.'

Wycliff was stunned. 'This is what Cummings had me sign? That investment account that never existed?' The pages slipped from his fingers to the floor. 'Where is that cocksucker, anyway?' he asked, enraged.

'Where you'll never find him,' she answered blithely. 'With his share of your money he can live nicely for a long time.'

He collapsed into himself. 'You stole everything! The house, the money. Everything!'

'No, darling,' she purred. 'I didn't steal anything. You *gave* it all to me. It was a straightforward business transaction.

He was shaking now, both from rage and despair. 'I knew from the beginning you were a scam artist! Why in God's name did I ever trust you?'

'Because you wanted to be a player, Wycliff,' she answered with ruthless brutality. 'You had dreams. For a low-rent shit-kicker like you, that's fatal.'

She went on with her story. After swallowing the bitter pill that she was too old to snare wealthy benefactors, she had to reinvent herself. She took up with male partners, preferably gay. She wasn't a fag hag, but it was less complicated to do business with men who didn't want to sleep with her.

She and John Cummings met a few days after she arrived in LA. It takes one to know one, as the saying goes, and they honed in on each other right off the bat, kindred spirits. John needed a partner who would lend an aura of legitimacy to his scams, and who could fill the role better than an attractive, worldly older woman?

'We chose marks who wouldn't come after us when they found out they had been cheated.

318

Suckers who couldn't afford to have their stupidity exposed to their businesses or relatives, or would rather take a financial hit than suffer public humiliation. We weren't greedy. We kept the scams small, usually under a few hundred thousand dollars. We left our victims with some money and some dignity. It's not smart to rob people of all their dignity. I know that, all too well.' She smiled. 'We had never gone for a really big score, until now. You were our first whale.'

He groaned. 'You fucking bitch.'

'Sticks and stones. I'm just like you, Wycliff. Vultures of a feather. Except I pulled my scam off, and you fucked yours up.'

'I didn't have a scam.'

'Of course you did. You wanted your brother's fortune. It's why you came here, it's why you took care of him. For this.'

She picked up the papers and put them back in her purse. 'You have an hour to pack up and leave. If you're not gone by then, I'm calling the police.'

His jaw dropped. *'You'll* call the police? Are you shitting me? Someone with your record? They'll throw you in a cell and swallow the key.'

'I don't have a record,' she answered with infuriating calmness. She reached over and picked up the gun. 'Even this is clean,' she said, hefting it. 'I bought it from a licensed dealer in Vegas. Federal gun check, everything on the up and up. You can't register a gun if you have a criminal record,' she said. 'For instance, I'm sure you couldn't buy one. Not legally.' She stroked the

319

trigger with her forefinger. 'Although if you needed a gun you could easily get hold of one, couldn't you?'

He stared at the gun in her hand. 'Be careful with that,' he cautioned her. 'Those things sometimes go off when you don't want them to.'

She rotated the gun back and forth, as if measuring its weight and solidity. 'Don't worry,' she said. 'I'm very careful with this. I would never fire at anyone I didn't want to hit. Would you?'

He flinched. 'Put the gun away, Charlotte.'

'I always make sure it's handy, in case I ever need it. Until now, I've never had to, fortunately. So you can imagine my surprise that when I looked for it recently, it was missing. Do you have any idea how that could have happened?'

Wycliff forced himself to breathe. 'No.'

'I thought you might, because I'm the only one who knows where it's hidden.' She hefted the gun again. 'The only one except you.'

'Put it away.'

'How many people did you shoot, Wycliff? Did you kill any of them?'

His voice was sandpaper in his throat. 'I didn't shoot anyone.'

'If I turn this gun over to the police and they match it to any killings that took place when it wasn't in my possession, you could be in a lot of trouble. The recent killings in Beverly Hills, for example. The woman and her psychiatrist. The woman Laurie Abramowitz hired you to kill, and the poor innocent bystander who was in the wrong place at the wrong time.'

His mouth had gone completely dry. 'Laurie Abramowitz,' he chocked out, his voice a hollow echo of hers.

Charlotte nodded. 'You didn't know Laurie and I were friends, did you?' Without waiting for an answer, she continued, 'Of course you didn't. If you had, you never would have gone through with it. And you would have dropped me like a hot rock before I could complete my work with you. My work,' she said, finally allowing herself to gloat, 'that has, at long last, set me free.'

That first encounter with Laurie at the iPhone store, Charlotte explained, was no accident. It was premeditated, carefully thought out.

'Laurie and I met socially, and over a period of time we became close. One evening, we got together for drinks. We got a little tipsy, and let our hair down.' She corrected herself. 'She let hers down. I didn't. You know me. I never reveal what's in my hand.'

The gun she was holding rocked back in forth like a metronome. 'By now, Wycliff, you should be able to guess what that problem was.'

He was mute, listening to her. He felt like a prisoner standing before a judge as his death sentence was handed down.

'Her partner was her problem. They'd had a bad falling out, professionally and personally. They had to go their separate ways. Which was a problem for Laurie. She couldn't afford a breakup.'

Wycliff kept his eyes on the gun as Charlotte fondled it. He was too far from her to make a move.

'But she did have a way out. They had taken out million-dollar life insurance policies on each other. If one of them died, the other would be the beneficiary. Their policies had double indemnity clauses. Do you know what that is, Wycliff? Did you ever see the movie? It's the best work Barbara Stanwyck ever did.' She smiled. 'That reminds me. You remember the first time we met, at the Chateau Marmont bar? Of course you do. You were trying to figure out the name of the movie star you thought I was. Barbara Stanwyck, of course, has been dead and gone these many years, poor angel. But if she was still alive and closer to my age, she would have been my model. You might be calling me Barbara instead of Charlotte.' She smiled. 'Although I prefer Charlotte. There are a lot of Barbaras in the world my age. Not so many Charlottes.'

She continued. 'A double-indemnity clause, my dear protégé, states that if a person dies under certain circumstances, one of which is murder, the beneficiary gets paid double. The million-dollar policy is doubled to two million. That's good money, Wycliff. A woman can live a nice life on two million dollars.'

So could a man, Wycliff thought, as he listened to Charlotte spinning her story. *I was going to live great on a lot less.*

'But to collect, Laurie needed her former partner dead. And that's where you came in.'

You pathetic asshole, Wycliff thought. *You knew the deal with Laurie stank like last week's garbage, and you went ahead with it anyway. Charlotte was right: you're a loser.*

'It was a calculated risk, Laurie giving you the first hundred thousand,' Charlotte said. 'You could have taken it and run for the hills. She was worried that you would. But I knew my Wycliff. I knew he wouldn't run. Like I knew he would give that money to John. And Billy's, too.

'A share of the pot of gold wasn't enough for you. You wanted it all.' She pointed the gun at him again, like a schoolmarm pointing a ruler at an unruly student. 'Pigs get rich, Wycliff, and hogs get slaughtered.'

Amelia warned me. And I didn't listen.

'It's a win-win all around, Wycliff. Laurie collected her two million dollars, and gave me a nice finder's fee. I got the house, and John and I split Billy's money. Win-win.' She paused and smiled. 'Except for you. Because if there's a winner, there has to be a loser, too, doesn't there? Tag. You're it.'

She trained the gun at his chest, holding it steady with both hands. 'One hour, Wycliff. Start packing.'

Keeping his eyes riveted to the weapon in her hand, he stood up. Moving in tandem to keep her distance from him, she also rose, maintaining her tight grip on the gun. 'Don't do anything stupid, Wycliff,' she warned him. 'I don't want to shoot you, but I will if you force me to. The police will believe me, of course. A small woman against a big man who has already killed two people. I had to defend myself. Thank God I had this gun. The gun that was used to murder two innocent people.'

Her eyes were on his, unblinking. 'I don't want

to shoot you, Wycliff. It would be messy and complicated. But I will if you force me to. It wasn't a five-foot-four woman running away from those Beverly Hills murders. It was a six-foot two-inch man.'

Wycliff started towards the bedroom, moving carefully so as not to spook her. 'Hey, Charlotte,' he said, keeping his voice disarmingly low and calm, 'if you're really going to shoot me with that gun, you should have remembered to reload it.'

He took a step towards her. She backed away from him and pulled the trigger.

The *click* on the empty chamber was as deafening as it would have been if an actual bullet had been detonated. Before she could recover from her shock and pull the trigger again Wycliff was on her, his hand grabbing for the gun to rip it from her hand. Their bodies were pressed together, so the sound of the discharge was muted. Any passer-by hearing the shot would think it was a car backfiring.

'Oh, God!' she cried out, as she staggered away from him and collapsed onto the floor. 'It burns.'

Wycliff knelt down and pried the weapon from her fingers. 'Where does it hurt?' he asked her, almost tenderly.

Her hand touched her abdomen. 'Here.'

Her blouse was already seeping blood. He pulled the wet material away. The bullet entered her soft belly below her navel. The wound oozed steadily, in rhythm with her heartbeat.

'You've been gut shot,' he told her.

'It hurts,' she whispered. Tears were forming in her eyes. 'It hurts really badly.'

'I know it does,' he said. 'That's a nasty wound to get.' He had treated gunshot wounds like this one when he did his time in the jail infirmary. Left untreated, they killed slowly and painfully.

'Call an ambulance,' she begged him. 'I don't want to die.'

'I don't want you to, either.' That was true, despite everything she had done to him. She had fucked him over completely and ripped his life to shreds, but she had changed him, as well. And she had been wrong. He was a player.

'I can't call for help,' he told her. 'I would if I could. But if I save your life, I'll be giving up mine.'

'You're going to let me die.'

He cradled her head in his lap, making sure she didn't bleed on him. 'I wish I could help you, Charlotte, I really do. But it's too late for that now.'

THIRTY

He took a bundle of towels from the linen closet and slid them under Charlotte's body, so the bleeding wouldn't stain the rug. She clung to life for almost an hour. Mercifully, she passed out long before she died. When he was sure it was over he laid her out on the floor, curled up in the fetal position. To the casual eye, she might have been sleeping. Until you noticed all the blood.

Wycliff was thinking clearly now. He got a sheet from the bedroom closet and lifted her body and the bloody towels onto it. The lower side of her body was turning dark, while the top was losing color, looking like muddled marble. She was becoming a statue, frozen in time. 'Goodbye, Charlotte,' he said softly to the corpse. 'You did me good before you did me bad, so thanks for the good times.'

He wrapped the body and towels in the sheet and secured the bloody package with duct tape. Then he stuffed all his belongings into garbage bags, making sure he didn't leave anything behind. There was no point in wiping the place clean of his fingerprints. He had lived here for months, it was logical he would leave some spoor. But it was not his house anymore, he had signed it over to Charlotte.

It was late now, past midnight. The street was quiet and dark. He carried the corpse outside and placed it in the trunk of the rental car. Then he went back into the house and brought out the garbage bags containing his stuff, which he tossed into the back seat. There wasn't much, mostly the clothing and accessories Charlotte had bought for him. Once he got on the road he'd get rid of everything, so there would be no trace left behind of their connection to each other.

The lawn mower and the other gardening tools were neatly stacked against the far wall of the garage. He picked up a shovel and carried it outside. He put the shovel in the trunk of the car, alongside the wrapped body.

One last reconnoiter of the house. He turned out the lights, locked up, and drove away forever.

The construction site had been readied for the foundation to be poured. Early in the morning, cement trucks would arrive and discharge their tons of concrete. The cement would harden within hours. Wycliff had driven by a few days earlier, He had done foundation work a few months before, back in Arizona. He could see that the walls of the molds for the cement had been dug several feet below ground level. He lifted Charlotte's wrapped corpse out of the trunk of the car and dropped it into one of the holes. Then he grabbed the shovel, jumped down, and went to work. It didn't take long to dig a hole big enough to stuff the grisly package into. He shoveled the loose dirt back over it and smoothed it out. No one would pay attention to any irregularity. By mid-morning, the body would be buried under several tons of industrial mud. If they couldn't find Jimmy Hoffa, they wouldn't find an old-lady grifter, either.

As soon as the bank opened in the morning, he closed his account. He was moving out of state, he explained to the bank representative, and this bank didn't have offices where he was going. He agreed that a wire transfer would be the proper way to go, but he didn't have his new account yet, so that wasn't feasible. He filled out the necessary IRS forms and took the money in five-thousand-dollar checks, four of which he cashed back on the spot.

Exiting the bank, he rubbed the stubble on the top of his head, which he had shaved down earlier in the day. It would grow out fast, back to his natural, dull color. He would grow his beard back, too, but this time he would keep it trimmer. He couldn't go the full bad-ass look anymore. Charlotte had civilized that out of him. To a point.

He returned the rental car to Enterprise and got a ride to the Honda dealership in North Hollywood, which had a low-mileage Volvo sedan for sale on its used-car lot. Car dealers don't like to keep inventory that isn't their brand, so a smart buyer can get a good bargain. He forked over $11,500 in cash, which included tax and license, and drove off the lot in his new ride to the North Hollywood Metro train station, where he retrieved the garbage bags with his belongings from the locker he had stashed them in.

He took the 405 over the pass, got off at Wilshire Boulevard, and drove into Santa Monica. He spent the afternoon in the English Pub. After the obligatory Guinness, he drank Cokes. He needed to be clean and sober, he had a long way to go.

It was time to hit the road, but he had one more stop to make. Amelia's shift ended at eight. Wycliff knew her schedule because she had left him numerous text and phone messages. *What was going on, why wasn't he answering, was he all*

*right, please get in touch, I miss you, I'm wor-
ried.* He hadn't responded to any of them.

He parked down the block from her apartment.
He rolled down the window and smoked a
cigarette while he waited for her to come home.
At eight thirty her little red Civic came puttering
down the street and pulled into its spot in the
exterior parking area next to her apartment
house. Still wearing her hospital scrubs, she got
out of the car and stretched. There was enough
illumination from the overhead street lamps that
he was able to see her clearly. Her face was
drawn, her body slumped over from fatigue.

She dug her cell phone out of her purse and
dialed, and as he watched, he knew she was
calling him. He wasn't that far from her, he
realized; from this distance, she might hear his
phone ringing. He grabbed the phone out of his
pocket and switched from ring to vibrate just in
time, because immediately his phone was
quivering. It felt like a live grenade in his hand.
He looked at the caller ID. It was her. Of course
it was her.

He slouched down and spied on her through
the windshield. She was listening to his phone
ringing, then his voice message. He could see
her talking into her phone to him.

She finished leaving her message, and hung
up. One more discouraged stretch, then she took
a bag of groceries out of her back seat, closed
and locked her car, and trudged on weary legs
into her building. A moment later, a light came
on in her apartment's bay window.

He played her message back. *Wycliff, what's*

going on? Please call me. There was a brief silence. Then she ended it with *I love you.*

He sat and watched her window and there she was, standing in front of it. She stared out into the street, as if by some miracle he would materialize there.

There weren't going to be any miracles. He waited until she drifted away from the window, out of sight. Then he started his new wheels and drove away.

He cruised up California Highway 1 through Malibu, past his favorite beach spot at Leo Carrillo State Park, crossing the LA line into Ventura County. The next ten miles were flat-out beautiful, the narrow two-lane blacktop hugging the coastline, the moonlight shimmering on the ocean. He had driven up here before, by himself. He wished Amelia had been with him then. She would have loved it.

He was going to miss her. She was the best woman he had ever known. Loving, kind, honest, everything a man wants and needs. But he wasn't the man for her. She might have thought he was, but he knew better. She was marriage, a house with a white picket fence, rose bushes, the whole nine yards. He was none of those things. Setting down roots was not in his DNA. He was a wanderer, a loner, a misfit. He definitely wasn't cut out to be in a permanent relationship. He didn't have the stamina for it, or the courage.

Amelia would miss him for a little while, then she would get angry, then she would get over him, and in time she would forget about him.

Not literally, she would remember him, but as a brief interlude in her life, not as a substantial part of it. She didn't know that tonight, but eventually she would. She was a good woman. She deserved a better man than him. Someday, he hoped, she would find one.

Once he was past Santa Barbara, the traffic thinned out to practically nothing. The Volvo was equipped with satellite radio. He found a classic rock station, and the music washed over him as he motored up the coast.

Three people were dead because of him. Others – Amelia – were hurt and broken.

He had wanted to be a player, and although he had tried like hell to become one, in his heart he knew he hadn't made it and never would. He couldn't deny who he was: a drifter, a petty schemer, a man who, in the end, couldn't connect.

And yet, he had enabled his dying brother to live his final days in peace and dignity. That counted for something.

He thought back to where he had been only a few short months ago. He had arrived in Los Angeles with nothing more than the clothes on his back, a hot car, and eight hundred dollars of stolen money in his pocket. Now he was driving a legal set of wheels and had over fifteen thousand dollars in his pocket. Maybe he wasn't a player, but he wasn't a complete loser anymore, either. From where he had started to now, he was ahead of the game.

The road stretched ahead of him and he followed it through Big Sur and Monterey, up to

San Francisco in the darkest part of the night, onward past Mendocino and Fort Bragg, along the rugged coast, wild and beautiful. He stopped at an all-night AMPM Minimart to fuel up, take a leak, and buy a carton of smokes and a six-pack.

Then he was on the road again. The first faint rays of gray-pink pre-dawn sunlight broke through the heavy clouds above the mountains to the east. A sign at the edge of the highway read *Welcome to Oregon, The Beaver State.*

He had never been to Oregon. He had heard it was nice up there. Maybe he would take a square job. They probably needed qualified plumbers, welders, and painters there as much as they did in Los Angeles.

He would find out, soon enough.

ACKNOWLEDGEMENTS

Thanks to Steve Kasdin and Kate Lyall Grant
for their support.